SACRAMENTO PUBLIC LIBRARY
828 "I" Street
Sacramento, CA 95814

D0470265

LADY CASTLE ™

DAWSON · WOODS · FARROW · NALTY

Ross Richie	CEO & Founder	Chris Rosa	Associate Editor
Matt Gagnon	Editor-In-Chief	Alex Galer	Associate Editor
Filip Sablik	President of Publishing & Marketing	Cameron Chittock	Associate Editor
Stephen Christy	President of Development	Matthew Levine	Assistant Editor
Lance Kreiter	VP of Licensing & Merchandising	Sophie Philips-Roberts	Assistant Editor
Phil Barbaro	VP of Finance	Jillian Crab	Production Designer
Arune Singh	VP of Marketing	Michelle Ankley	Production Designer
Bryce Carlson	Managing Editor	Kara Leopard	Production Designer
Mel Caylo	Marketing Manager	Grace Park	Production Design Assistant
Scott Newman	Production Design Manager	Elizabeth Loughridge	Accounting Coordinator
Kate Henning	Operations Manager	Stephanie Hocutt	Social Media Coordinator
Sierra Hahn	Senior Editor	José Meza	Event Coordinator
Dafna Pleban	Editor, Talent Development	James Arriola	Mailroom Assistant
Shannon Watters	Editor	Holly Aitchison	Operations Assistant
Eric Harburn	Editor	Megan Christopher	Operations Assistant
Whitney Leopard	Editor	Morgan Perry	Direct Market Representative
Jasmine Amiri	Editor		

BOOM! STUDIOS

LADYCASTLE, October 2017. Published by BOOM! Studios, a division of Boom Entertainment, Inc. Ladycastle is ™ & © 2017 Delores S. Dawson. Originally published in single magazine form as LADYCASTLE No. 1-4. ™ & © 2017 Delores S. Dawson. All rights reserved. BOOM! Studios™ and the BOOM! Studios logo are trademarks of Boom Entertainment, Inc., registered in various countries and categories. All characters, events, and institutions depicted herein are fictional. Any similarity between any of the names, characters, persons, events, and/or institutions in this publication to actual names, characters, and persons, whether living or dead, events, and/or institutions is unintended and purely coincidental. BOOM! Studios does not read or accept unsolicited submissions of ideas, stories, or artwork.

BOOM! Studios, 5670 Wilshire Boulevard, Suite 450, Los Angeles, CA 90036-5679. Printed in China. First Printing.

ISBN: 978-1-68415-032-8, eISBN: 978-1-61398-709-4

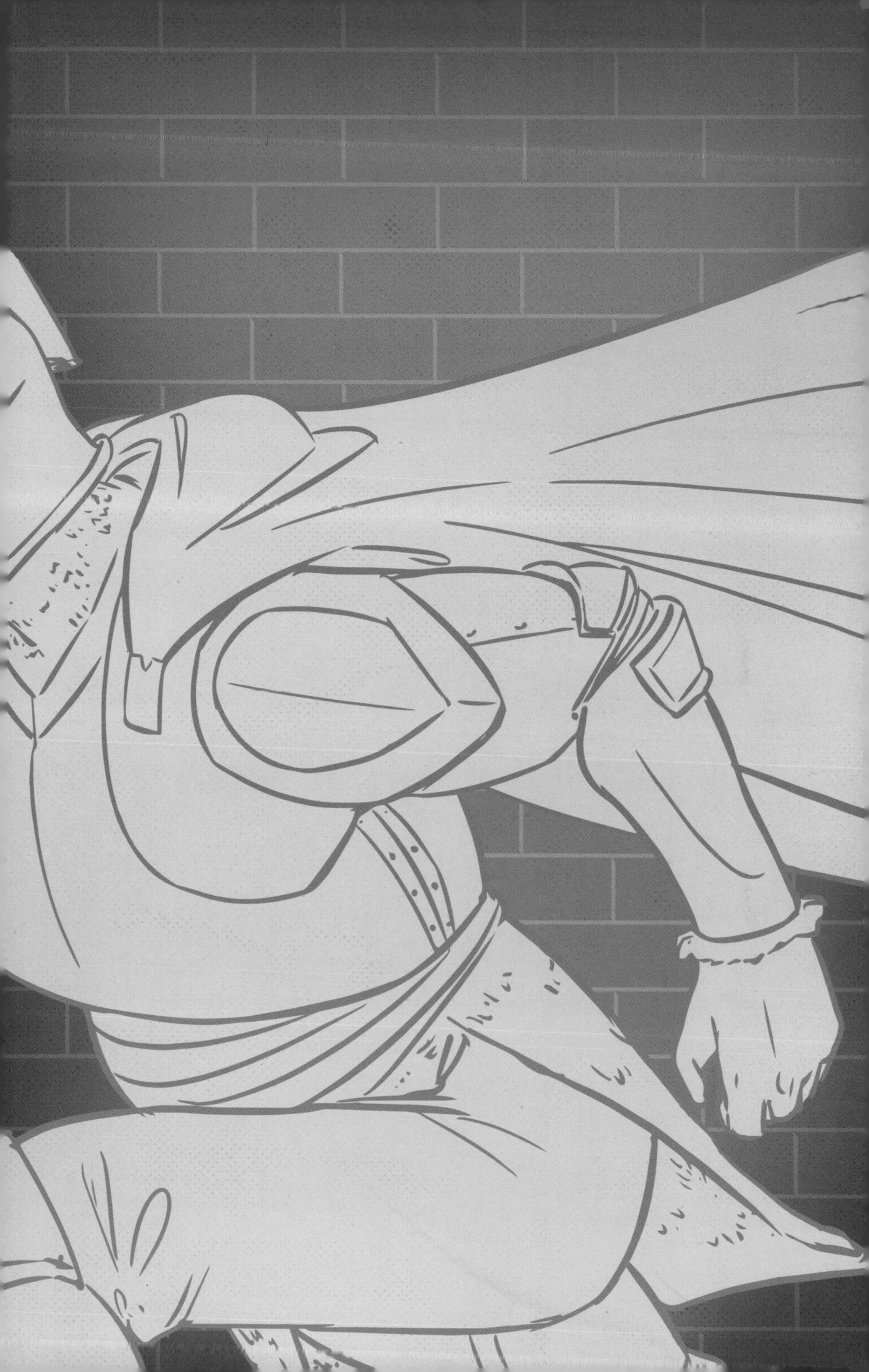

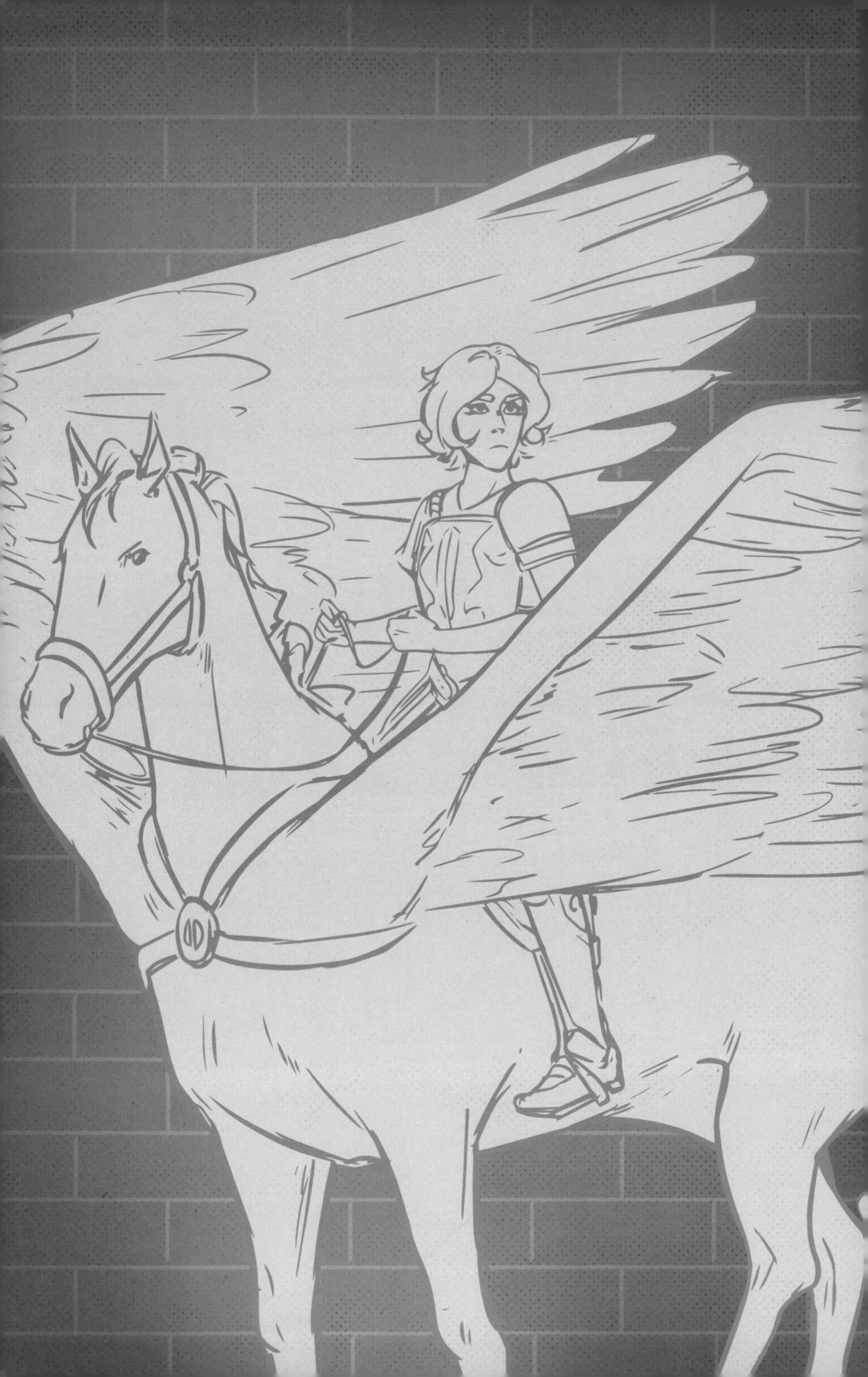

WRITTEN & CREATED BY **DELILAH S. DAWSON**

ILLUSTRATED BY **ASHLEY A. WOODS**
(CHAPTER 1)

BECCA FARROW
(CHAPTERS 2-4)

COLORED BY **REBECCA NALTY**
(CHAPTERS 2-4)

LETTERED BY **JIM CAMPBELL**

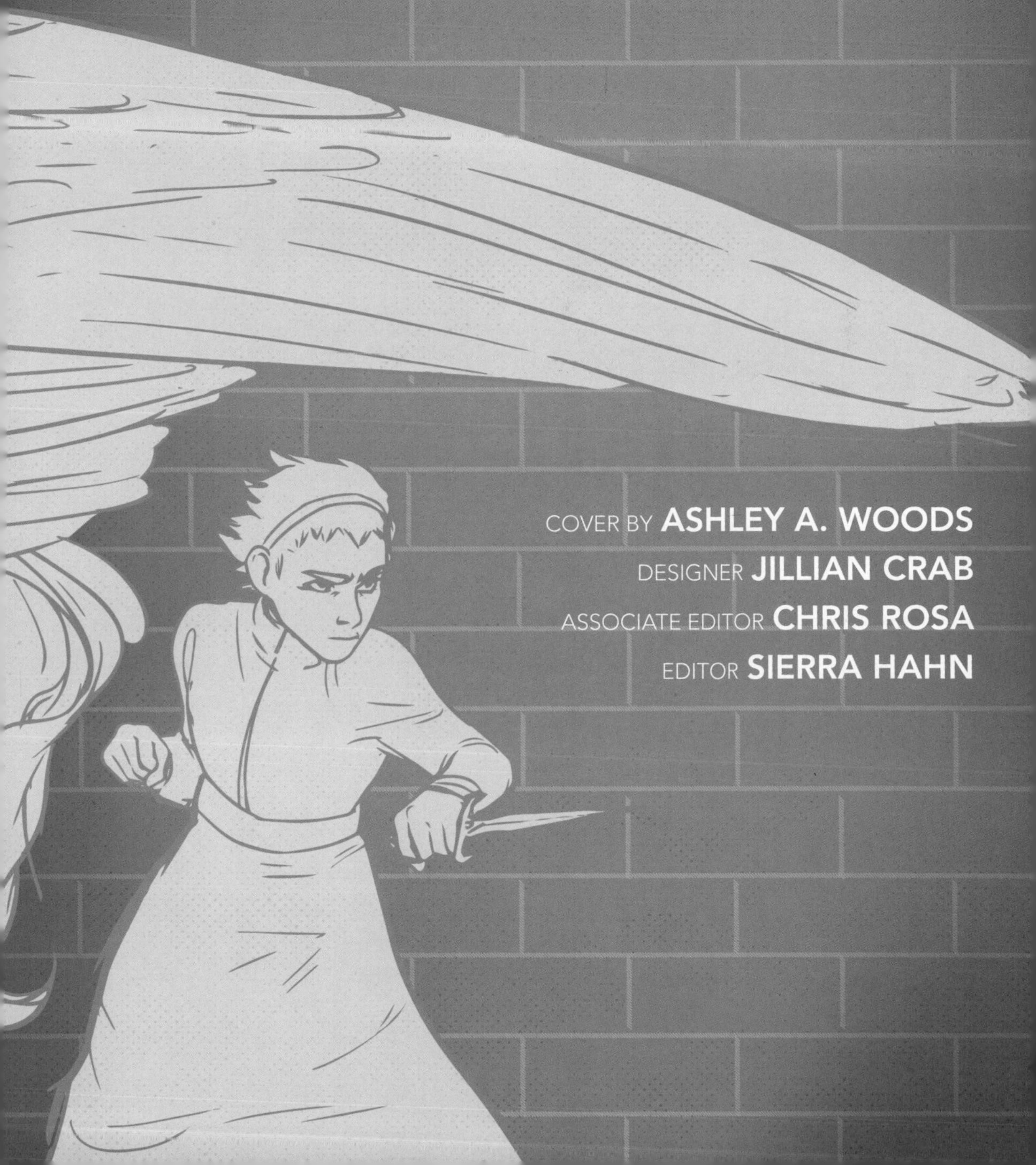

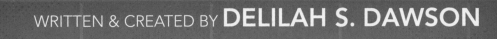

COVER BY **ASHLEY A. WOODS**

DESIGNER **JILLIAN CRAB**

ASSOCIATE EDITOR **CHRIS ROSA**

EDITOR **SIERRA HAHN**

CHAPTER ONE

WELCOME TO LADYCASTLE

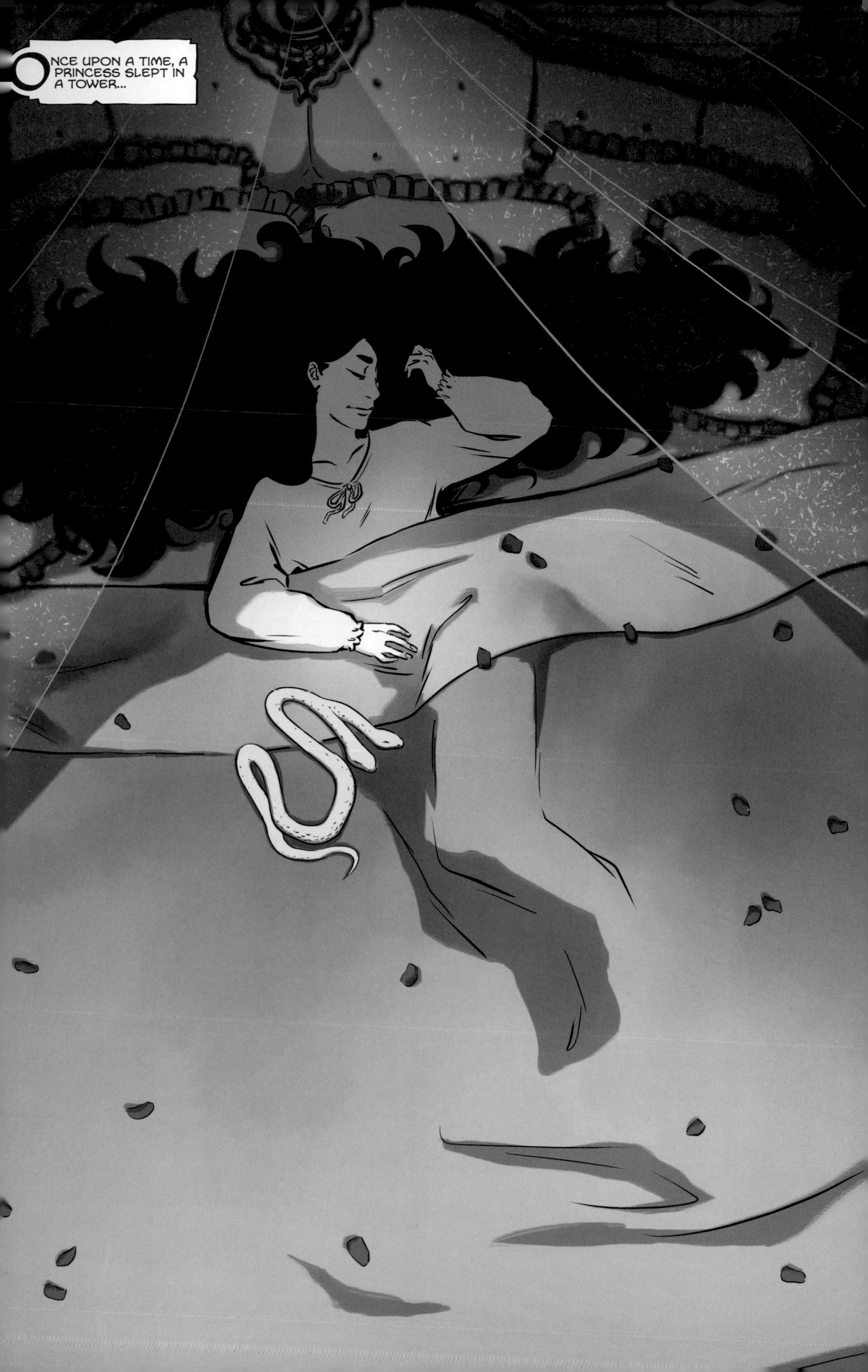
ONCE UPON A TIME, A PRINCESS SLEPT IN A TOWER...

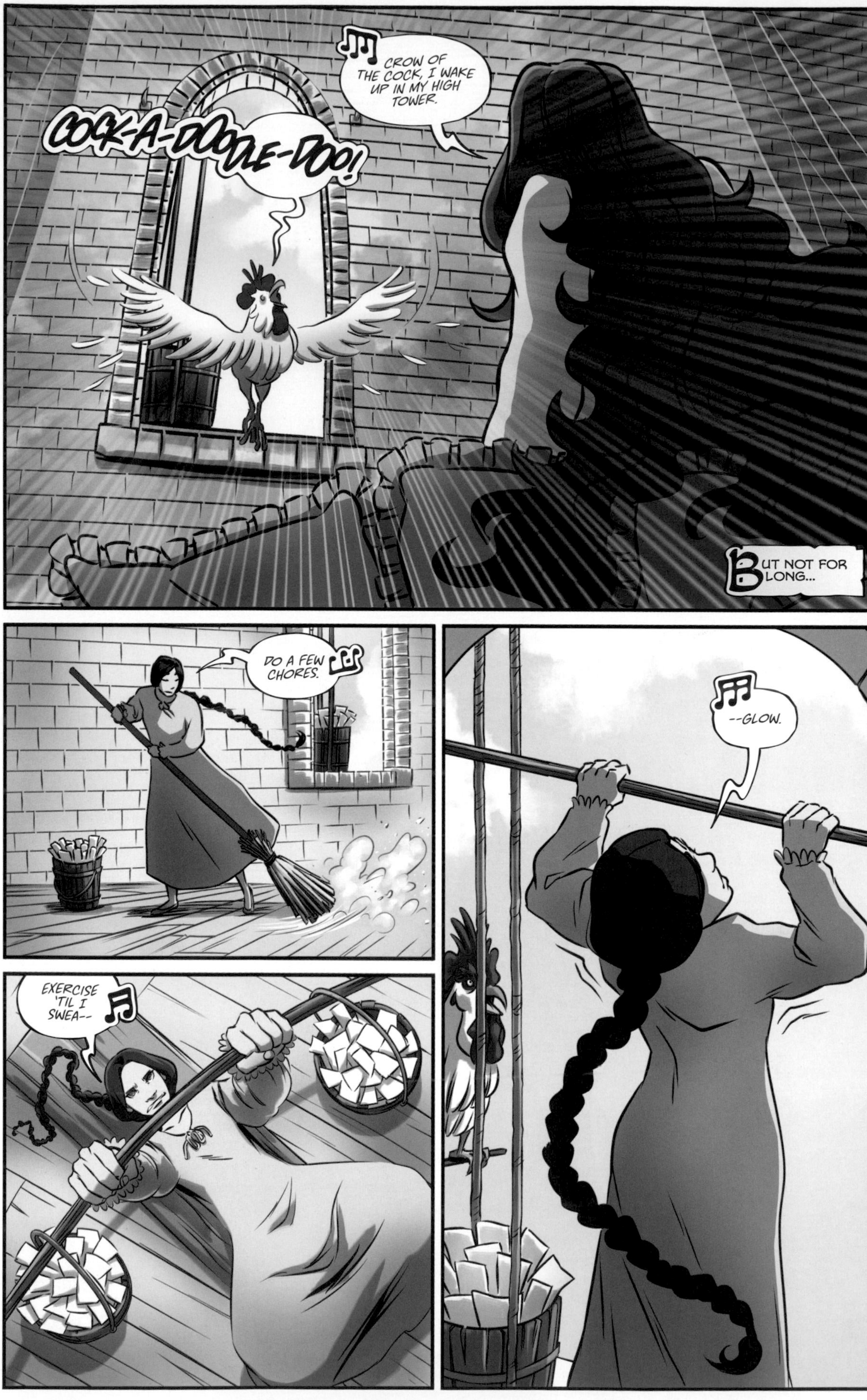
CROW OF THE COCK, I WAKE UP IN MY HIGH TOWER.
COCK-A-DOODLE-DOO!
BUT NOT FOR LONG...
DO A FEW CHORES.
EXERCISE 'TIL I SWEA--
--GLOW.

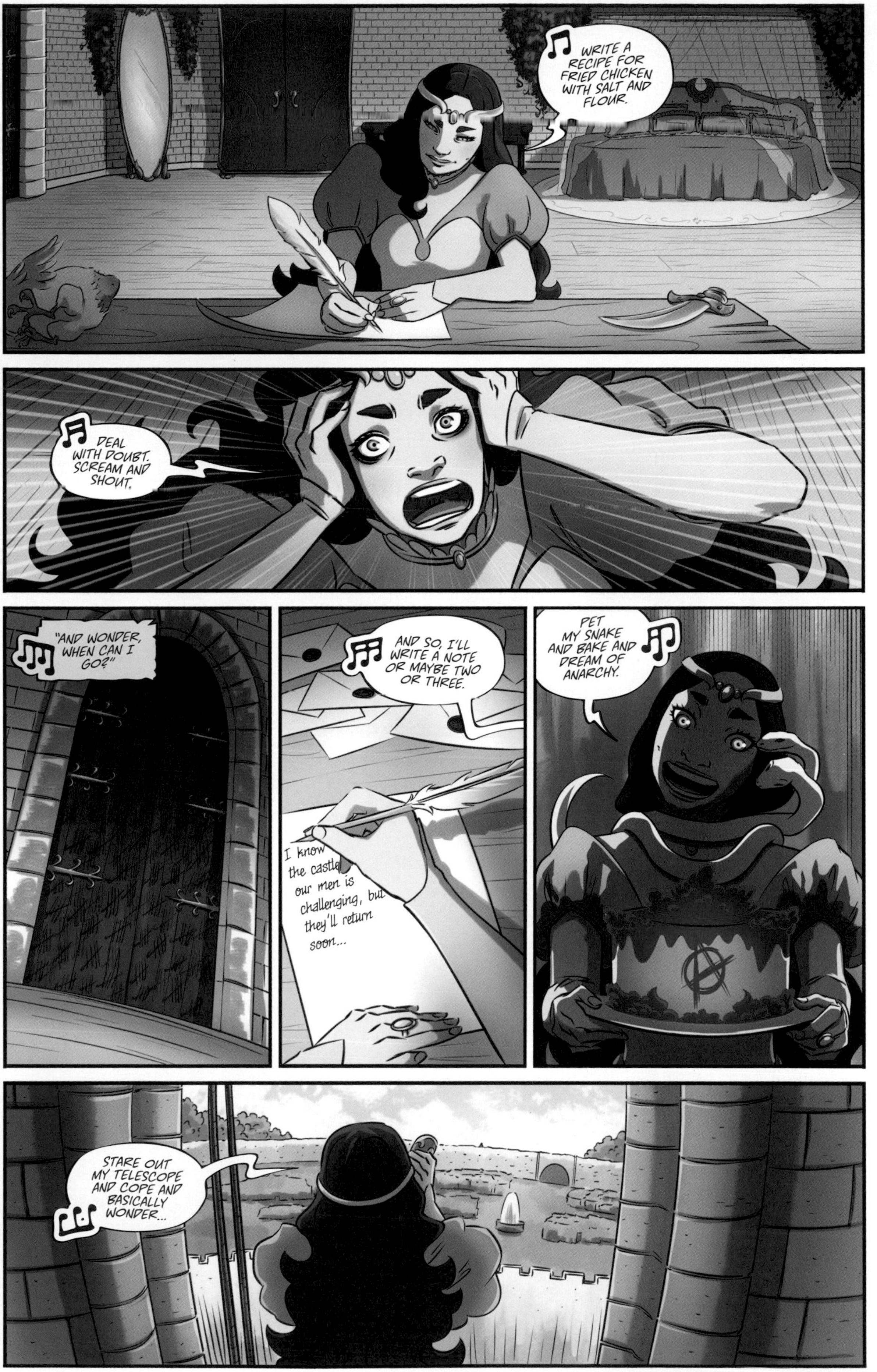
WRITE A RECIPE FOR FRIED CHICKEN WITH SALT AND FLOUR.
DEAL WITH DOUBT. SCREAM AND SHOUT.
"AND WONDER, WHEN CAN I GO?"
AND SO, I'LL WRITE A NOTE OR MAYBE TWO OR THREE.
I know the castle our men is challenging, but they'll return soon...
PET MY SNAKE AND BAKE AND DREAM OF ANARCHY.
STARE OUT MY TELESCOPE AND COPE AND BASICALLY WONDER...

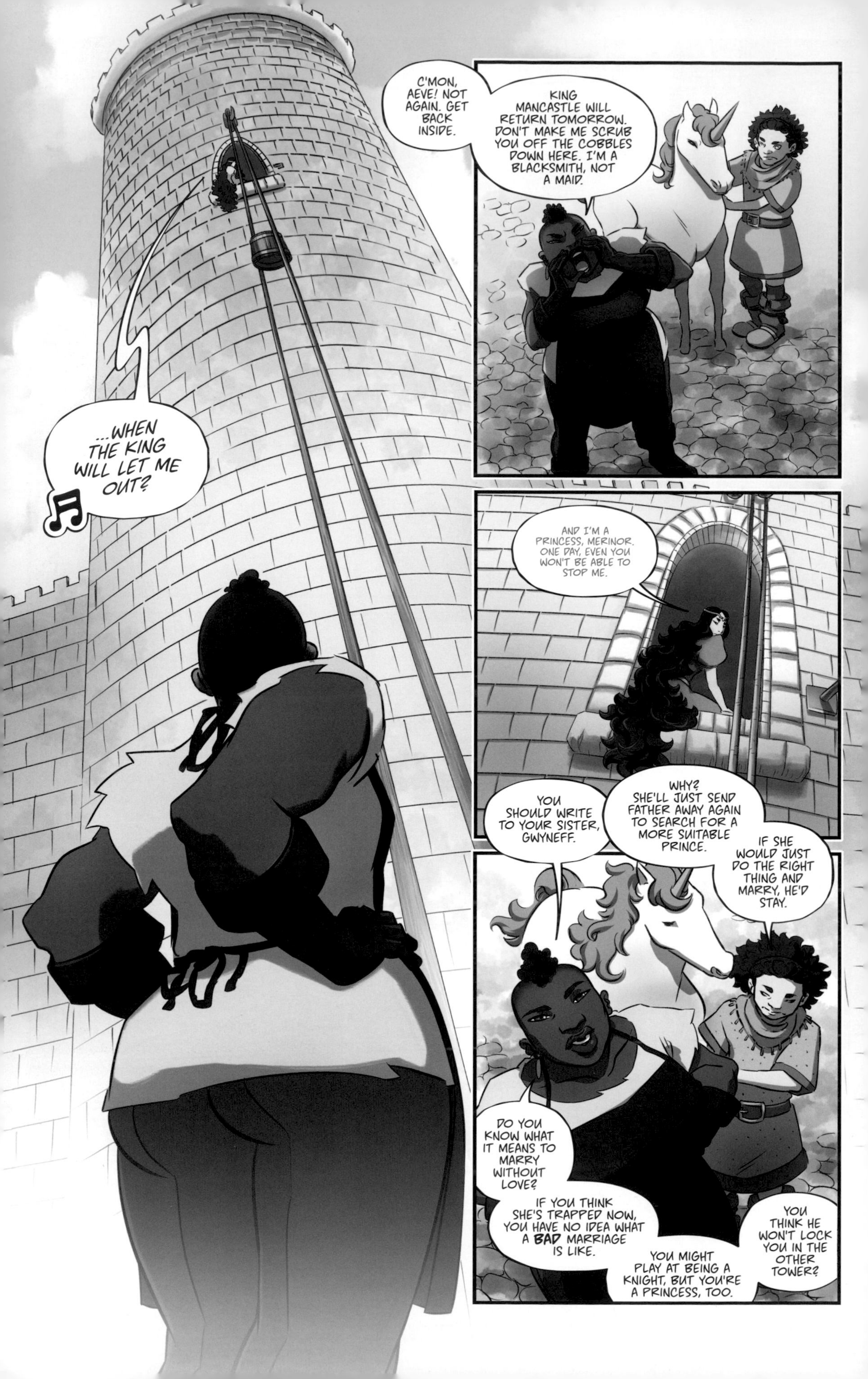
...WHEN THE KING WILL LET ME OUT?
C'MON, AEVE! NOT AGAIN. GET BACK INSIDE.
KING MANCASTLE WILL RETURN TOMORROW. DON'T MAKE ME SCRUB YOU OFF THE COBBLES DOWN HERE. I'M A BLACKSMITH, NOT A MAID.
AND I'M A PRINCESS, MERINOR. ONE DAY, EVEN YOU WON'T BE ABLE TO STOP ME.
YOU SHOULD WRITE TO YOUR SISTER, GWYNEFF.
WHY? SHE'LL JUST SEND FATHER AWAY AGAIN TO SEARCH FOR A MORE SUITABLE PRINCE.
IF SHE WOULD JUST DO THE RIGHT THING AND MARRY, HE'D STAY.
DO YOU KNOW WHAT IT MEANS TO MARRY WITHOUT LOVE?
IF YOU THINK SHE'S TRAPPED NOW, YOU HAVE NO IDEA WHAT A BAD MARRIAGE IS LIKE.
YOU MIGHT PLAY AT BEING A KNIGHT, BUT YOU'RE A PRINCESS, TOO.
YOU THINK HE WON'T LOCK YOU IN THE OTHER TOWER?

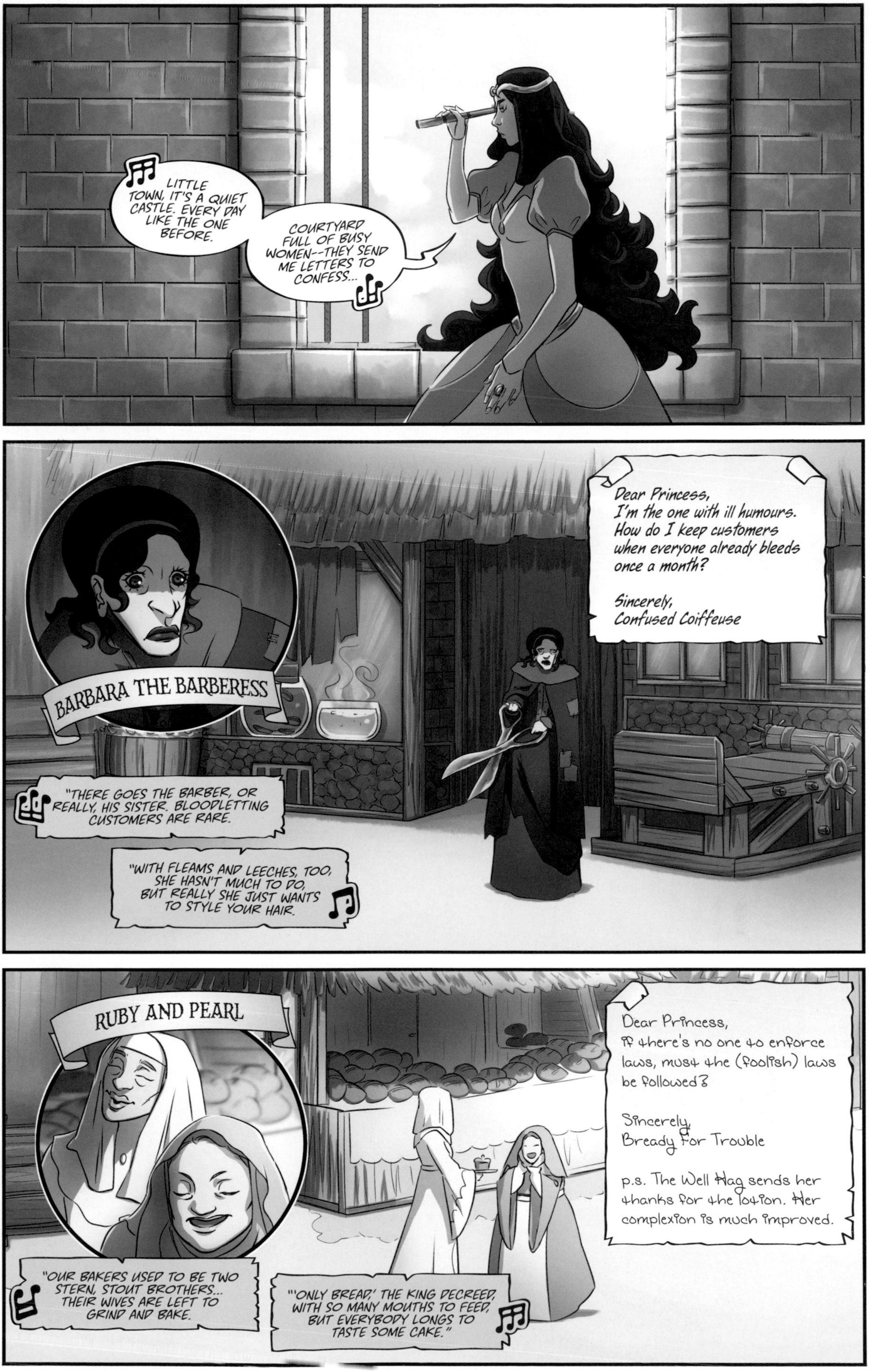
LITTLE TOWN, IT'S A QUIET CASTLE. EVERY DAY LIKE THE ONE BEFORE.
COURTYARD FULL OF BUSY WOMEN--THEY SEND ME LETTERS TO CONFESS...
BARBARA THE BARBERESS
Dear Princess,
I'm the one with ill humours. How do I keep customers when everyone already bleeds once a month?
Sincerely,
Confused Coiffeuse
"THERE GOES THE BARBER, OR REALLY, HIS SISTER. BLOODLETTING CUSTOMERS ARE RARE.
"WITH FLEAMS AND LEECHES, TOO, SHE HASN'T MUCH TO DO, BUT REALLY SHE JUST WANTS TO STYLE YOUR HAIR.
RUBY AND PEARL
Dear Princess,
If there's no one to enforce laws, must the (foolish) laws be followed?
Sincerely,
Bready for Trouble
p.s. The Well Hag sends her thanks for the lotion. Her complexion is much improved.
"OUR BAKERS USED TO BE TWO STERN, STOUT BROTHERS... THEIR WIVES ARE LEFT TO GRIND AND BAKE.
"'ONLY BREAD,' THE KING DECREED, WITH SO MANY MOUTHS TO FEED, BUT EVERYBODY LONGS TO TASTE SOME CAKE."

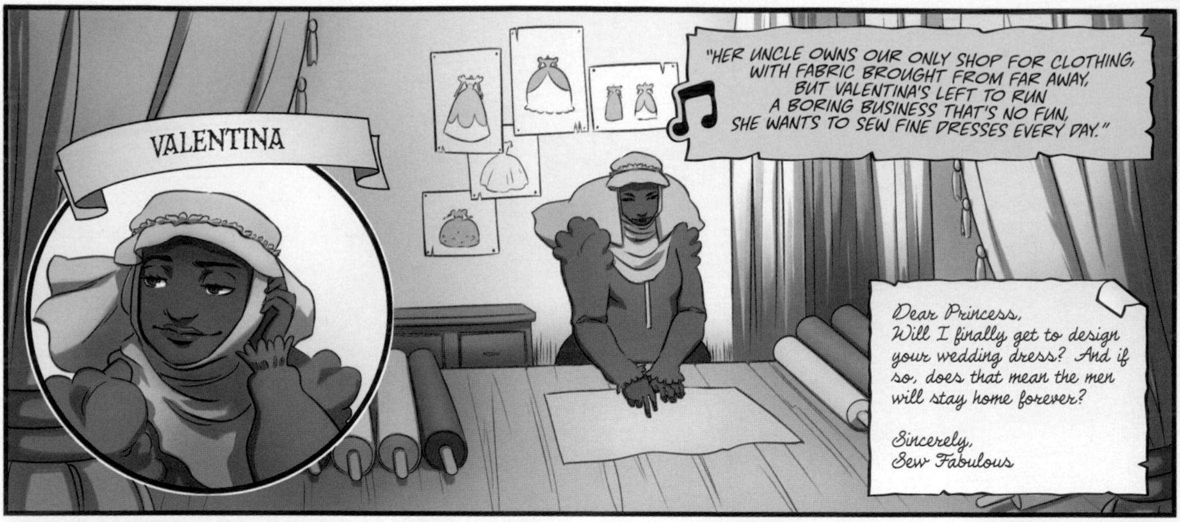
VALENTINA
"HER UNCLE OWNS OUR ONLY SHOP FOR CLOTHING, WITH FABRIC BROUGHT FROM FAR AWAY, BUT VALENTINA'S LEFT TO RUN A BORING BUSINESS THAT'S NO FUN, SHE WANTS TO SEW FINE DRESSES EVERY DAY."
Dear Princess, Will I finally get to design your wedding dress? And if so, does that mean the men will stay home forever? Sincerely, Sew Fabulous

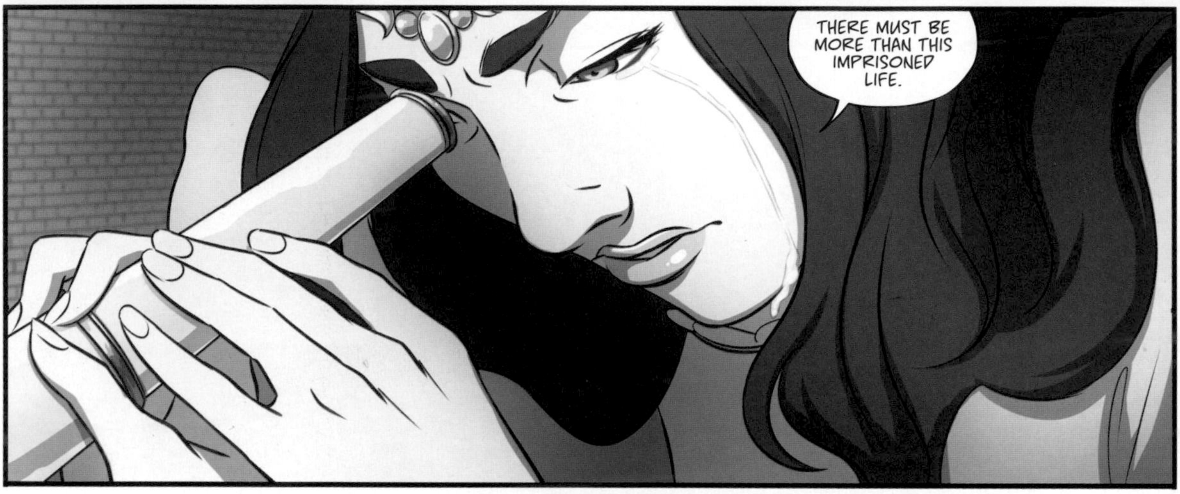
THERE MUST BE MORE THAN THIS IMPRISONED LIFE.

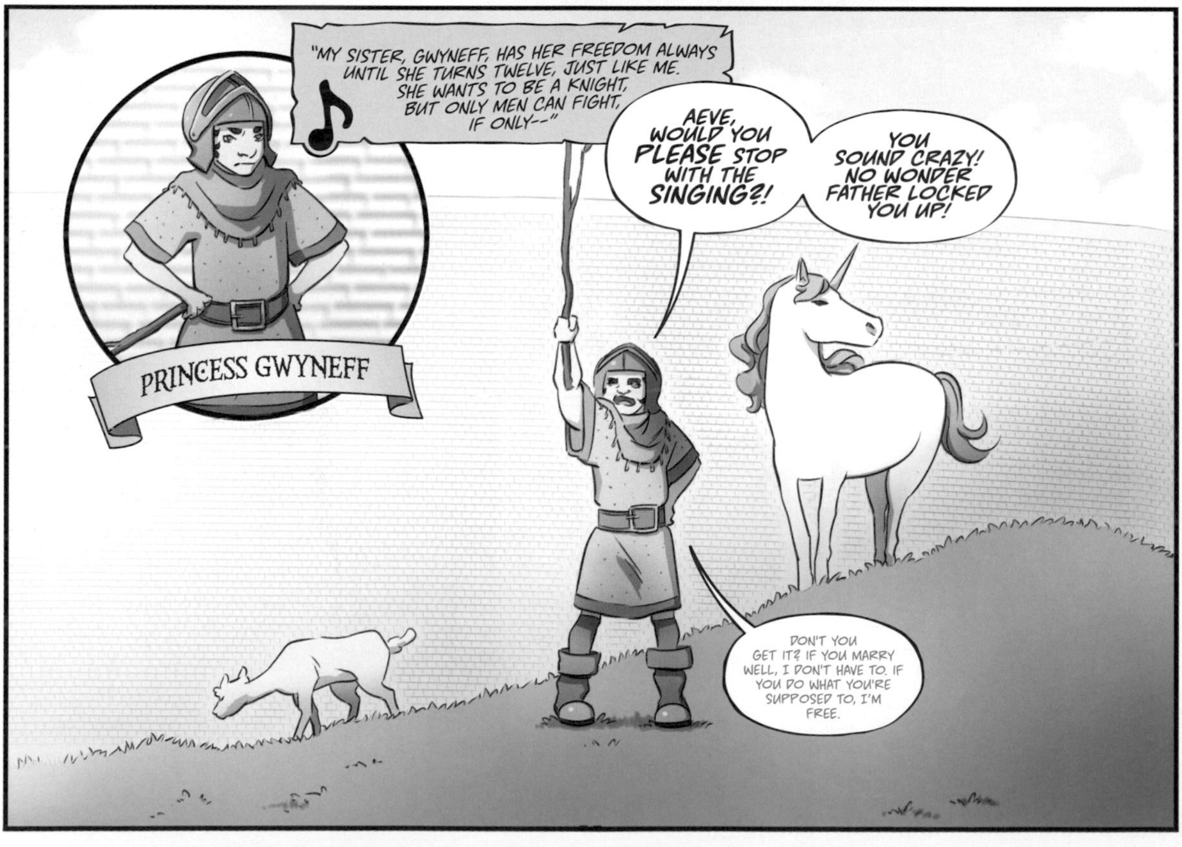
"MY SISTER, GWYNEFF, HAS HER FREEDOM ALWAYS UNTIL SHE TURNS TWELVE, JUST LIKE ME. SHE WANTS TO BE A KNIGHT, BUT ONLY MEN CAN FIGHT, IF ONLY--"
PRINCESS GWYNEFF
AEVE, WOULD YOU PLEASE STOP WITH THE SINGING?!
YOU SOUND CRAZY! NO WONDER FATHER LOCKED YOU UP!
DON'T YOU GET IT? IF YOU MARRY WELL, I DON'T HAVE TO. IF YOU DO WHAT YOU'RE SUPPOSED TO, I'M FREE.

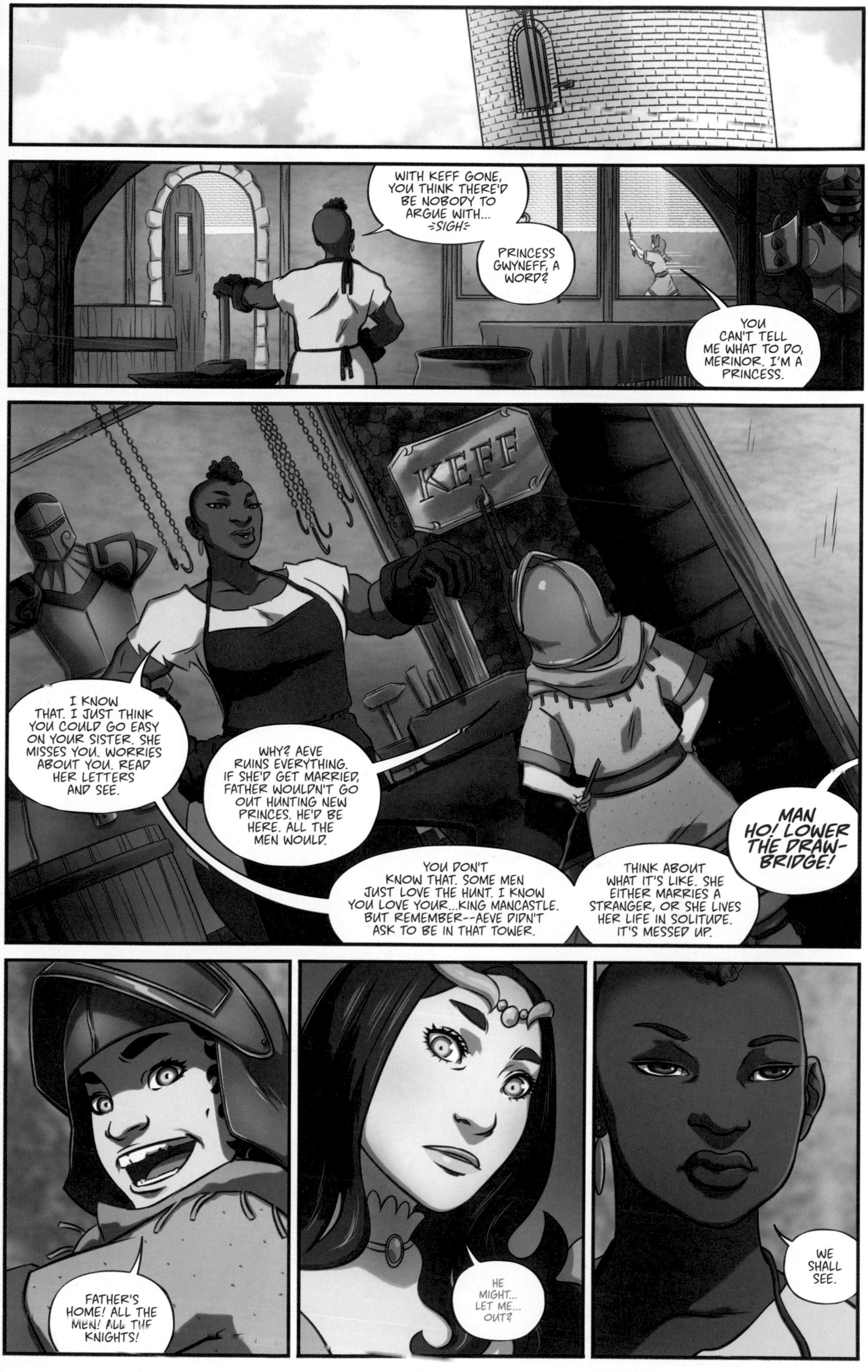
WITH KEFF GONE, YOU THINK THERE'D BE NOBODY TO ARGUE WITH... =SIGH=
PRINCESS GWYNEFF, A WORD?
YOU CAN'T TELL ME WHAT TO DO, MERINOR. I'M A PRINCESS.
KEFF
I KNOW THAT. I JUST THINK YOU COULD GO EASY ON YOUR SISTER. SHE MISSES YOU. WORRIES ABOUT YOU. READ HER LETTERS AND SEE.
WHY? AEVE RUINS EVERYTHING. IF SHE'D GET MARRIED, FATHER WOULDN'T GO OUT HUNTING NEW PRINCES. HE'D BE HERE. ALL THE MEN WOULD.
YOU DON'T KNOW THAT. SOME MEN JUST LOVE THE HUNT. I KNOW YOU LOVE YOUR...KING MANCASTLE. BUT REMEMBER--AEVE DIDN'T ASK TO BE IN THAT TOWER.
THINK ABOUT WHAT IT'S LIKE. SHE EITHER MARRIES A STRANGER, OR SHE LIVES HER LIFE IN SOLITUDE. IT'S MESSED UP.
MAN HO! LOWER THE DRAW-BRIDGE!
FATHER'S HOME! ALL THE MEN! ALL THE KNIGHTS!
HE MIGHT... LET ME... OUT?
WE SHALL SEE.

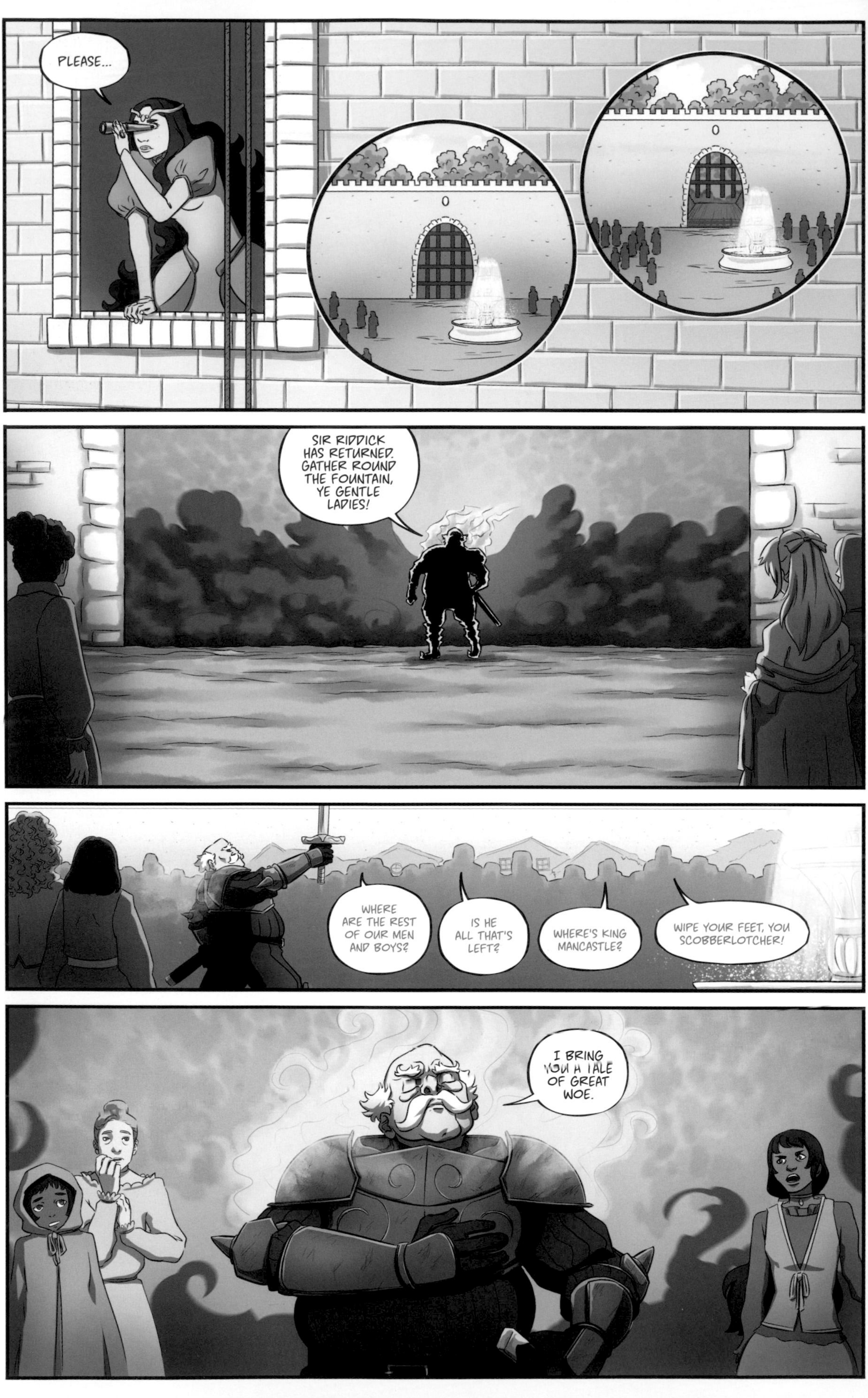
PLEASE...
SIR RIDDICK HAS RETURNED. GATHER ROUND THE FOUNTAIN, YE GENTLE LADIES!
WHERE ARE THE REST OF OUR MEN AND BOYS?
IS HE ALL THAT'S LEFT?
WHERE'S KING MANCASTLE?
WIPE YOUR FEET, YOU SCOBBERLOTCHER!
I BRING YOU A TALE OF GREAT WOE.

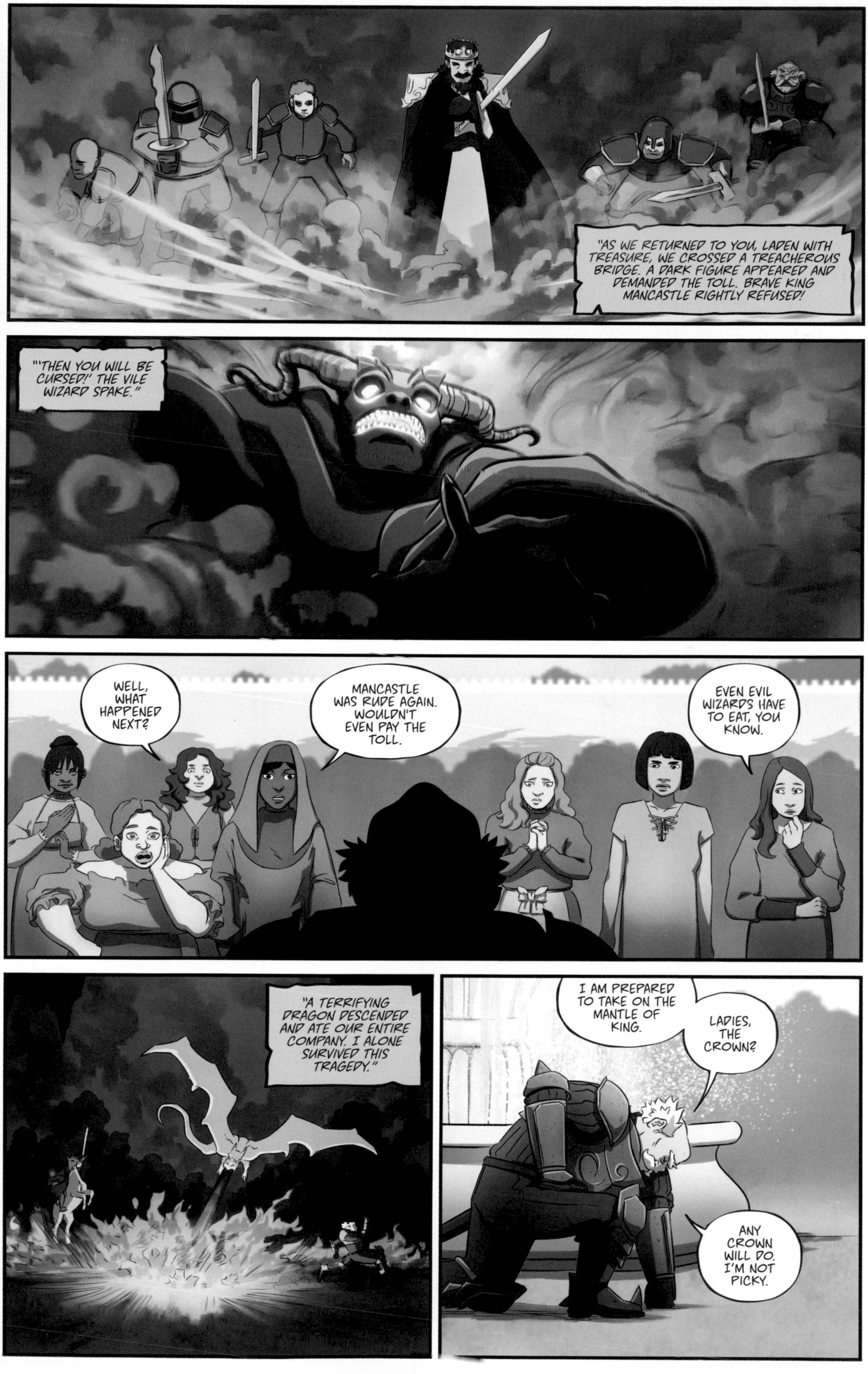
"AS WE RETURNED TO YOU, LADEN WITH TREASURE, WE CROSSED A TREACHEROUS BRIDGE. A DARK FIGURE APPEARED AND DEMANDED THE TOLL. BRAVE KING MANCASTLE RIGHTLY REFUSED!
"'THEN YOU WILL BE CURSED!' THE VILE WIZARD SPAKE."
WELL, WHAT HAPPENED NEXT?
MANCASTLE WAS RUDE AGAIN. WOULDN'T EVEN PAY THE TOLL.
EVEN EVIL WIZARDS HAVE TO EAT, YOU KNOW.
"A TERRIFYING DRAGON DESCENDED AND ATE OUR ENTIRE COMPANY. I ALONE SURVIVED THIS TRAGEDY."
I AM PREPARED TO TAKE ON THE MANTLE OF KING.
LADIES, THE CROWN?
ANY CROWN WILL DO. I'M NOT PICKY.

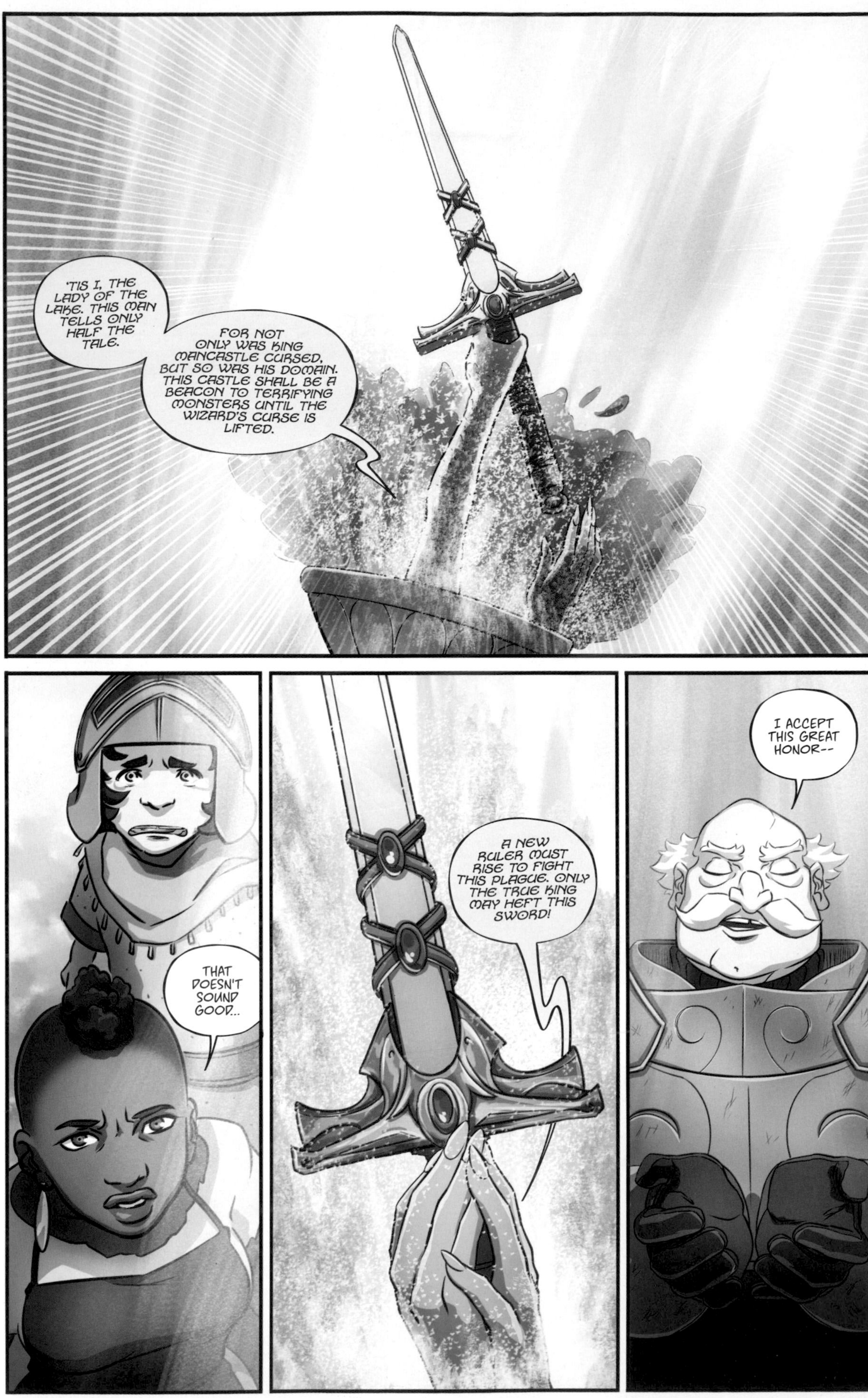
'TIS I, THE LADY OF THE LAKE. THIS MAN TELLS ONLY HALF THE TALE.
FOR NOT ONLY WAS KING MANCASTLE CURSED, BUT SO WAS HIS DOMAIN. THIS CASTLE SHALL BE A BEACON TO TERRIFYING MONSTERS UNTIL THE WIZARD'S CURSE IS LIFTED.
THAT DOESN'T SOUND GOOD...
A NEW RULER MUST RISE TO FIGHT THIS PLAGUE. ONLY THE TRUE KING MAY HEFT THIS SWORD!
I ACCEPT THIS GREAT HONOR--

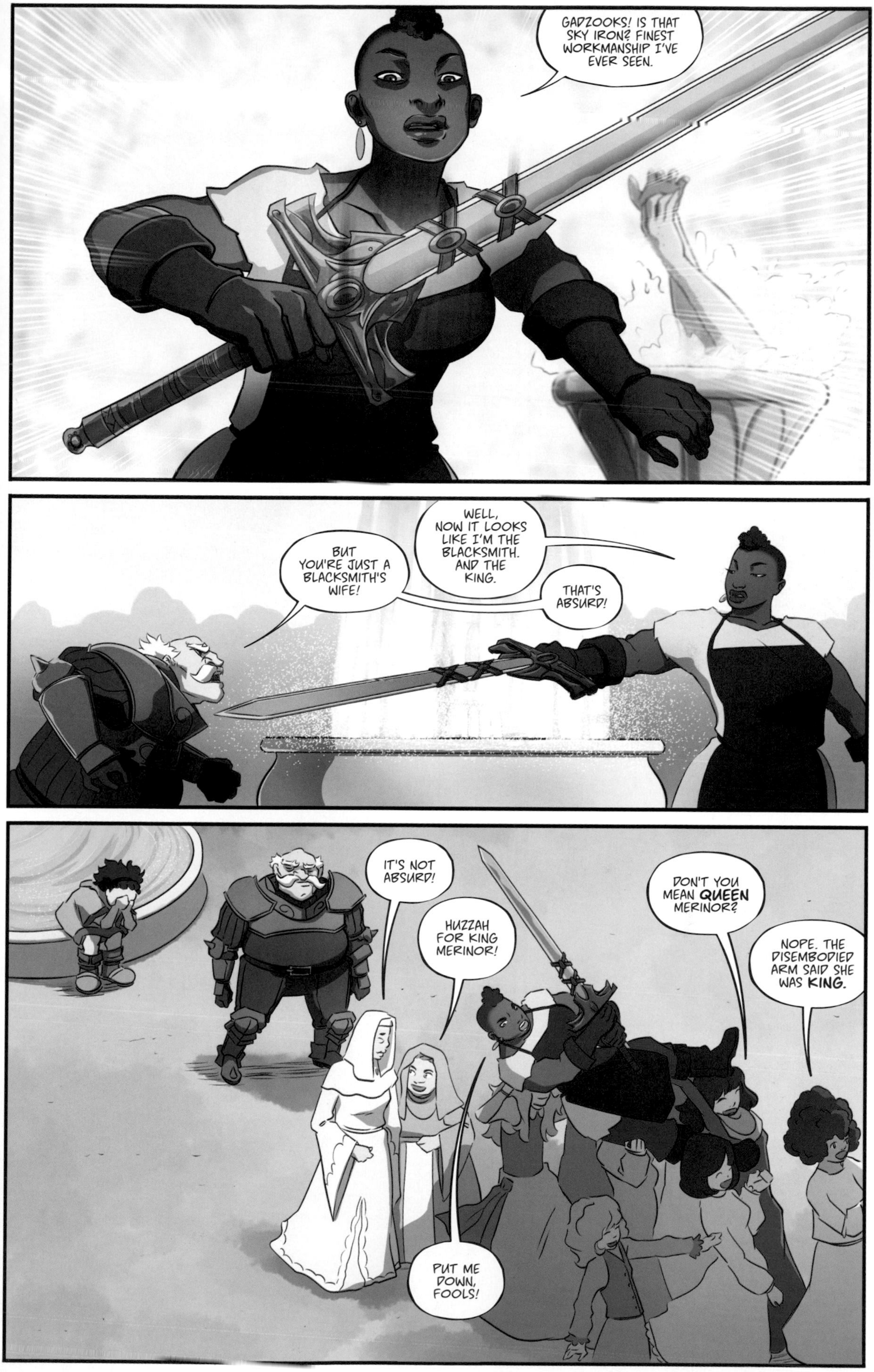
GADZOOKS! IS THAT SKY IRON? FINEST WORKMANSHIP I'VE EVER SEEN.
WELL, NOW IT LOOKS LIKE I'M THE BLACKSMITH. AND THE KING.
BUT YOU'RE JUST A BLACKSMITH'S WIFE!
THAT'S ABSURD!
IT'S NOT ABSURD!
HUZZAH FOR KING MERINOR!
DON'T YOU MEAN QUEEN MERINOR?
NOPE. THE DISEMBODIED ARM SAID SHE WAS KING.
PUT ME DOWN, FOOLS!

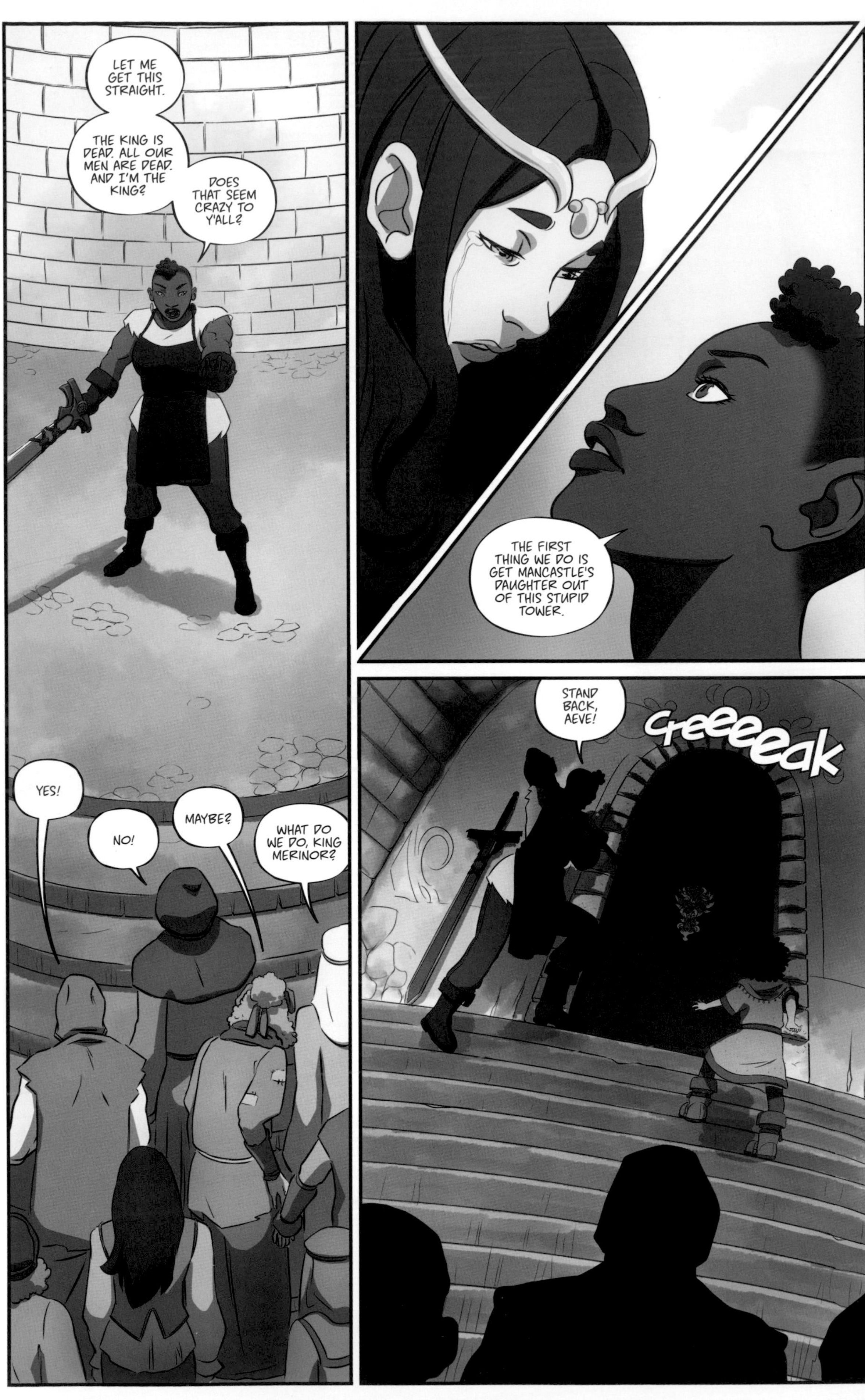
LET ME GET THIS STRAIGHT.
THE KING IS DEAD. ALL OUR MEN ARE DEAD. AND I'M THE KING?
DOES THAT SEEM CRAZY TO Y'ALL?
YES!
NO!
MAYBE?
WHAT DO WE DO, KING MERINOR?
THE FIRST THING WE DO IS GET MANCASTLE'S DAUGHTER OUT OF THIS STUPID TOWER.
STAND BACK, AEVE!
CREEEEAK

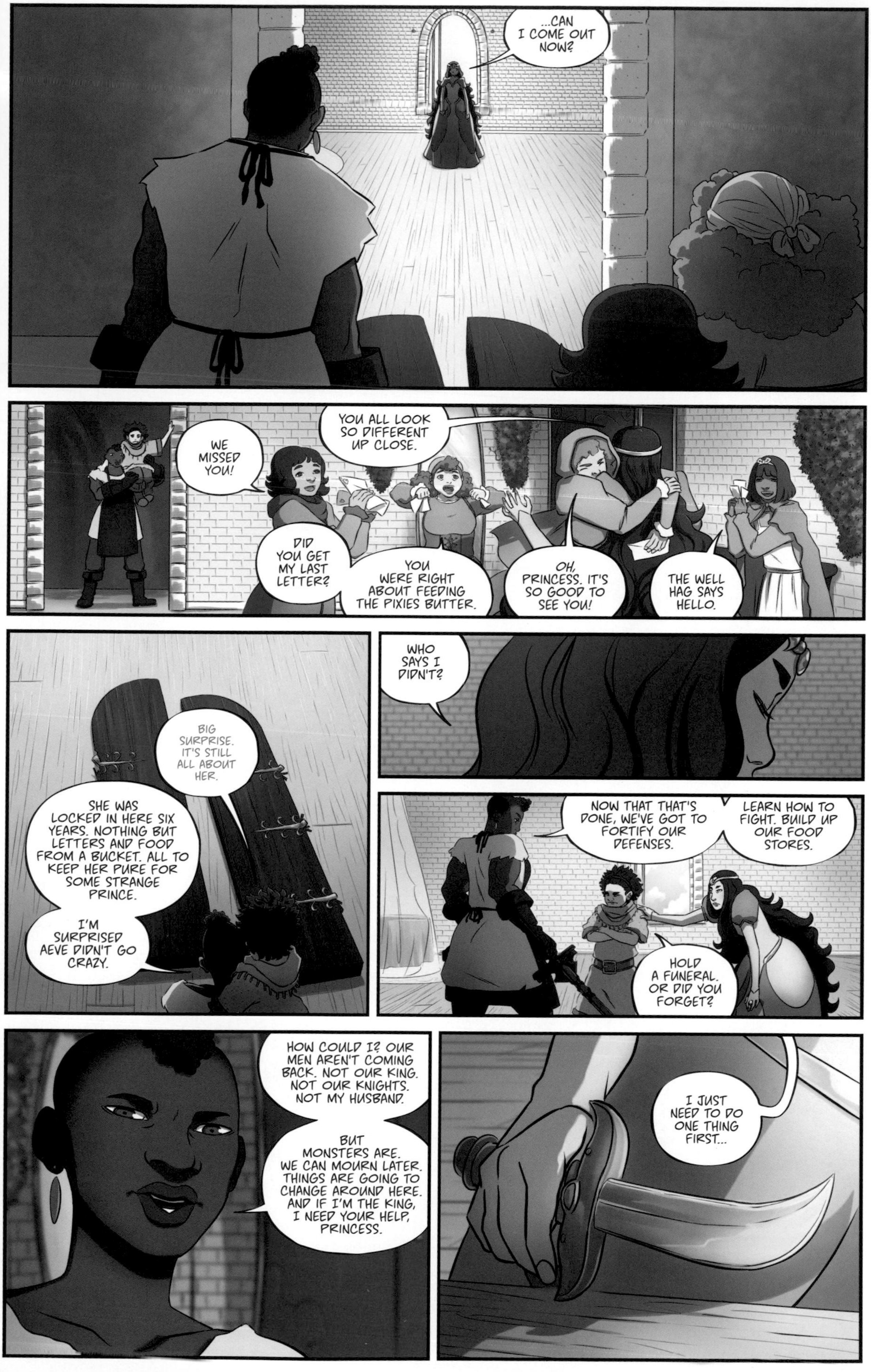
...CAN I COME OUT NOW?
WE MISSED YOU!
YOU ALL LOOK SO DIFFERENT UP CLOSE.
DID YOU GET MY LAST LETTER?
YOU WERE RIGHT ABOUT FEEDING THE PIXIES BUTTER.
OH, PRINCESS. IT'S SO GOOD TO SEE YOU!
THE WELL HAG SAYS HELLO.
BIG SURPRISE. IT'S STILL ALL ABOUT HER.
SHE WAS LOCKED IN HERE SIX YEARS. NOTHING BUT LETTERS AND FOOD FROM A BUCKET. ALL TO KEEP HER PURE FOR SOME STRANGE PRINCE.
I'M SURPRISED AEVE DIDN'T GO CRAZY.
WHO SAYS I DIDN'T?
NOW THAT THAT'S DONE, WE'VE GOT TO FORTIFY OUR DEFENSES.
LEARN HOW TO FIGHT. BUILD UP OUR FOOD STORES.
HOLD A FUNERAL. OR DID YOU FORGET?
HOW COULD I? OUR MEN AREN'T COMING BACK. NOT OUR KING. NOT OUR KNIGHTS. NOT MY HUSBAND.
BUT MONSTERS ARE. WE CAN MOURN LATER. THINGS ARE GOING TO CHANGE AROUND HERE. AND IF I'M THE KING, I NEED YOUR HELP, PRINCESS.
I JUST NEED TO DO ONE THING FIRST...

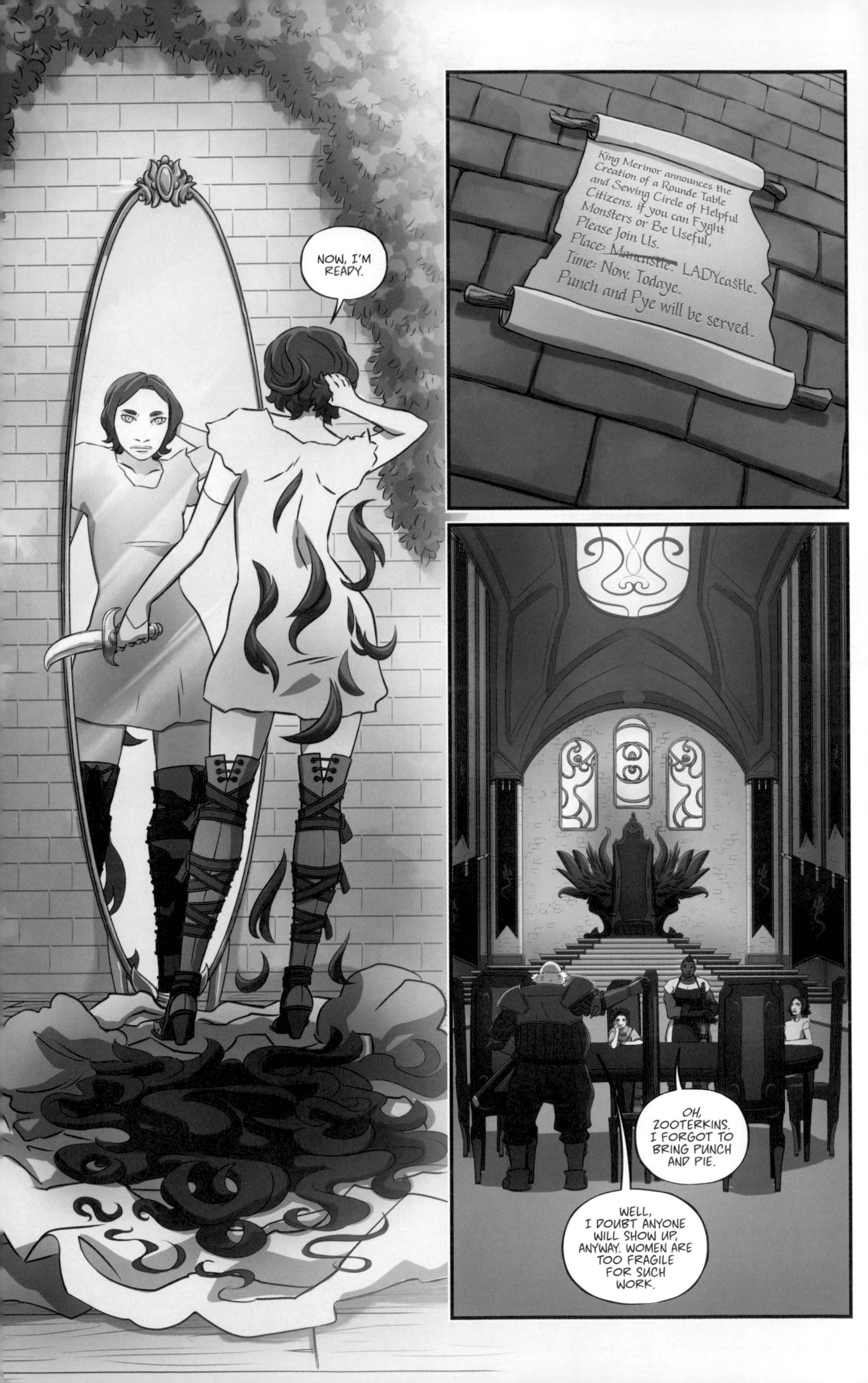
NOW, I'M READY.
King Merinor announces the Creation of a Rounde Table and Sewing Circle of Helpful Citizens. if you can Fyght Monsters or Be Useful, Please Join Us.
Place: Mancastle. LADYcastle.
Time: Now. Todaye.
Punch and Pye will be served.
OH, ZOOTERKINS. I FORGOT TO BRING PUNCH AND PIE.
WELL, I DOUBT ANYONE WILL SHOW UP, ANYWAY. WOMEN ARE TOO FRAGILE FOR SUCH WORK.

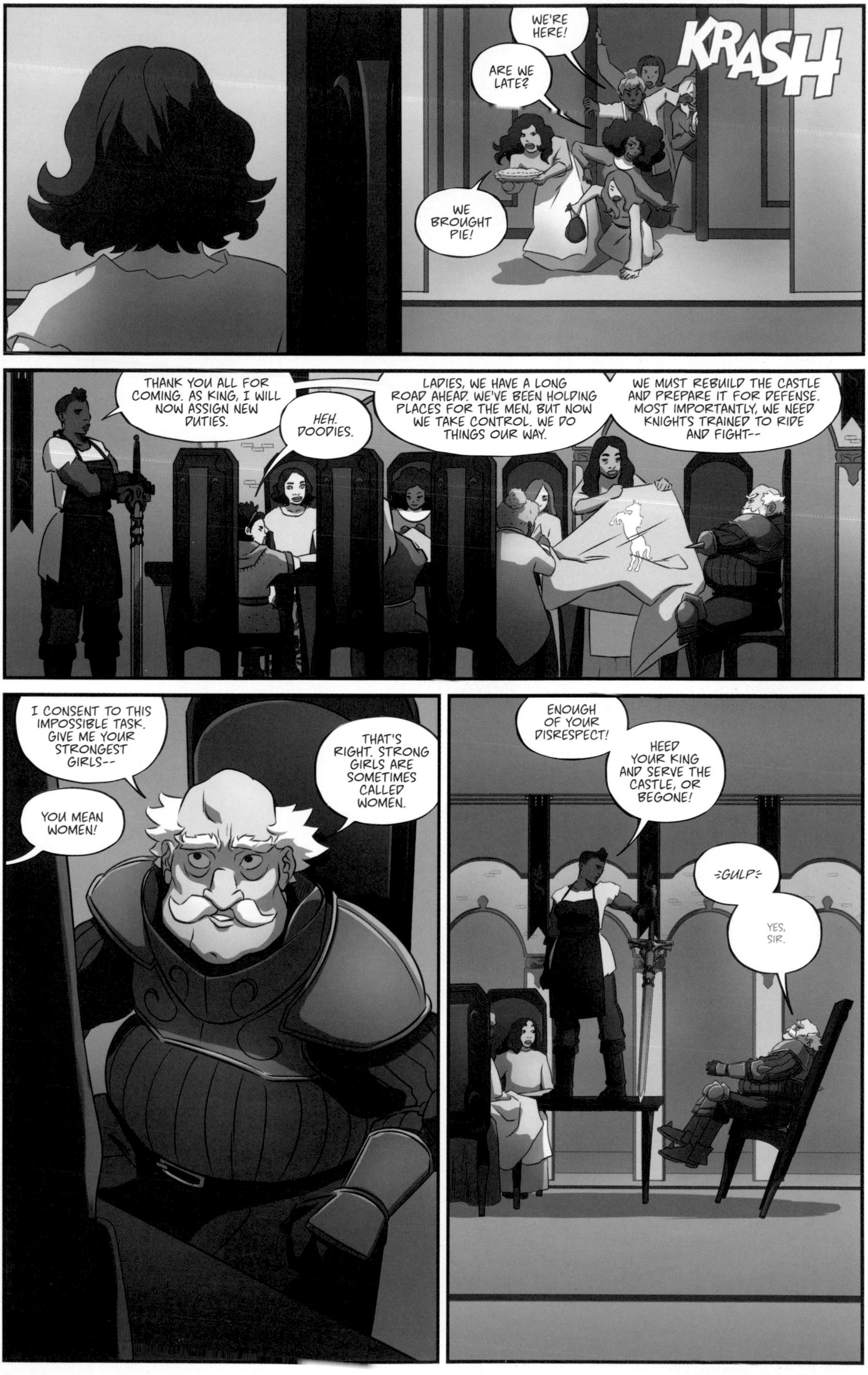
KRASH
WE'RE HERE!
ARE WE LATE?
WE BROUGHT PIE!
THANK YOU ALL FOR COMING. AS KING, I WILL NOW ASSIGN NEW DUTIES.
HEH. DOODIES.
LADIES, WE HAVE A LONG ROAD AHEAD. WE'VE BEEN HOLDING PLACES FOR THE MEN, BUT NOW WE TAKE CONTROL. WE DO THINGS OUR WAY.
WE MUST REBUILD THE CASTLE AND PREPARE IT FOR DEFENSE. MOST IMPORTANTLY, WE NEED KNIGHTS TRAINED TO RIDE AND FIGHT--
I CONSENT TO THIS IMPOSSIBLE TASK. GIVE ME YOUR STRONGEST GIRLS--
YOU MEAN WOMEN!
THAT'S RIGHT. STRONG GIRLS ARE SOMETIMES CALLED WOMEN.
ENOUGH OF YOUR DISRESPECT!
HEED YOUR KING AND SERVE THE CASTLE, OR BEGONE!
GULP
YES, SIR.

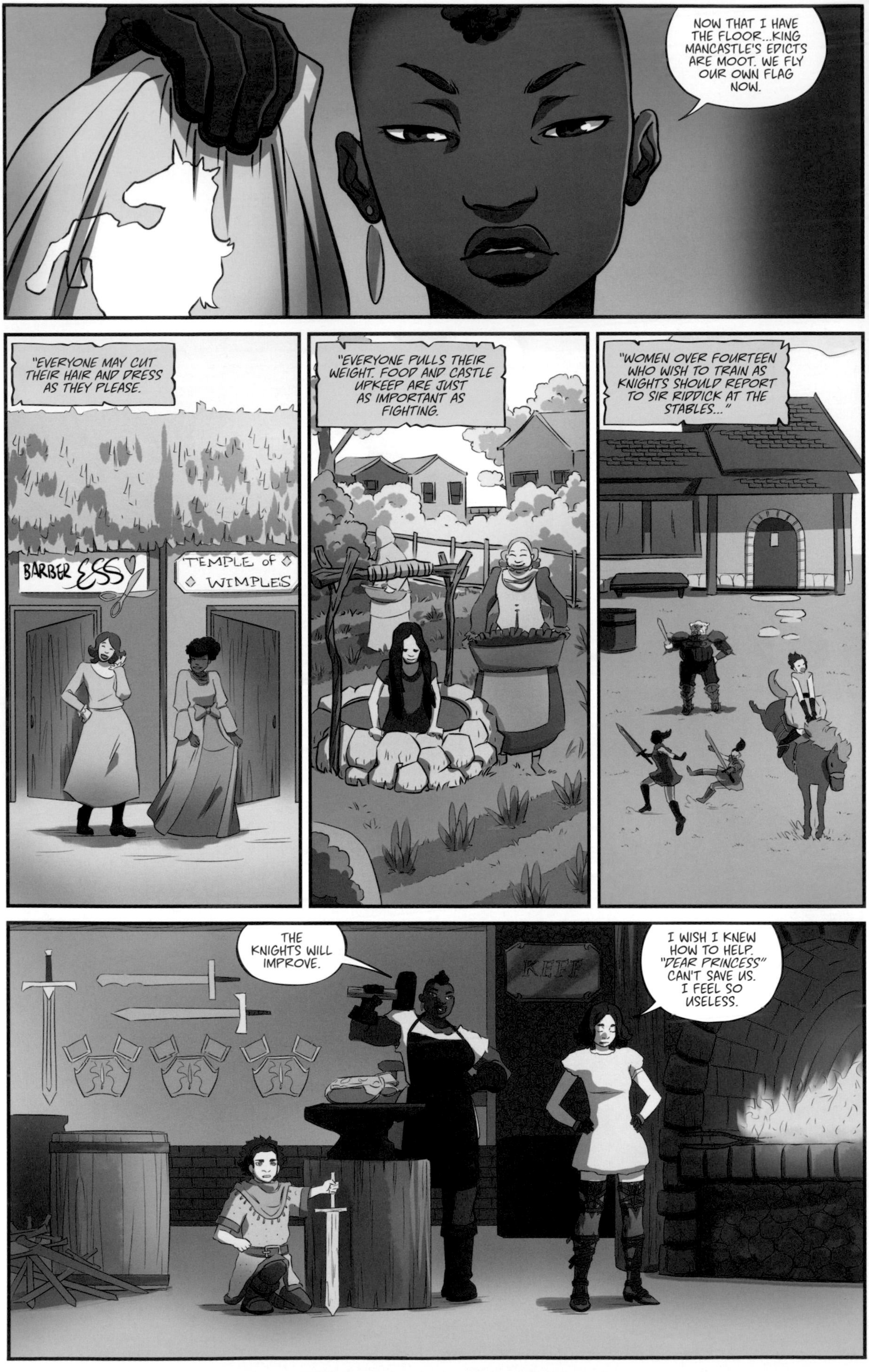
NOW THAT I HAVE THE FLOOR...KING MANCASTLE'S EDICTS ARE MOOT. WE FLY OUR OWN FLAG NOW.
"EVERYONE MAY CUT THEIR HAIR AND DRESS AS THEY PLEASE.
BARBER ESS
TEMPLE of WIMPLES
"EVERYONE PULLS THEIR WEIGHT. FOOD AND CASTLE UPKEEP ARE JUST AS IMPORTANT AS FIGHTING.
"WOMEN OVER FOURTEEN WHO WISH TO TRAIN AS KNIGHTS SHOULD REPORT TO SIR RIDDICK AT THE STABLES..."
THE KNIGHTS WILL IMPROVE.
KEFF
I WISH I KNEW HOW TO HELP. "DEAR PRINCESS" CAN'T SAVE US. I FEEL SO USELESS.

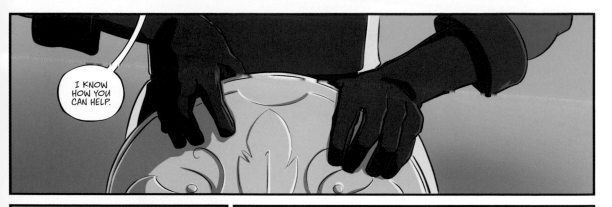

I KNOW HOW YOU CAN HELP.

LISTEN UP, ME --LADIES! CHIVALROUS CONDUCT MEANS BRAVERY, COURTESY, HONOR, AND GALLANTRY TOWARD...ER... YOURSELVES.

YOU MUST BE STRONG!

I AM! YOU TRY HAULING A BUCKET FULL OF BOOKS UP A TOWER EVERY DAY.

YOU MUST LEARN HOW TO FIGHT!

DOES VERBAL SPARRING WITH MY SISTER COUNT?

THE TRICK TO RIDING ASTRIDE? PUT ALL YOUR WEIGHT IN YOUR ARSE.

I DUB THEE, SIR AEVE. GREATEST AND BRAVEST OF KNIGHTS. THE KING'S CHAMPION!

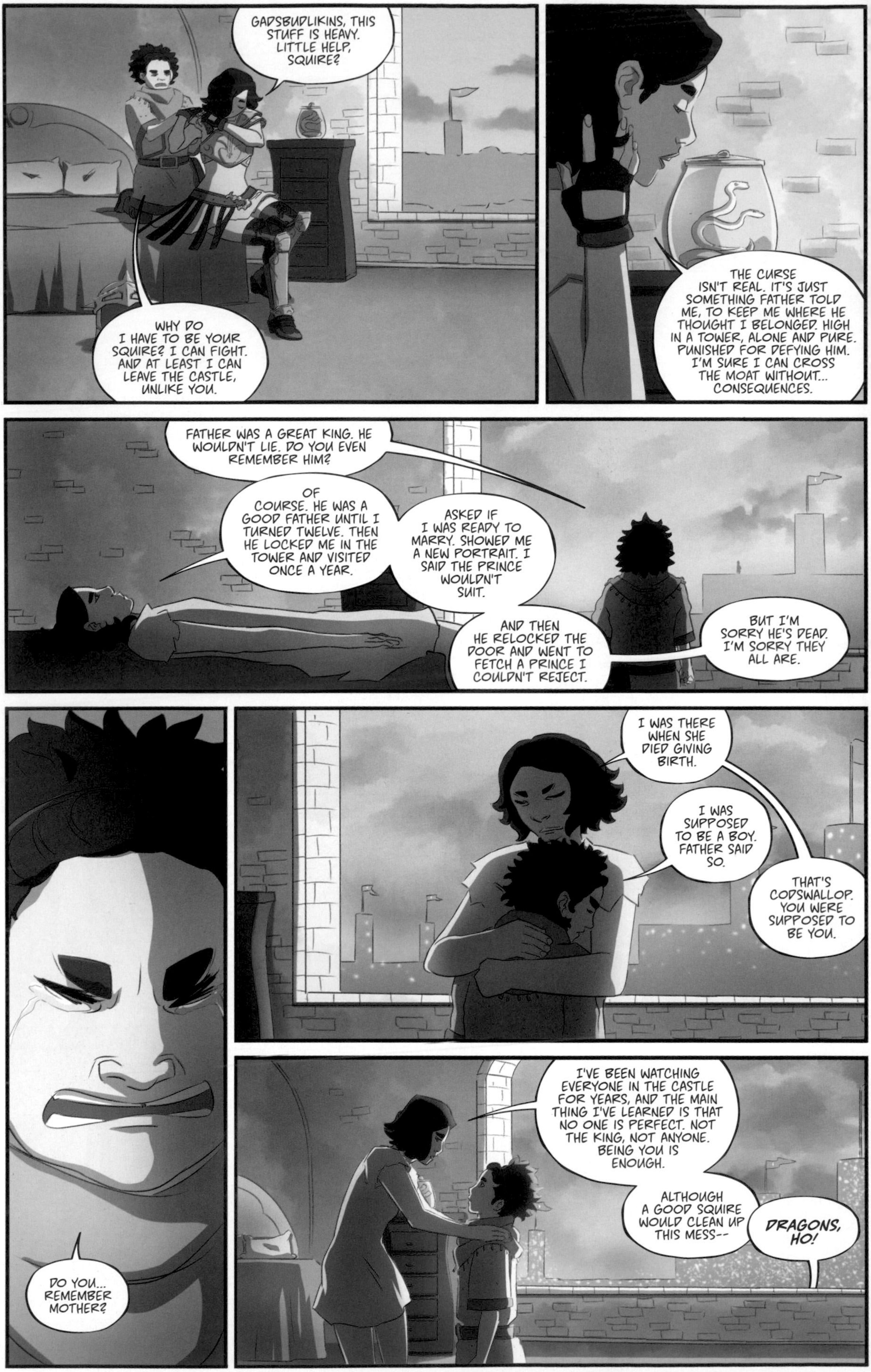
GADSBUDLIKINS, THIS STUFF IS HEAVY. LITTLE HELP, SQUIRE?
WHY DO I HAVE TO BE YOUR SQUIRE? I CAN FIGHT. AND AT LEAST I CAN LEAVE THE CASTLE, UNLIKE YOU.
THE CURSE ISN'T REAL. IT'S JUST SOMETHING FATHER TOLD ME, TO KEEP ME WHERE HE THOUGHT I BELONGED. HIGH IN A TOWER, ALONE AND PURE. PUNISHED FOR DEFYING HIM. I'M SURE I CAN CROSS THE MOAT WITHOUT... CONSEQUENCES.
FATHER WAS A GREAT KING. HE WOULDN'T LIE. DO YOU EVEN REMEMBER HIM?
OF COURSE. HE WAS A GOOD FATHER UNTIL I TURNED TWELVE. THEN HE LOCKED ME IN THE TOWER AND VISITED ONCE A YEAR.
ASKED IF I WAS READY TO MARRY. SHOWED ME A NEW PORTRAIT. I SAID THE PRINCE WOULDN'T SUIT.
AND THEN HE RELOCKED THE DOOR AND WENT TO FETCH A PRINCE I COULDN'T REJECT.
BUT I'M SORRY HE'S DEAD. I'M SORRY THEY ALL ARE.
DO YOU... REMEMBER MOTHER?
I WAS THERE WHEN SHE DIED GIVING BIRTH.
I WAS SUPPOSED TO BE A BOY. FATHER SAID SO.
THAT'S CODSWALLOP. YOU WERE SUPPOSED TO BE YOU.
I'VE BEEN WATCHING EVERYONE IN THE CASTLE FOR YEARS, AND THE MAIN THING I'VE LEARNED IS THAT NO ONE IS PERFECT. NOT THE KING, NOT ANYONE. BEING YOU IS ENOUGH.
ALTHOUGH A GOOD SQUIRE WOULD CLEAN UP THIS MESS--
DRAGONS, HO!

TIME TO KNIGHT UP.

SOME OF YOU LADIES ARE WONDERING WHETHER OR NOT YOU'LL CHICKEN OUT UNDER FIRE. DON'T WORRY ABOUT IT. I CAN ASSURE YOU THAT YOU'LL ALL DO YOUR DUTY.

DRAGON FIGHTING IS A BLOODY BUSINESS, A KILLING BUSINESS. THE DRAGONS ARE THE ENEMY.

I DON'T ACTUALLY THINK IT'S DRAGONS.

FINE. THE REST OF THE SPEECH IS THE SAME. YOU KNOW HOW I FEEL. KILL WHATEVER IT IS. JUST **KILL EVERYTHING.** THAT'S ALL.

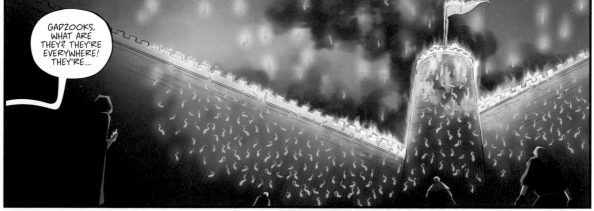

GADZOOKS, WHAT ARE THEY? THEY'RE EVERYWHERE! THEY'RE...

IT'S... *SALAMANDERS!*

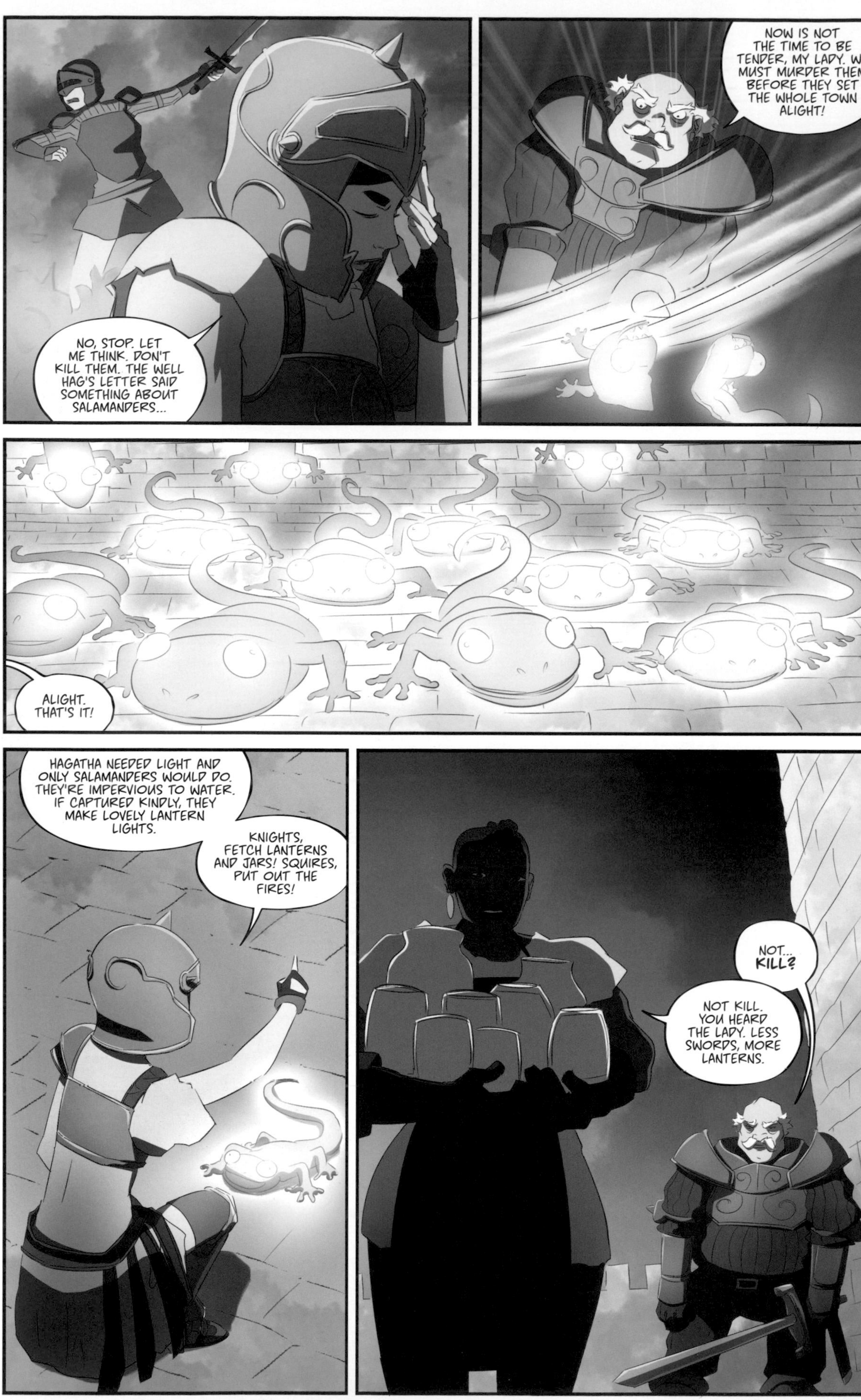
NO, STOP. LET ME THINK. DON'T KILL THEM. THE WELL HAG'S LETTER SAID SOMETHING ABOUT SALAMANDERS...
NOW IS NOT THE TIME TO BE TENDER, MY LADY. WE MUST MURDER THEM BEFORE THEY SET THE WHOLE TOWN ALIGHT!
ALIGHT. THAT'S IT!
HAGATHA NEEDED LIGHT AND ONLY SALAMANDERS WOULD DO. THEY'RE IMPERVIOUS TO WATER. IF CAPTURED KINDLY, THEY MAKE LOVELY LANTERN LIGHTS.
KNIGHTS, FETCH LANTERNS AND JARS! SQUIRES, PUT OUT THE FIRES!
NOT... **KILL?**
NOT KILL. YOU HEARD THE LADY. LESS SWORDS, MORE LANTERNS.

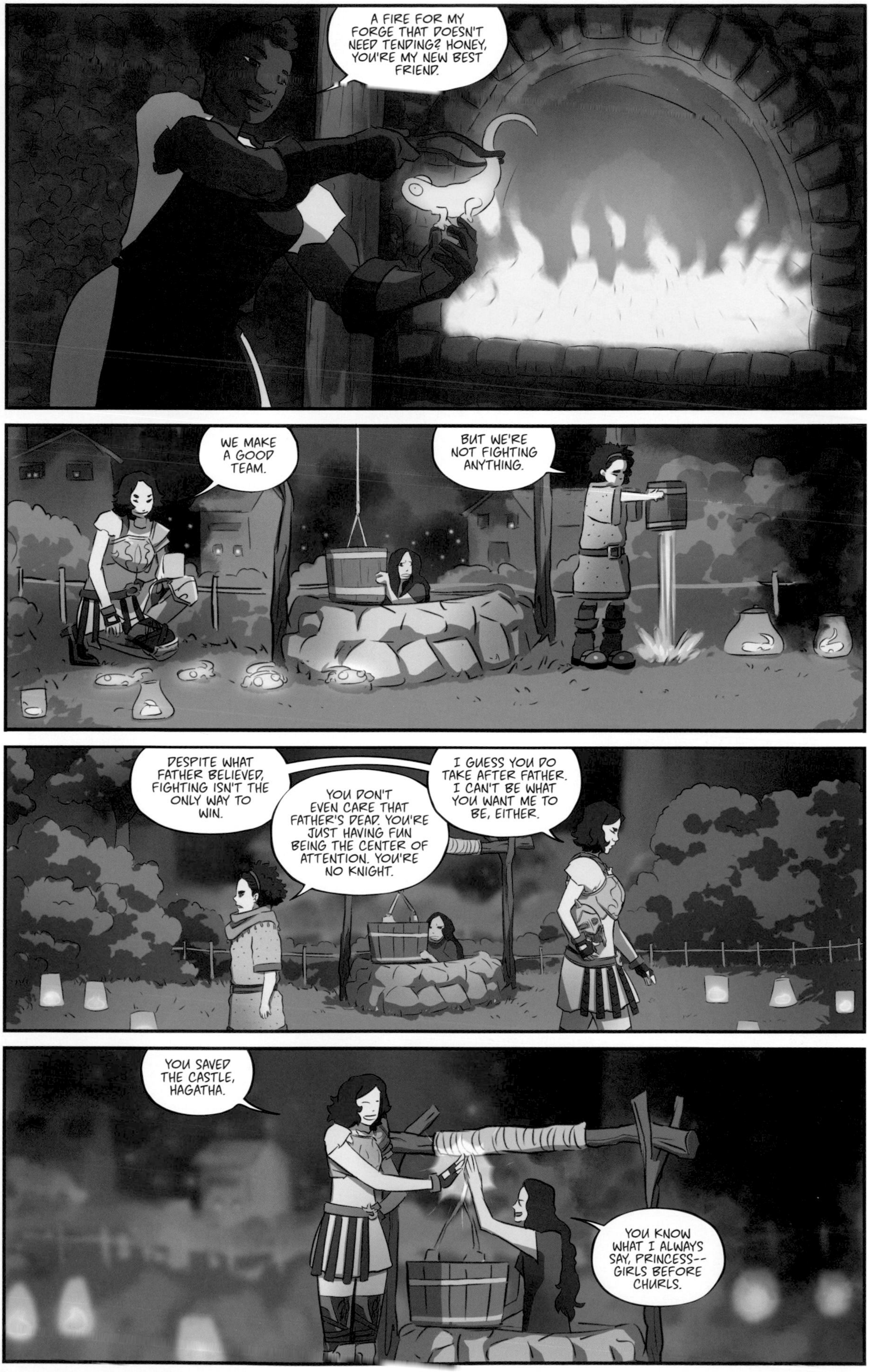
A FIRE FOR MY FORGE THAT DOESN'T NEED TENDING? HONEY, YOU'RE MY NEW BEST FRIEND.
WE MAKE A GOOD TEAM.
BUT WE'RE NOT FIGHTING ANYTHING.
DESPITE WHAT FATHER BELIEVED, FIGHTING ISN'T THE ONLY WAY TO WIN.
YOU DON'T EVEN CARE THAT FATHER'S DEAD. YOU'RE JUST HAVING FUN BEING THE CENTER OF ATTENTION. YOU'RE NO KNIGHT.
I GUESS YOU DO TAKE AFTER FATHER. I CAN'T BE WHAT YOU WANT ME TO BE, EITHER.
YOU SAVED THE CASTLE, HAGATHA.
YOU KNOW WHAT I ALWAYS SAY, PRINCESS-- GIRLS BEFORE CHURLS.

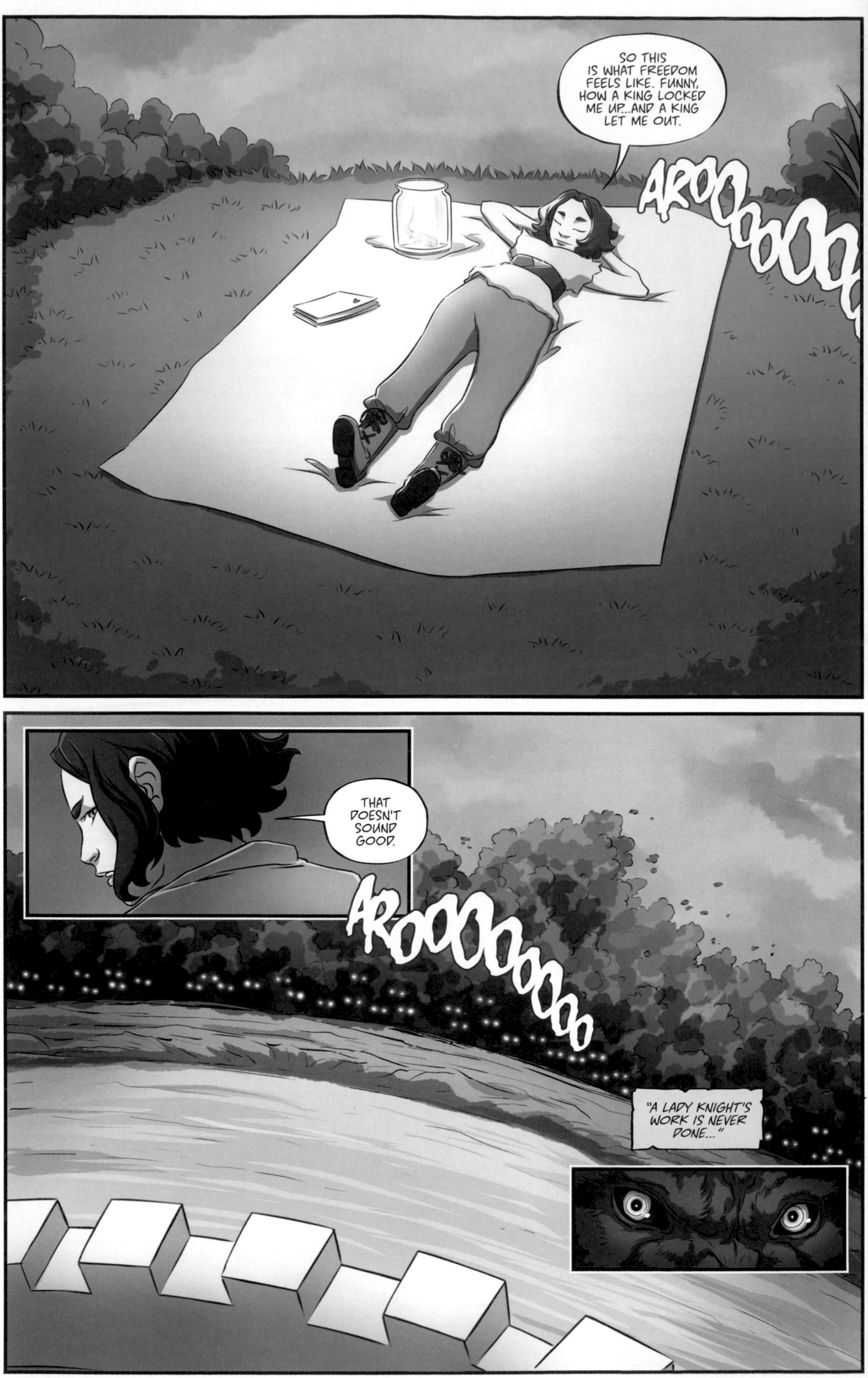
SO THIS IS WHAT FREEDOM FEELS LIKE. FUNNY, HOW A KING LOCKED ME UP...AND A KING LET ME OUT.
AROOOOOOOO
THAT DOESN'T SOUND GOOD.
AROOOOOOOOO
"A LADY KNIGHT'S WORK IS NEVER DONE..."

"LISTEN, *STRANGE WOMEN* LYIN' IN PONDS DISTRIBUTIN' **SWORDS** IS A *GREAT* BASIS FOR A SYSTEM OF **GOVERNMENT**."

CHAPTER TWO

THAT PESKY
WEREWOLF
PROBLEM

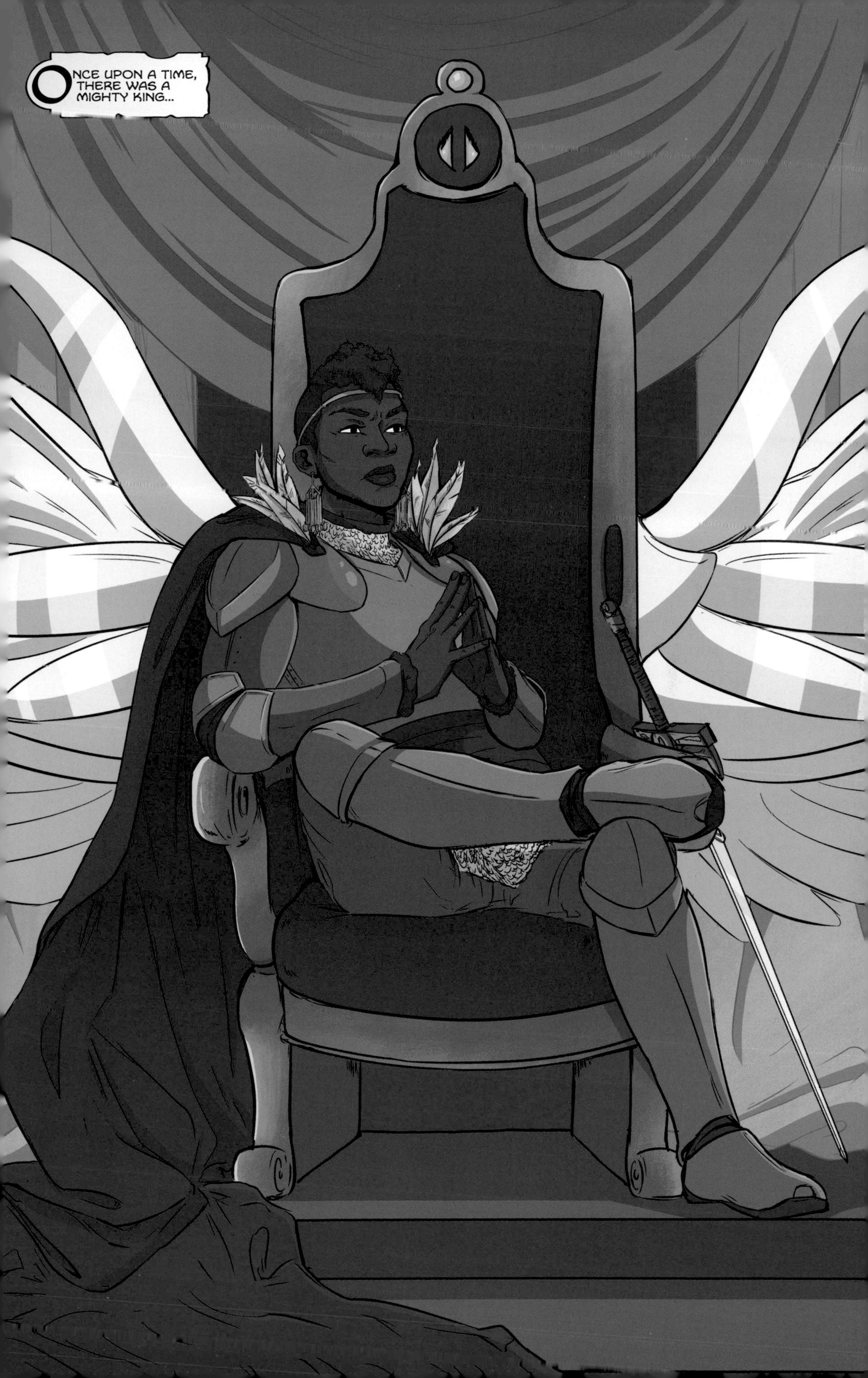
ONCE UPON A TIME, THERE WAS A MIGHTY KING...

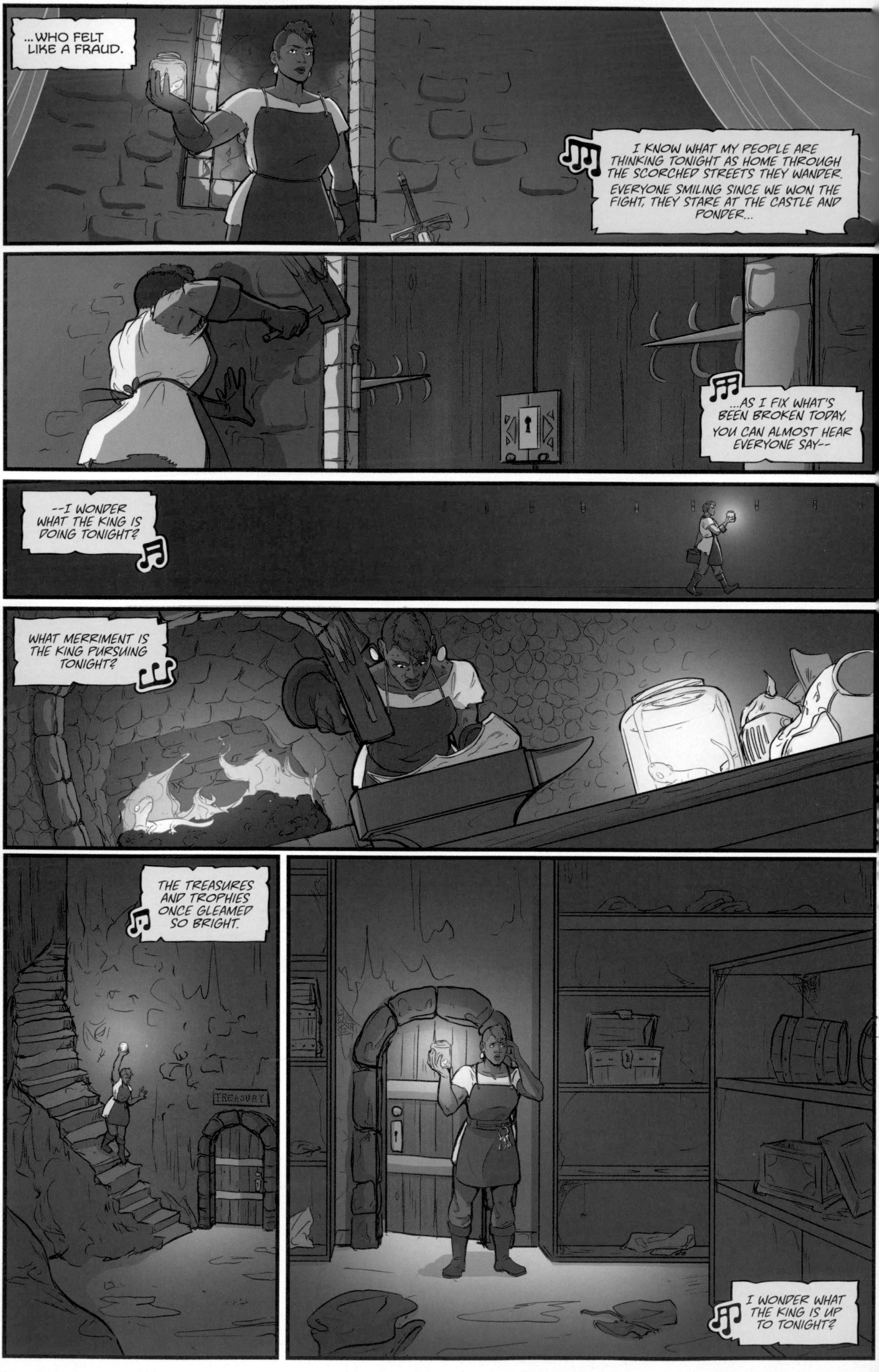
...WHO FELT LIKE A FRAUD.
I KNOW WHAT MY PEOPLE ARE THINKING TONIGHT AS HOME THROUGH THE SCORCHED STREETS THEY WANDER.
EVERYONE SMILING SINCE WE WON THE FIGHT, THEY STARE AT THE CASTLE AND PONDER...
...AS I FIX WHAT'S BEEN BROKEN TODAY,
YOU CAN ALMOST HEAR EVERYONE SAY--
--I WONDER WHAT THE KING IS DOING TONIGHT?
WHAT MERRIMENT IS THE KING PURSUING TONIGHT?
THE TREASURES AND TROPHIES ONCE GLEAMED SO BRIGHT.
TREASURY
I WONDER WHAT THE KING IS UP TO TONIGHT?

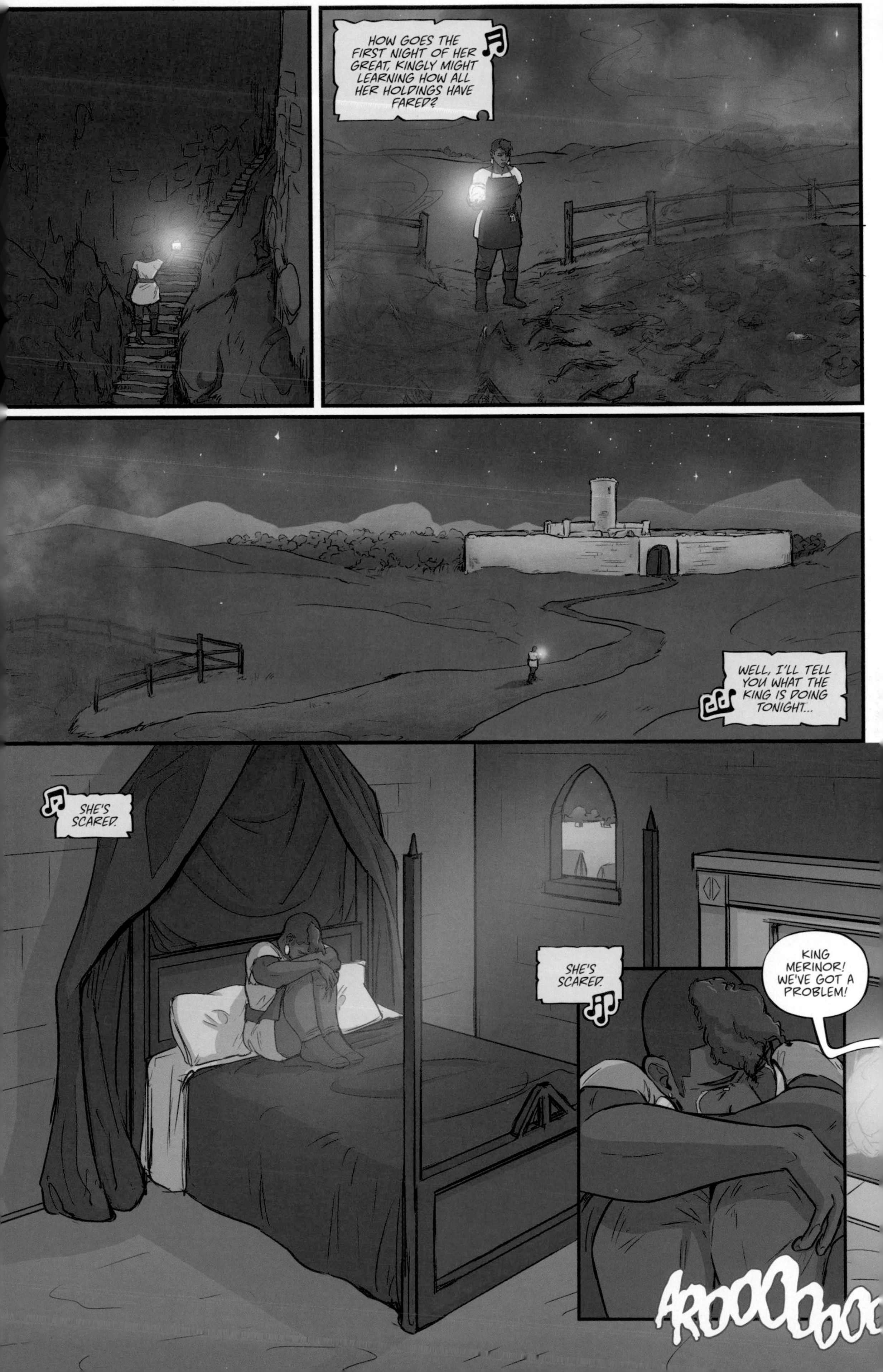

HOW GOES THE FIRST NIGHT OF HER GREAT, KINGLY MIGHT LEARNING HOW ALL HER HOLDINGS HAVE FARED?
WELL, I'LL TELL YOU WHAT THE KING IS DOING TONIGHT...
SHE'S SCARED.
SHE'S SCARED.
KING MERINOR! WE'VE GOT A PROBLEM!
AROOOOOOO

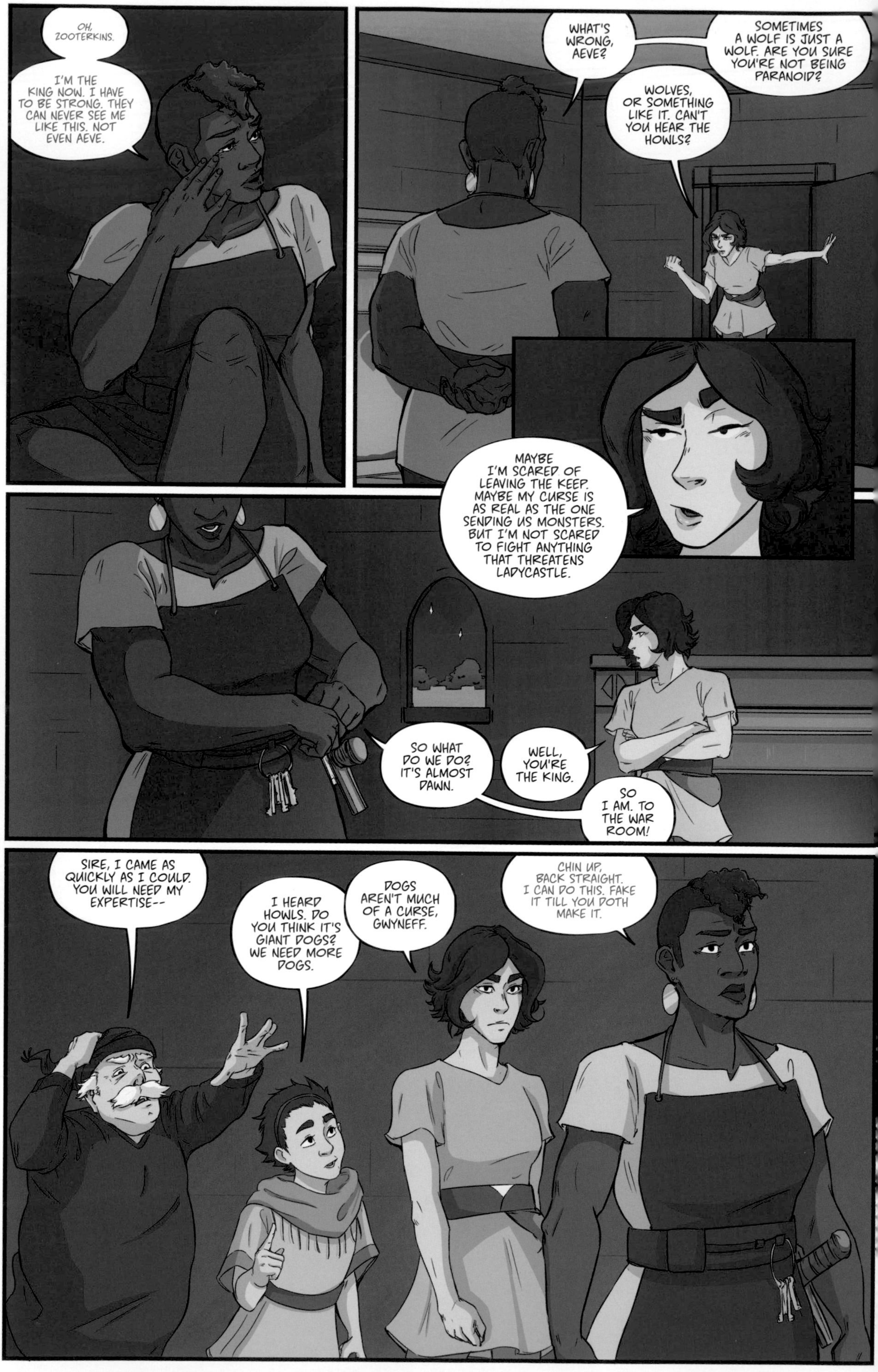
OH, ZOOTERKINS.
I'M THE KING NOW. I HAVE TO BE STRONG. THEY CAN NEVER SEE ME LIKE THIS. NOT EVEN AEVE.
WHAT'S WRONG, AEVE?
WOLVES, OR SOMETHING LIKE IT. CAN'T YOU HEAR THE HOWLS?
SOMETIMES A WOLF IS JUST A WOLF. ARE YOU SURE YOU'RE NOT BEING PARANOID?
MAYBE I'M SCARED OF LEAVING THE KEEP. MAYBE MY CURSE IS AS REAL AS THE ONE SENDING US MONSTERS. BUT I'M NOT SCARED TO FIGHT ANYTHING THAT THREATENS LADYCASTLE.
SO WHAT DO WE DO? IT'S ALMOST DAWN.
WELL, YOU'RE THE KING.
SO I AM. TO THE WAR ROOM!
SIRE, I CAME AS QUICKLY AS I COULD. YOU WILL NEED MY EXPERTISE--
I HEARD HOWLS. DO YOU THINK IT'S GIANT DOGS? WE NEED MORE DOGS.
DOGS AREN'T MUCH OF A CURSE, GWYNEFF.
CHIN UP, BACK STRAIGHT. I CAN DO THIS. FAKE IT TILL YOU DOTH MAKE IT.

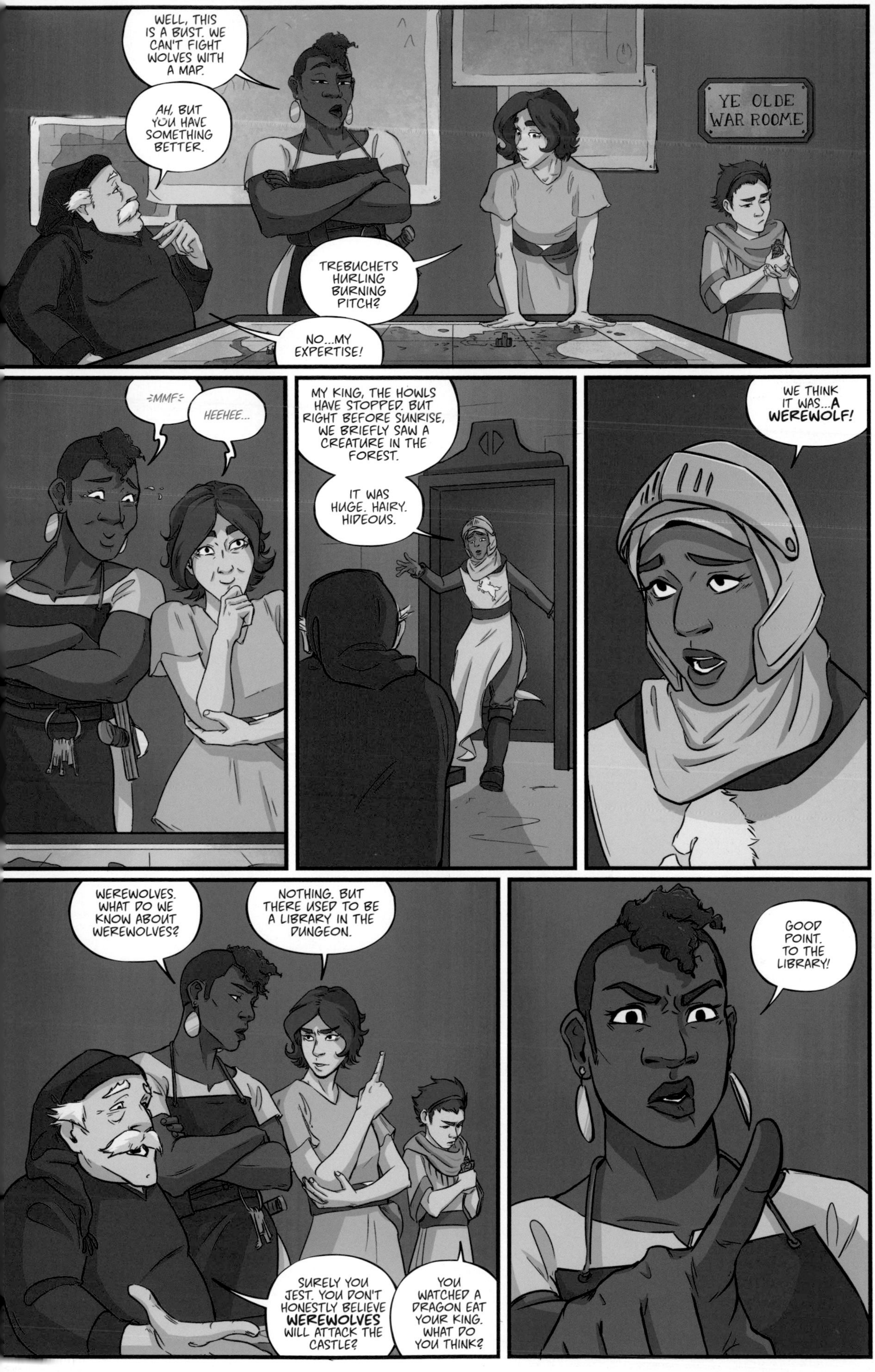

WELL, THIS IS A BUST. WE CAN'T FIGHT WOLVES WITH A MAP.
AH, BUT YOU HAVE SOMETHING BETTER.
YE OLDE WAR ROOME
TREBUCHETS HURLING BURNING PITCH?
NO...MY EXPERTISE!
MMF
HEEHEE...
MY KING, THE HOWLS HAVE STOPPED. BUT RIGHT BEFORE SUNRISE, WE BRIEFLY SAW A CREATURE IN THE FOREST.
IT WAS HUGE. HAIRY. HIDEOUS.
WE THINK IT WAS...A **WEREWOLF!**
WEREWOLVES. WHAT DO WE KNOW ABOUT WEREWOLVES?
NOTHING. BUT THERE USED TO BE A LIBRARY IN THE DUNGEON.
SURELY YOU JEST. YOU DON'T HONESTLY BELIEVE **WEREWOLVES** WILL ATTACK THE CASTLE?
YOU WATCHED A DRAGON EAT YOUR KING. WHAT DO YOU THINK?
GOOD POINT. TO THE LIBRARY!

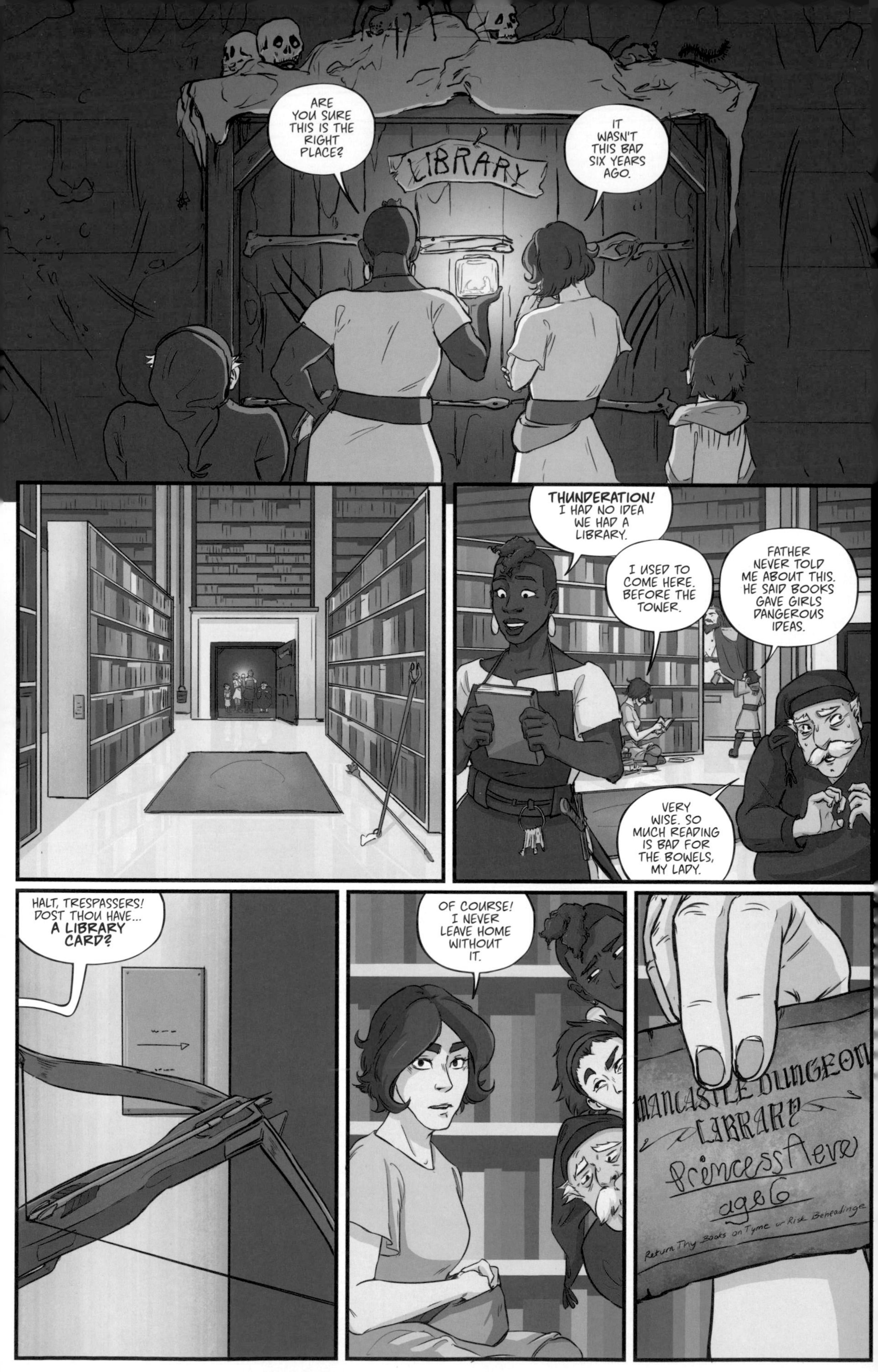

ARE YOU SURE THIS IS THE RIGHT PLACE?
LIBRARY
IT WASN'T THIS BAD SIX YEARS AGO.
THUNDERATION! I HAD NO IDEA WE HAD A LIBRARY.
I USED TO COME HERE. BEFORE THE TOWER.
FATHER NEVER TOLD ME ABOUT THIS. HE SAID BOOKS GAVE GIRLS DANGEROUS IDEAS.
VERY WISE. SO MUCH READING IS BAD FOR THE BOWELS, MY LADY.
HALT, TRESPASSERS! DOST THOU HAVE... A LIBRARY CARD?
OF COURSE! I NEVER LEAVE HOME WITHOUT IT.
MANCASTLE DUNGEON LIBRARY
Princess Aeve
age 6
Return Thy Books on Tyme or Risk Beheadinge

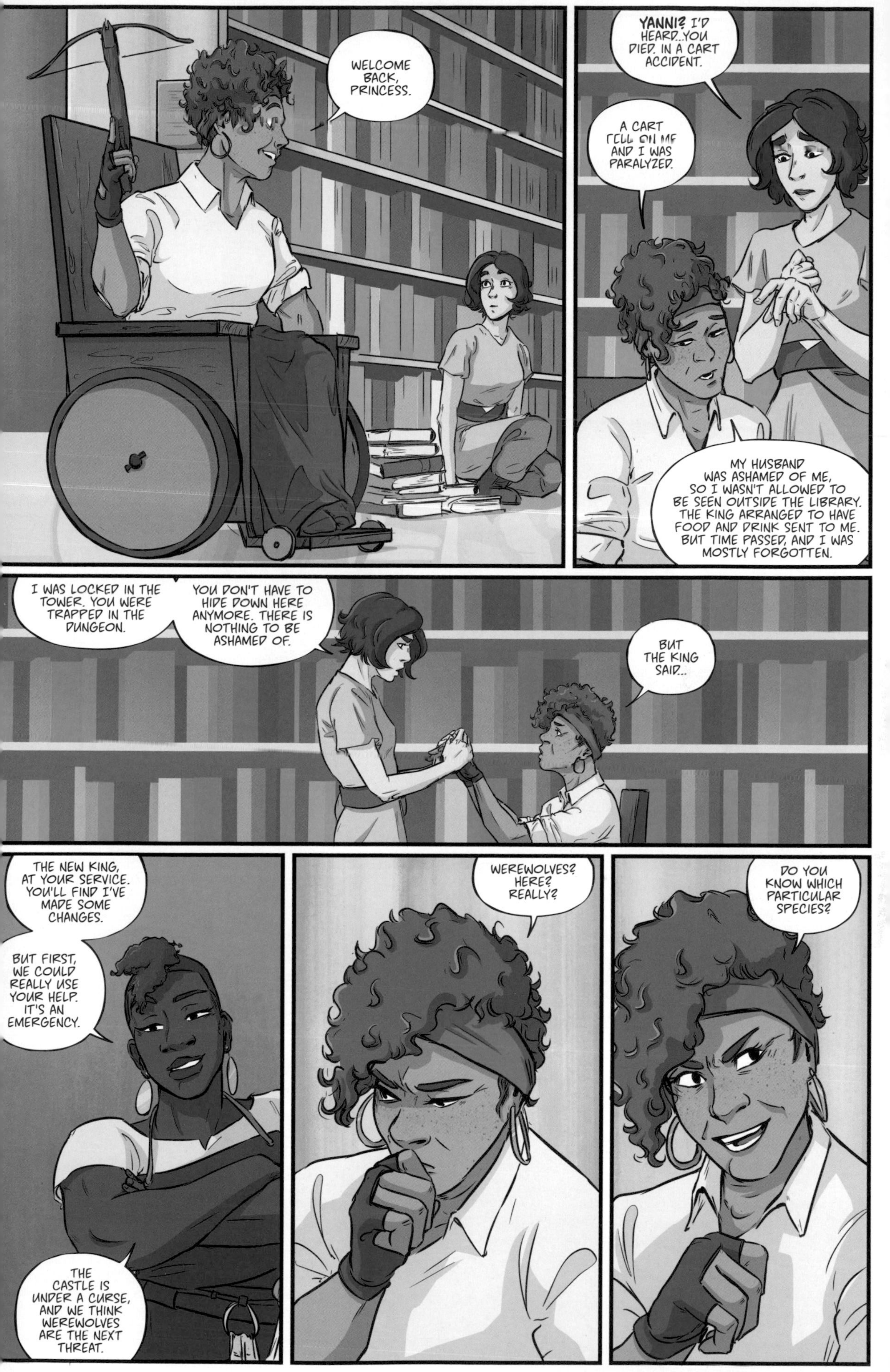
WELCOME BACK, PRINCESS.
YANNI? I'D HEARD...YOU DIED. IN A CART ACCIDENT.
A CART FELL ON ME AND I WAS PARALYZED.
MY HUSBAND WAS ASHAMED OF ME, SO I WASN'T ALLOWED TO BE SEEN OUTSIDE THE LIBRARY. THE KING ARRANGED TO HAVE FOOD AND DRINK SENT TO ME. BUT TIME PASSED, AND I WAS MOSTLY FORGOTTEN.
I WAS LOCKED IN THE TOWER. YOU WERE TRAPPED IN THE DUNGEON.
YOU DON'T HAVE TO HIDE DOWN HERE ANYMORE. THERE IS NOTHING TO BE ASHAMED OF.
BUT THE KING SAID...
THE NEW KING, AT YOUR SERVICE. YOU'LL FIND I'VE MADE SOME CHANGES.
BUT FIRST, WE COULD REALLY USE YOUR HELP. IT'S AN EMERGENCY.
THE CASTLE IS UNDER A CURSE, AND WE THINK WEREWOLVES ARE THE NEXT THREAT.
WEREWOLVES? HERE? REALLY?
DO YOU KNOW WHICH PARTICULAR SPECIES?

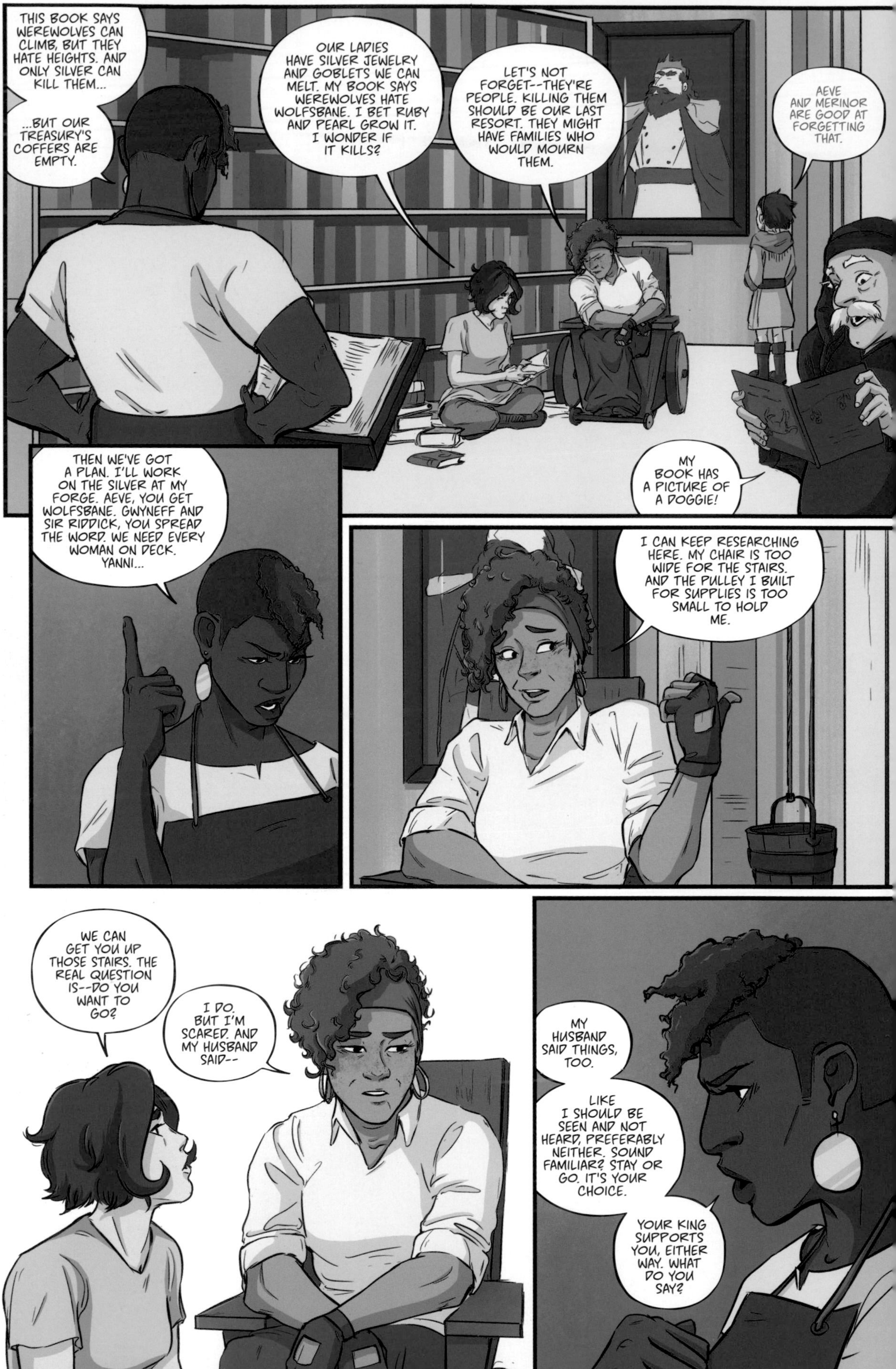
THIS BOOK SAYS WEREWOLVES CAN CLIMB, BUT THEY HATE HEIGHTS. AND ONLY SILVER CAN KILL THEM...
...BUT OUR TREASURY'S COFFERS ARE EMPTY.
OUR LADIES HAVE SILVER JEWELRY AND GOBLETS WE CAN MELT. MY BOOK SAYS WEREWOLVES HATE WOLFSBANE. I BET RUBY AND PEARL GROW IT. I WONDER IF IT KILLS?
LET'S NOT FORGET--THEY'RE PEOPLE. KILLING THEM SHOULD BE OUR LAST RESORT. THEY MIGHT HAVE FAMILIES WHO WOULD MOURN THEM.
AEVE AND MERINOR ARE GOOD AT FORGETTING THAT.
MY BOOK HAS A PICTURE OF A DOGGIE!
THEN WE'VE GOT A PLAN. I'LL WORK ON THE SILVER AT MY FORGE. AEVE, YOU GET WOLFSBANE. GWYNEFF AND SIR RIDDICK, YOU SPREAD THE WORD. WE NEED EVERY WOMAN ON DECK. YANNI...
I CAN KEEP RESEARCHING HERE. MY CHAIR IS TOO WIDE FOR THE STAIRS. AND THE PULLEY I BUILT FOR SUPPLIES IS TOO SMALL TO HOLD ME.
WE CAN GET YOU UP THOSE STAIRS. THE REAL QUESTION IS--DO YOU WANT TO GO?
I DO. BUT I'M SCARED. AND MY HUSBAND SAID--
MY HUSBAND SAID THINGS, TOO.
LIKE I SHOULD BE SEEN AND NOT HEARD, PREFERABLY NEITHER. SOUND FAMILIAR? STAY OR GO. IT'S YOUR CHOICE.
YOUR KING SUPPORTS YOU, EITHER WAY. WHAT DO YOU SAY?

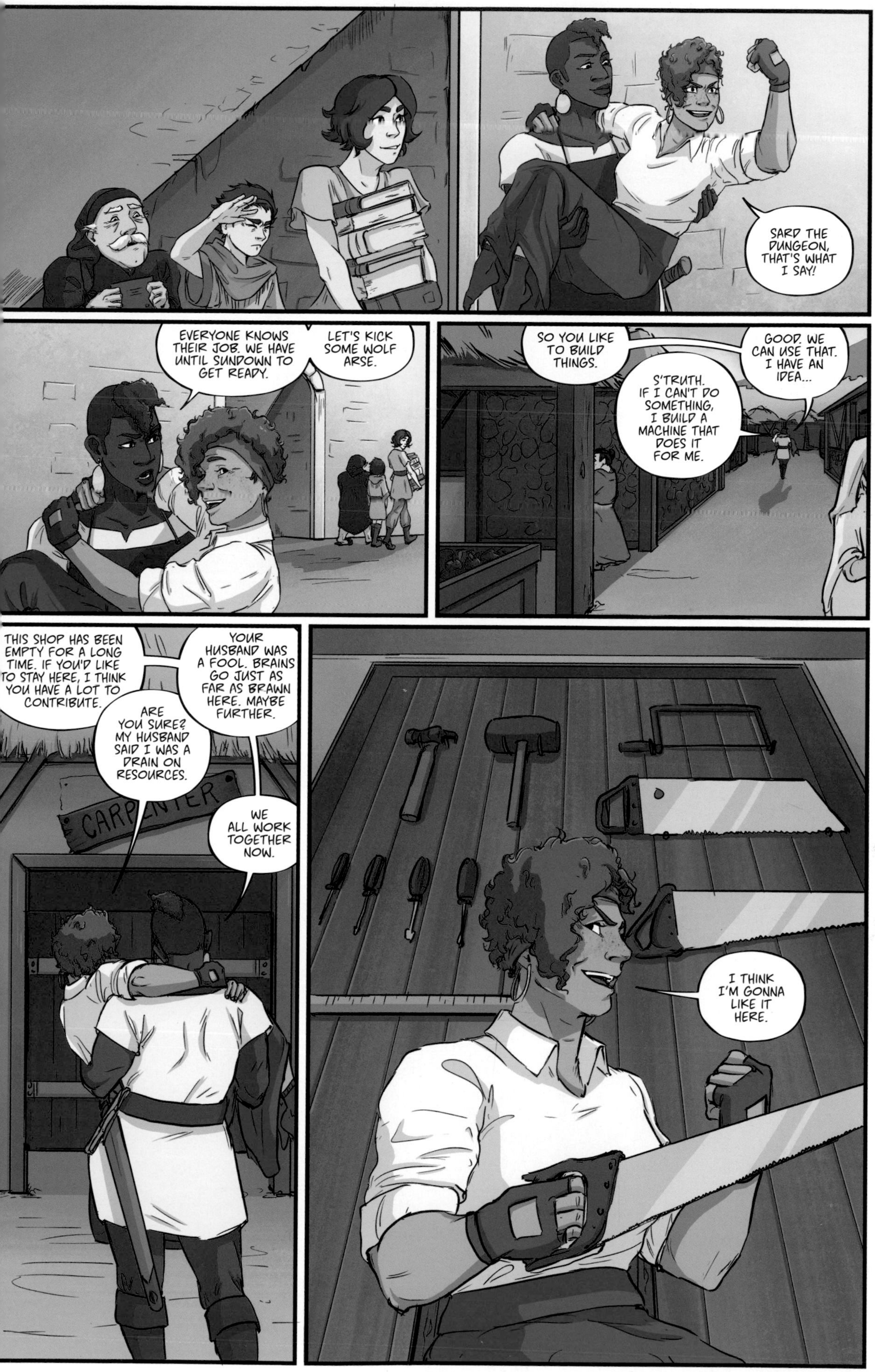
SARD THE DUNGEON, THAT'S WHAT I SAY!
EVERYONE KNOWS THEIR JOB. WE HAVE UNTIL SUNDOWN TO GET READY.
LET'S KICK SOME WOLF ARSE.
SO YOU LIKE TO BUILD THINGS.
S'TRUTH. IF I CAN'T DO SOMETHING, I BUILD A MACHINE THAT DOES IT FOR ME.
GOOD. WE CAN USE THAT. I HAVE AN IDEA...
THIS SHOP HAS BEEN EMPTY FOR A LONG TIME. IF YOU'D LIKE TO STAY HERE, I THINK YOU HAVE A LOT TO CONTRIBUTE.
ARE YOU SURE? MY HUSBAND SAID I WAS A DRAIN ON RESOURCES.
YOUR HUSBAND WAS A FOOL. BRAINS GO JUST AS FAR AS BRAWN HERE. MAYBE FURTHER.
WE ALL WORK TOGETHER NOW.
CARPENTER
I THINK I'M GONNA LIKE IT HERE.

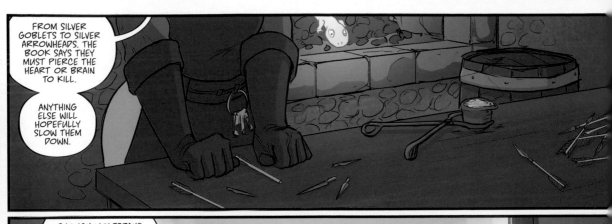

FROM SILVER GOBLETS TO SILVER ARROWHEADS. THE BOOK SAYS THEY MUST PIERCE THE HEART OR BRAIN TO KILL.

ANYTHING ELSE WILL HOPEFULLY SLOW THEM DOWN.

ENOUGH WOLFSBANE TO MAKE NEARLY A GALLON OF POTION. THANK GOODNESS FOR YOUR GREEN-- ER, PURPLE THUMBS!

HAGATHA SAYS IT WILL WEAKEN, NOT KILL THEM.

FOR THAT, WE'D NEED YOUR MEATLOAF, RUBY.

GENTLE LADIES, I BRING TERRIFYING NEWS!

WEREWOLVES APPROACH THE CASTLE, SLAVERING BEASTS WHO CRAVE YOUR BLOOD.

WE MUST FIGHT THEM. CITIZENS, SMEAR YOUR DOORS WITH WOLFSBANE AND HIDE. OR PUT ON YOUR SILVER JEWELRY AND PREPARE TO FIGHT!

FINALLY, YOU GET TO BE USEFUL! LEECHES LIKE WEREWOLF BLOOD, RIGHT?

LEECHE

FASHION IS ALWAYS THE BEST DEFENSE. THIS SITUATION CALLS FOR HOUNDSTOOTH.

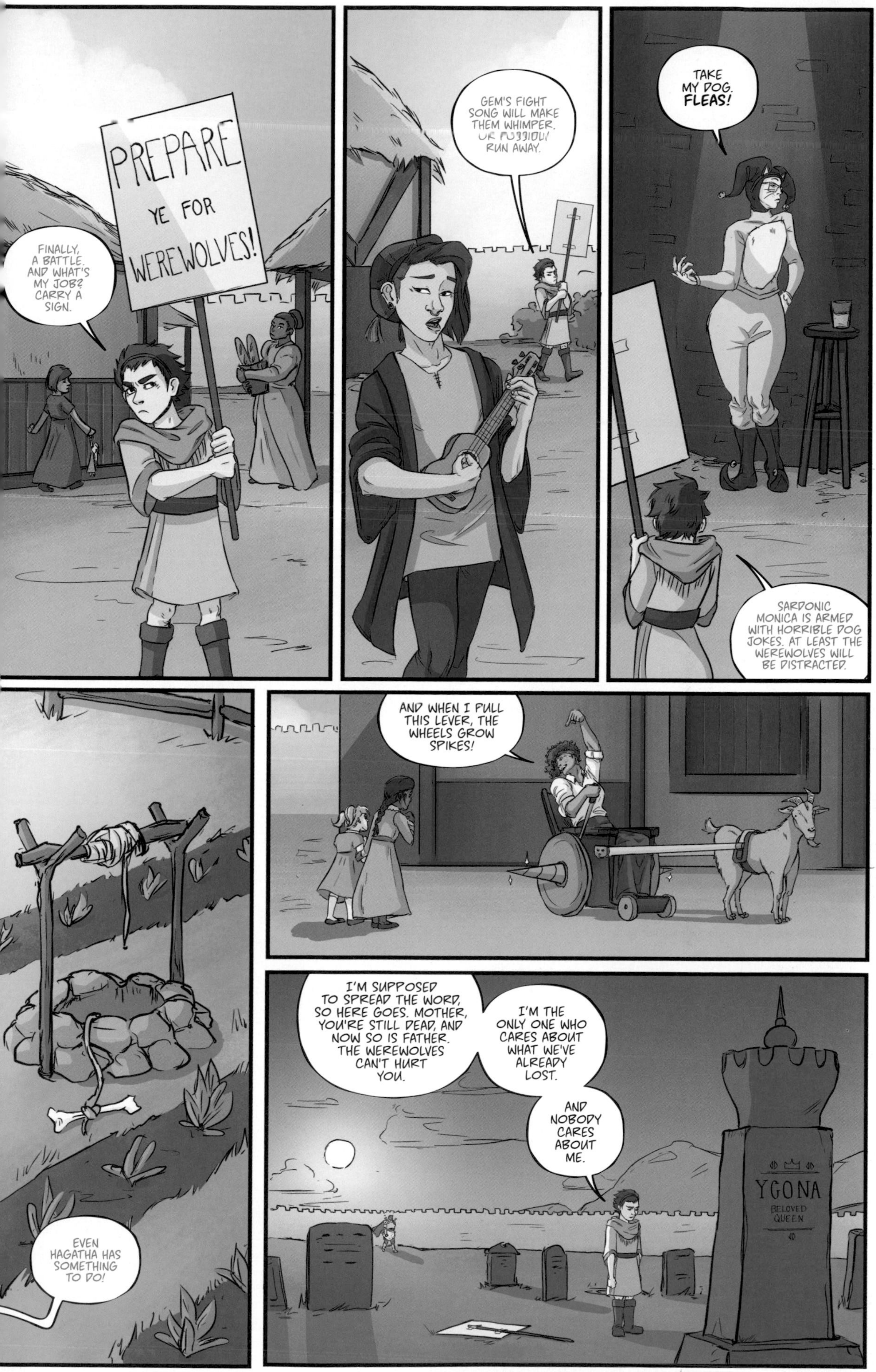
PREPARE YE FOR WEREWOLVES!
FINALLY, A BATTLE. AND WHAT'S MY JOB? CARRY A SIGN.
GEM'S FIGHT SONG WILL MAKE THEM WHIMPER. OR POSSIBLY RUN AWAY.
TAKE MY DOG. FLEAS!
SARDONIC MONICA IS ARMED WITH HORRIBLE DOG JOKES. AT LEAST THE WEREWOLVES WILL BE DISTRACTED.
EVEN HAGATHA HAS SOMETHING TO DO!
AND WHEN I PULL THIS LEVER, THE WHEELS GROW SPIKES!
I'M SUPPOSED TO SPREAD THE WORD, SO HERE GOES. MOTHER, YOU'RE STILL DEAD, AND NOW SO IS FATHER. THE WEREWOLVES CAN'T HURT YOU.
I'M THE ONLY ONE WHO CARES ABOUT WHAT WE'VE ALREADY LOST.
AND NOBODY CARES ABOUT ME.
YGONA
BELOVED QUEEN

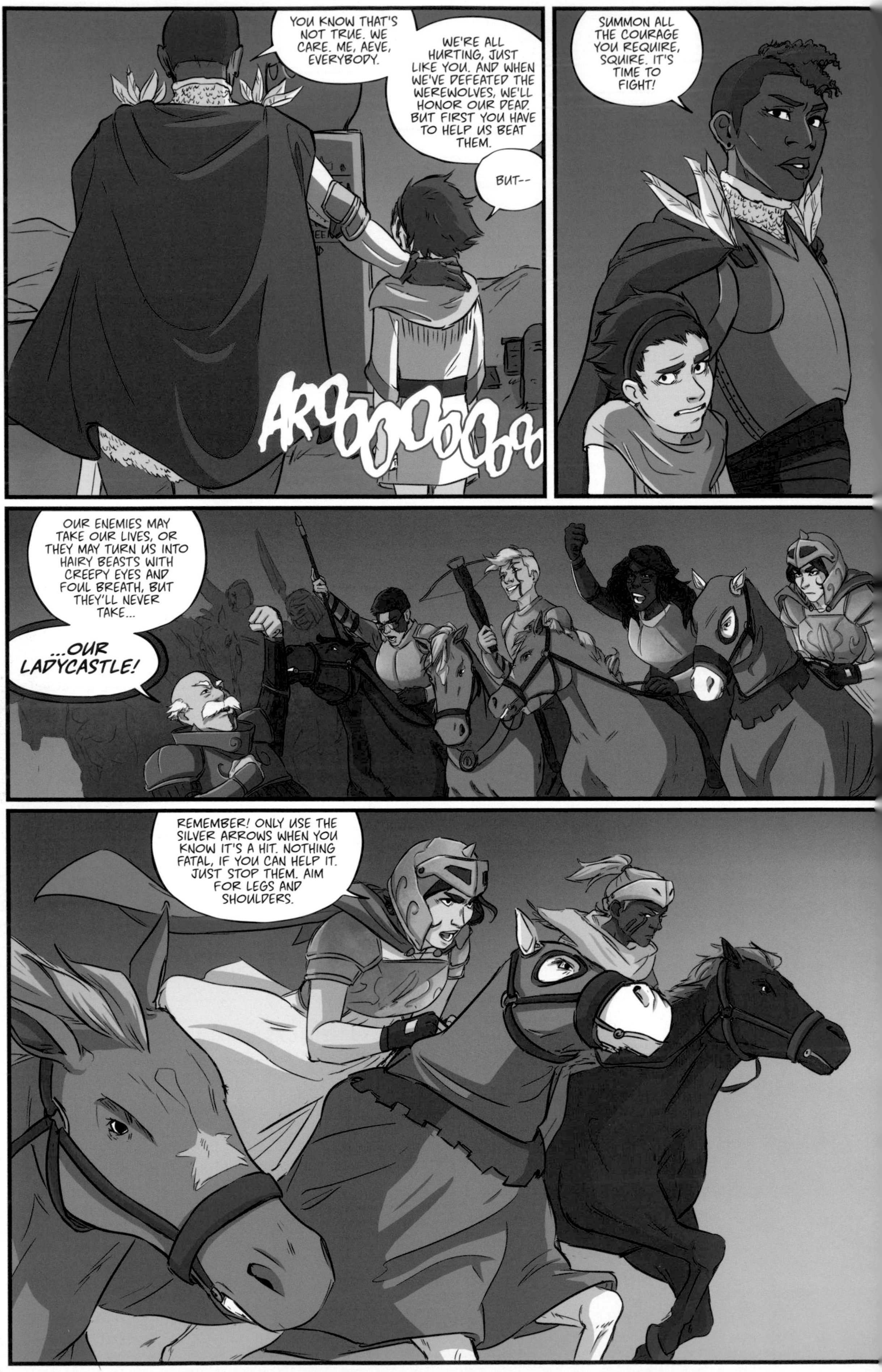
YOU KNOW THAT'S NOT TRUE. WE CARE. ME, AEVE, EVERYBODY.
WE'RE ALL HURTING, JUST LIKE YOU. AND WHEN WE'VE DEFEATED THE WEREWOLVES, WE'LL HONOR OUR DEAD. BUT FIRST YOU HAVE TO HELP US BEAT THEM.
BUT--
AROOOOOOOOO
SUMMON ALL THE COURAGE YOU REQUIRE, SQUIRE. IT'S TIME TO FIGHT!
OUR ENEMIES MAY TAKE OUR LIVES, OR THEY MAY TURN US INTO HAIRY BEASTS WITH CREEPY EYES AND FOUL BREATH, BUT THEY'LL NEVER TAKE...
...OUR LADYCASTLE!
REMEMBER! ONLY USE THE SILVER ARROWS WHEN YOU KNOW IT'S A HIT. NOTHING FATAL, IF YOU CAN HELP IT. JUST STOP THEM. AIM FOR LEGS AND SHOULDERS.

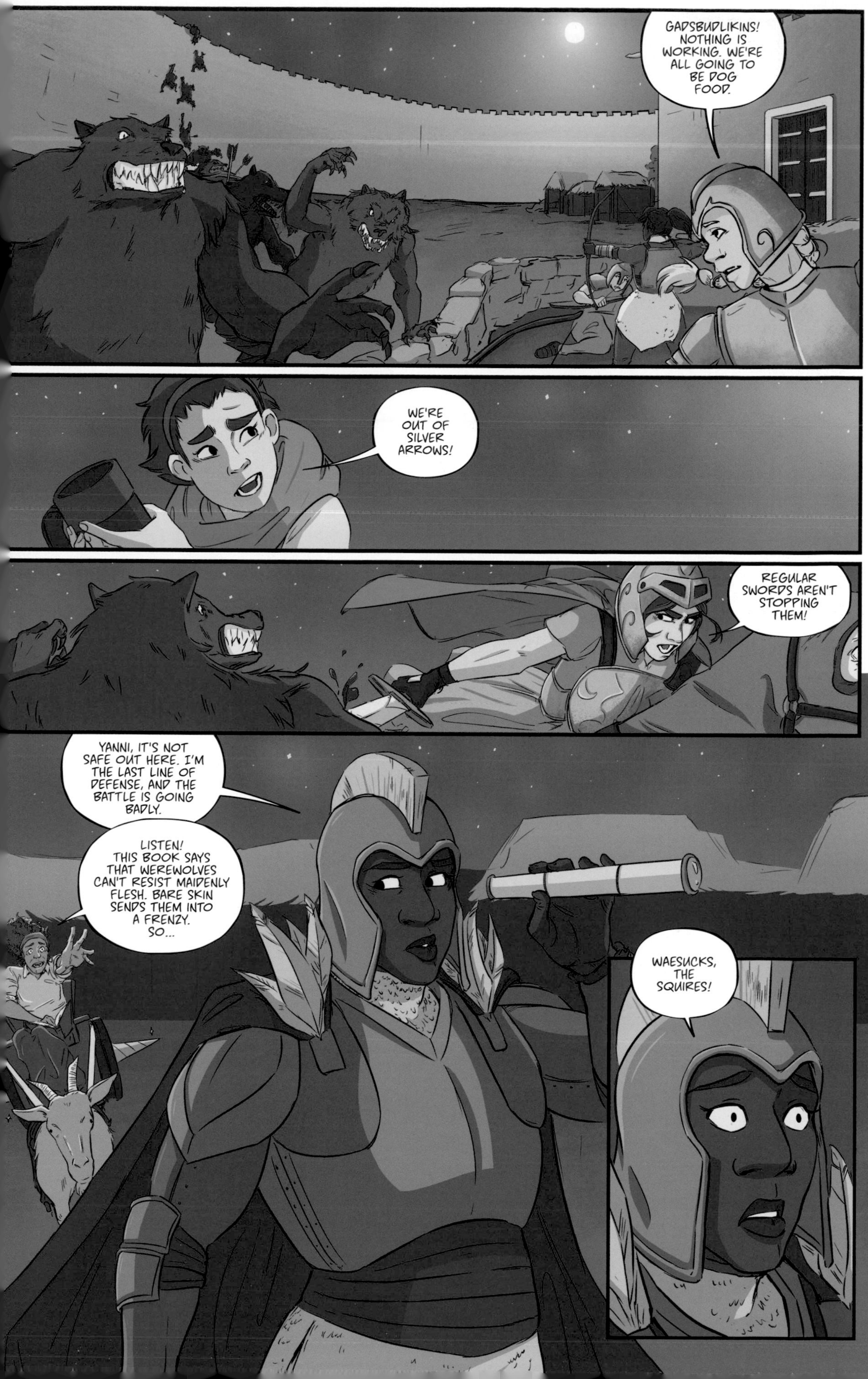
GADSBUDLIKINS! NOTHING IS WORKING. WE'RE ALL GOING TO BE DOG FOOD.
WE'RE OUT OF SILVER ARROWS!
REGULAR SWORDS AREN'T STOPPING THEM!
YANNI, IT'S NOT SAFE OUT HERE. I'M THE LAST LINE OF DEFENSE, AND THE BATTLE IS GOING BADLY.
LISTEN! THIS BOOK SAYS THAT WEREWOLVES CAN'T RESIST MAIDENLY FLESH. BARE SKIN SENDS THEM INTO A FRENZY. SO...
WAESUCKS, THE SQUIRES!

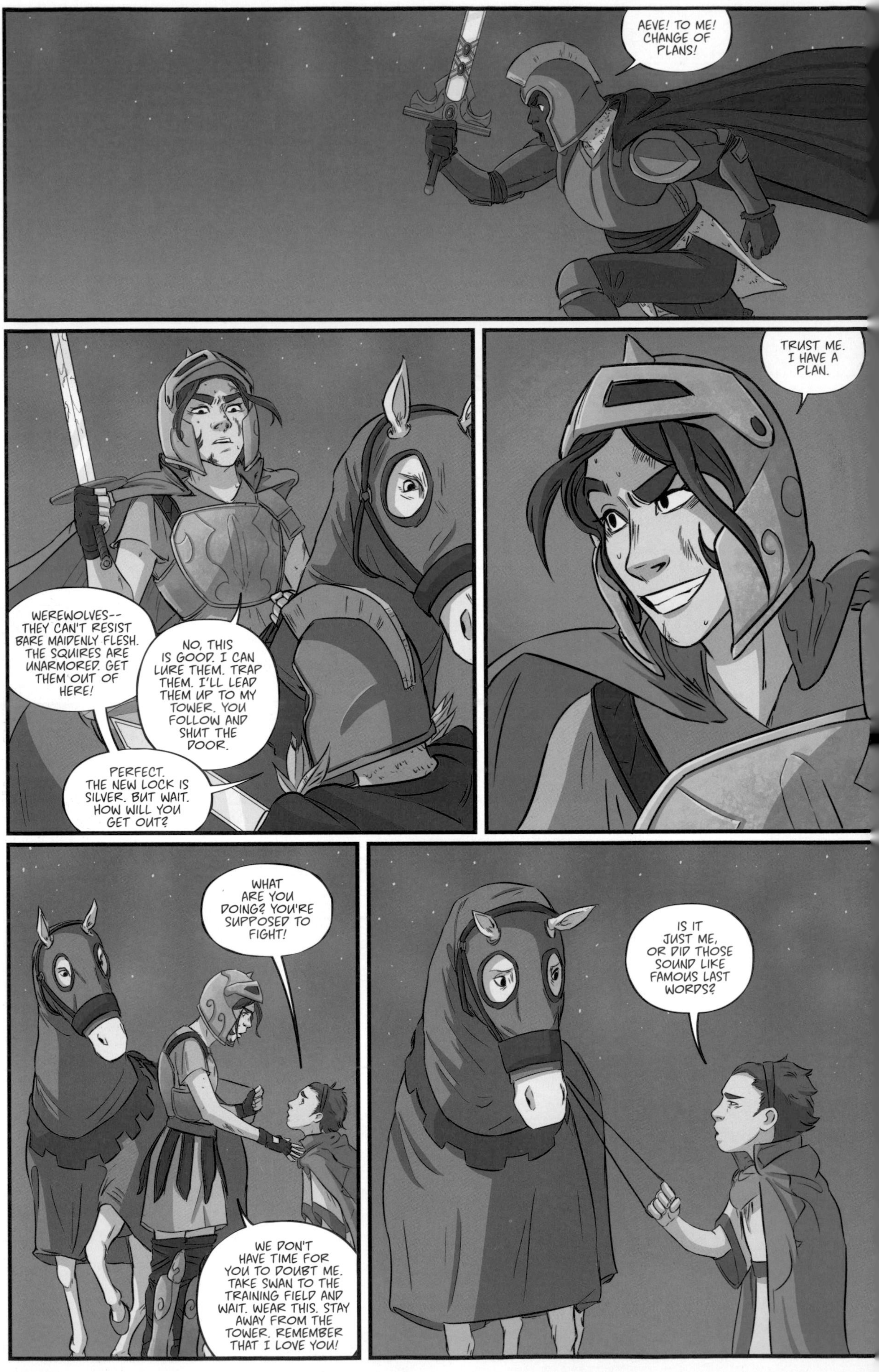
AEVE! TO ME! CHANGE OF PLANS!
WEREWOLVES-- THEY CAN'T RESIST BARE MAIDENLY FLESH. THE SQUIRES ARE UNARMORED. GET THEM OUT OF HERE!
NO, THIS IS GOOD. I CAN LURE THEM. TRAP THEM. I'LL LEAD THEM UP TO MY TOWER. YOU FOLLOW AND SHUT THE DOOR.
PERFECT. THE NEW LOCK IS SILVER. BUT WAIT. HOW WILL YOU GET OUT?
TRUST ME. I HAVE A PLAN.
WHAT ARE YOU DOING? YOU'RE SUPPOSED TO FIGHT!
WE DON'T HAVE TIME FOR YOU TO DOUBT ME. TAKE SWAN TO THE TRAINING FIELD AND WAIT. WEAR THIS. STAY AWAY FROM THE TOWER. REMEMBER THAT I LOVE YOU!
IS IT JUST ME, OR DID THOSE SOUND LIKE FAMOUS LAST WORDS?

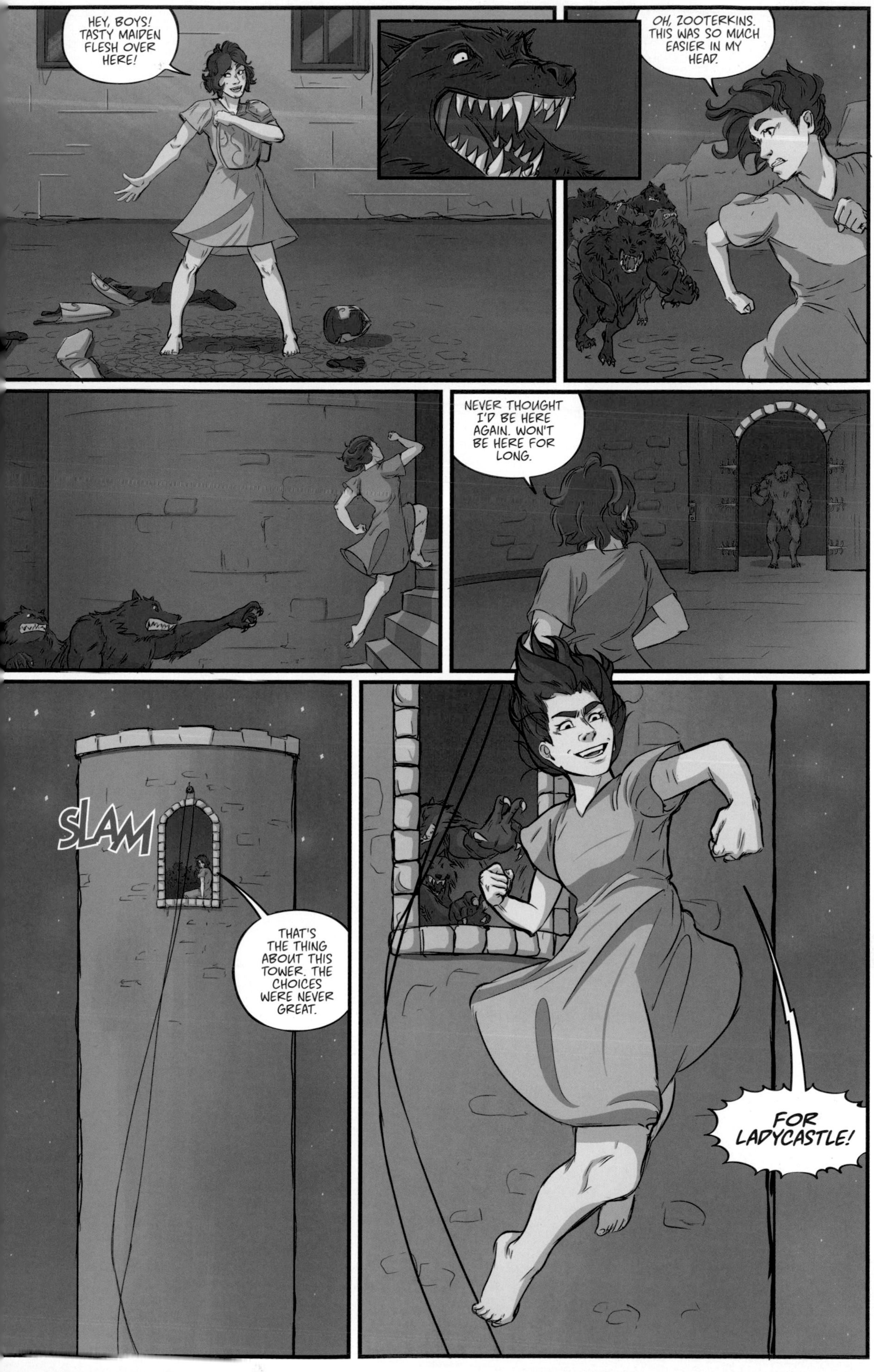
HEY, BOYS! TASTY MAIDEN FLESH OVER HERE!
OH, ZOOTERKINS. THIS WAS SO MUCH EASIER IN MY HEAD.
NEVER THOUGHT I'D BE HERE AGAIN. WON'T BE HERE FOR LONG.
SLAM
THAT'S THE THING ABOUT THIS TOWER. THE CHOICES WERE NEVER GREAT.
FOR LADYCASTLE!

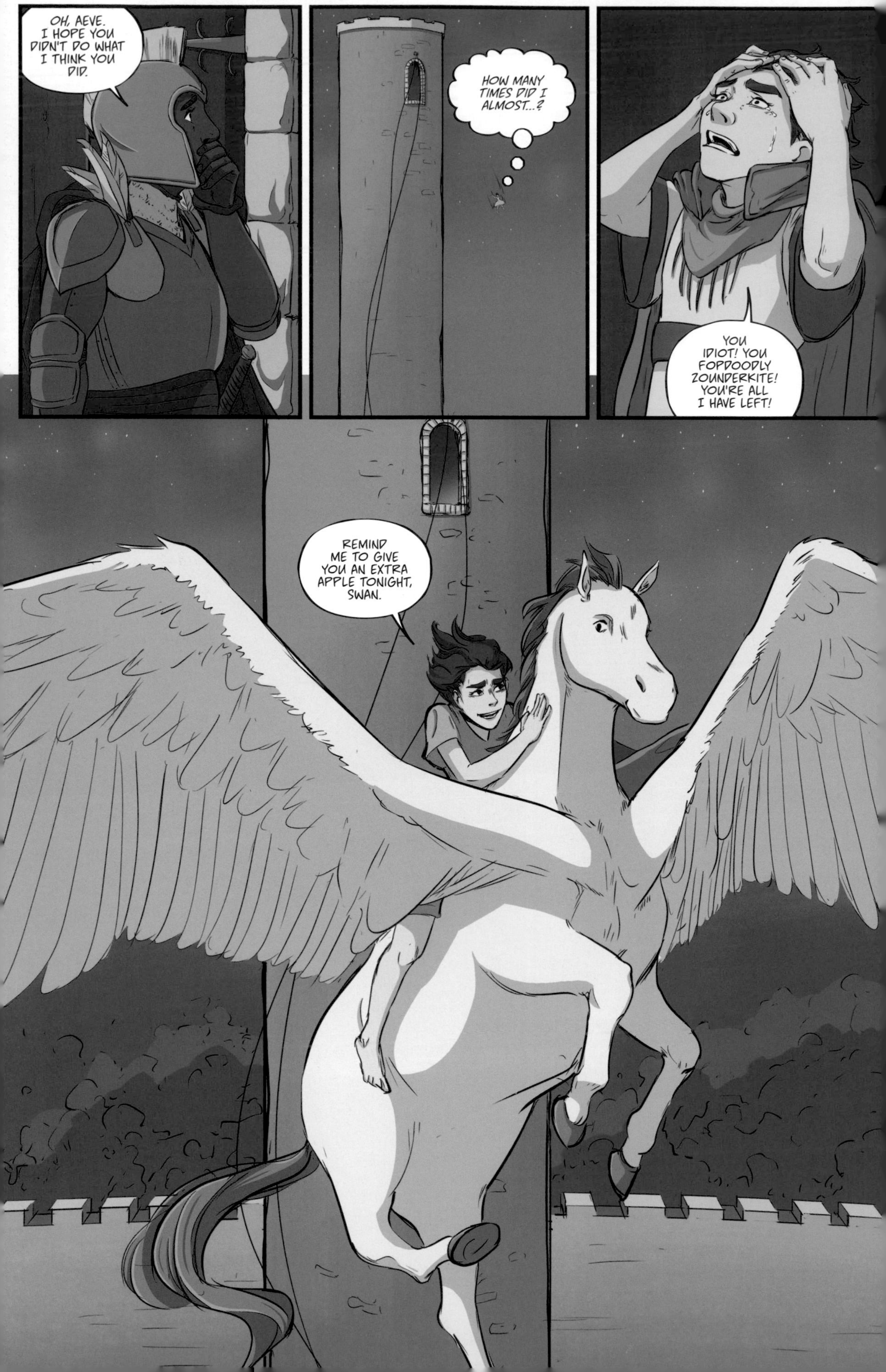
OH, AEVE. I HOPE YOU DIDN'T DO WHAT I THINK YOU DID.
HOW MANY TIMES DID I ALMOST...?
YOU IDIOT! YOU FOPDOODLY ZOUNDERKITE! YOU'RE ALL I HAVE LEFT!
REMIND ME TO GIVE YOU AN EXTRA APPLE TONIGHT, SWAN.

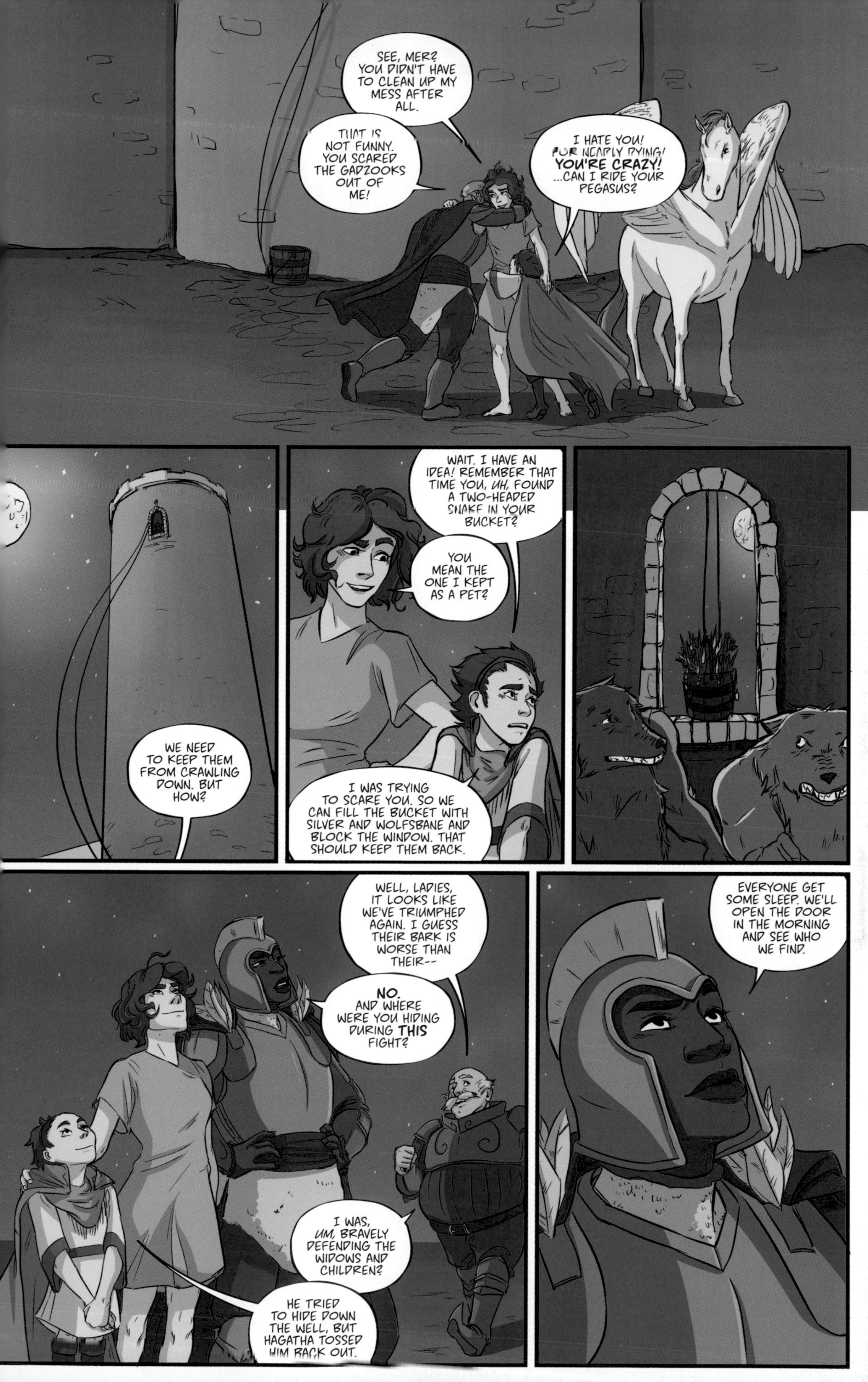
SEE, MER? YOU DIDN'T HAVE TO CLEAN UP MY MESS AFTER ALL.
THAT IS NOT FUNNY. YOU SCARED THE GADZOOKS OUT OF ME!
I HATE YOU! FOR NEARLY DYING! YOU'RE CRAZY! ...CAN I RIDE YOUR PEGASUS?
WE NEED TO KEEP THEM FROM CRAWLING DOWN. BUT HOW?
WAIT. I HAVE AN IDEA! REMEMBER THAT TIME YOU, UH, FOUND A TWO-HEADED SNAKE IN YOUR BUCKET?
YOU MEAN THE ONE I KEPT AS A PET?
I WAS TRYING TO SCARE YOU. SO WE CAN FILL THE BUCKET WITH SILVER AND WOLFSBANE AND BLOCK THE WINDOW. THAT SHOULD KEEP THEM BACK.
WELL, LADIES, IT LOOKS LIKE WE'VE TRIUMPHED AGAIN. I GUESS THEIR BARK IS WORSE THAN THEIR--
NO. AND WHERE WERE YOU HIDING DURING THIS FIGHT?
I WAS, UM, BRAVELY DEFENDING THE WIDOWS AND CHILDREN?
HE TRIED TO HIDE DOWN THE WELL, BUT HAGATHA TOSSED HIM BACK OUT.
EVERYONE GET SOME SLEEP. WE'LL OPEN THE DOOR IN THE MORNING AND SEE WHO WE FIND.

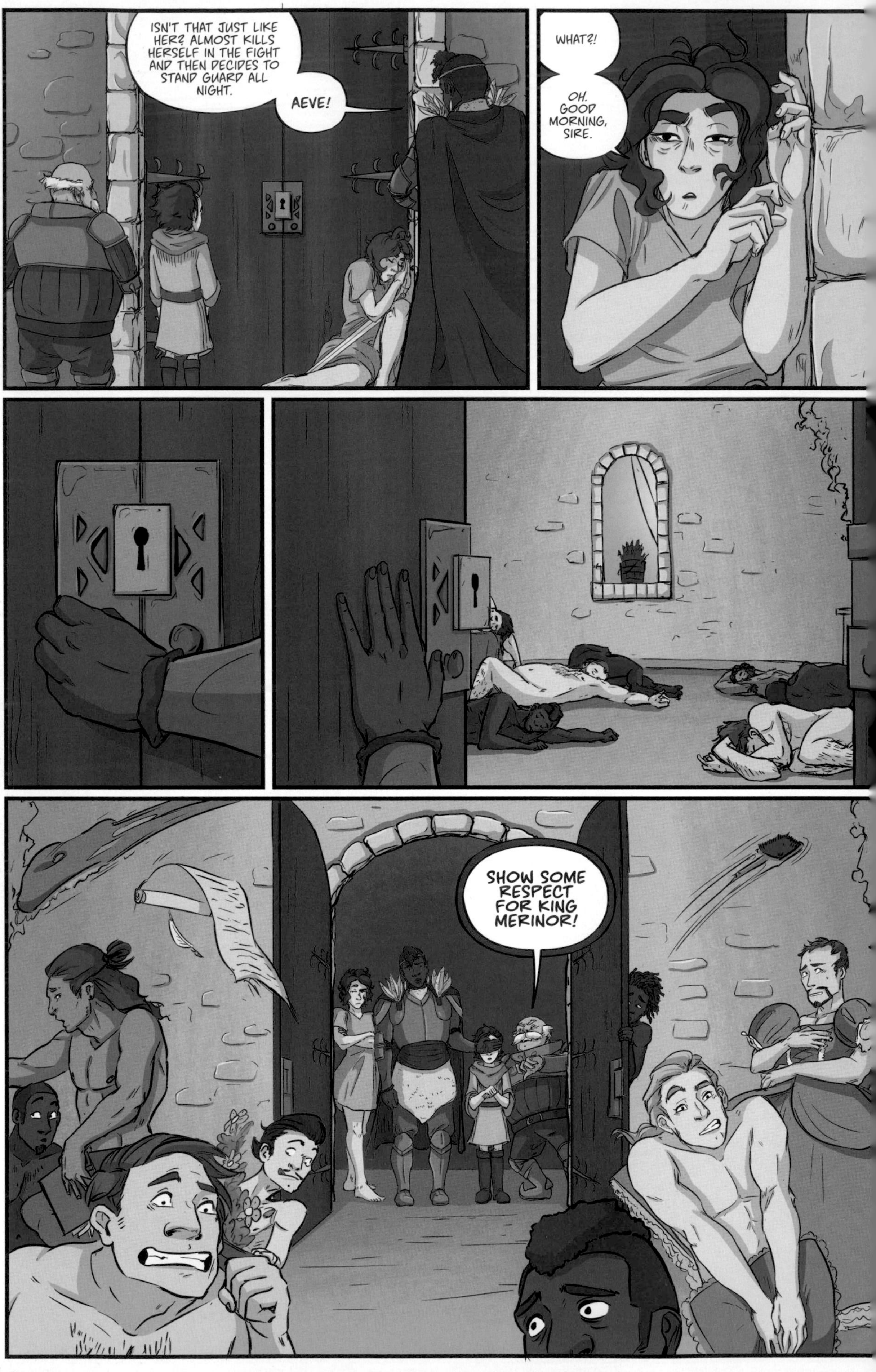
ISN'T THAT JUST LIKE HER? ALMOST KILLS HERSELF IN THE FIGHT AND THEN DECIDES TO STAND GUARD ALL NIGHT.
AEVE!
WHAT?!
OH. GOOD MORNING, SIRE.
SHOW SOME RESPECT FOR KING MERINOR!

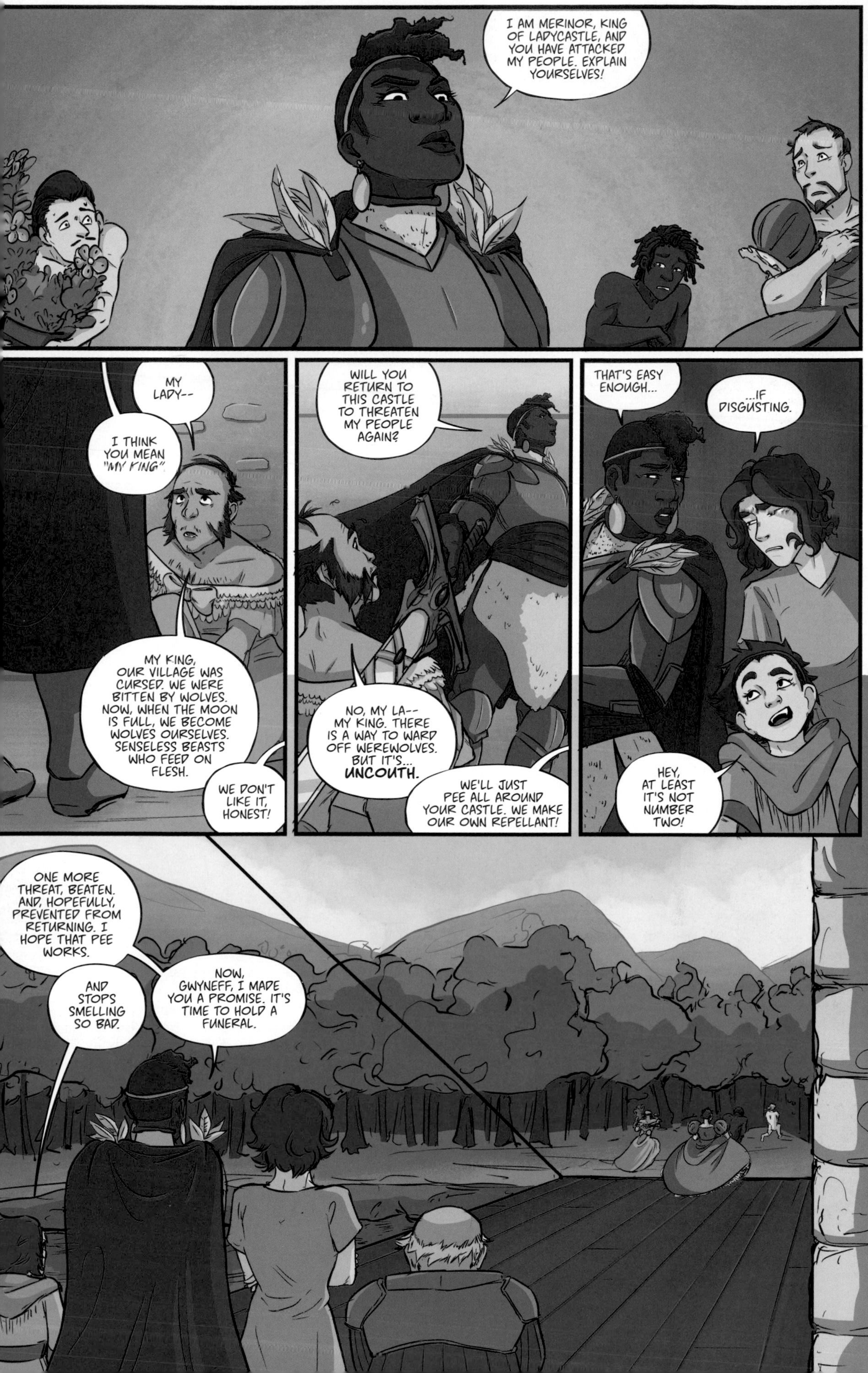

I AM MERINOR, KING OF LADYCASTLE, AND YOU HAVE ATTACKED MY PEOPLE. EXPLAIN YOURSELVES!
MY LADY--
I THINK YOU MEAN "MY KING".
MY KING, OUR VILLAGE WAS CURSED. WE WERE BITTEN BY WOLVES. NOW, WHEN THE MOON IS FULL, WE BECOME WOLVES OURSELVES. SENSELESS BEASTS WHO FEED ON FLESH.
WE DON'T LIKE IT, HONEST!
WILL YOU RETURN TO THIS CASTLE TO THREATEN MY PEOPLE AGAIN?
NO, MY LA-- MY KING. THERE IS A WAY TO WARD OFF WEREWOLVES. BUT IT'S... UNCOUTH.
WE'LL JUST PEE ALL AROUND YOUR CASTLE. WE MAKE OUR OWN REPELLANT!
THAT'S EASY ENOUGH...
...IF DISGUSTING.
HEY, AT LEAST IT'S NOT NUMBER TWO!
ONE MORE THREAT, BEATEN. AND, HOPEFULLY, PREVENTED FROM RETURNING. I HOPE THAT PEE WORKS.
AND STOPS SMELLING SO BAD.
NOW, GWYNEFF, I MADE YOU A PROMISE. IT'S TIME TO HOLD A FUNERAL.

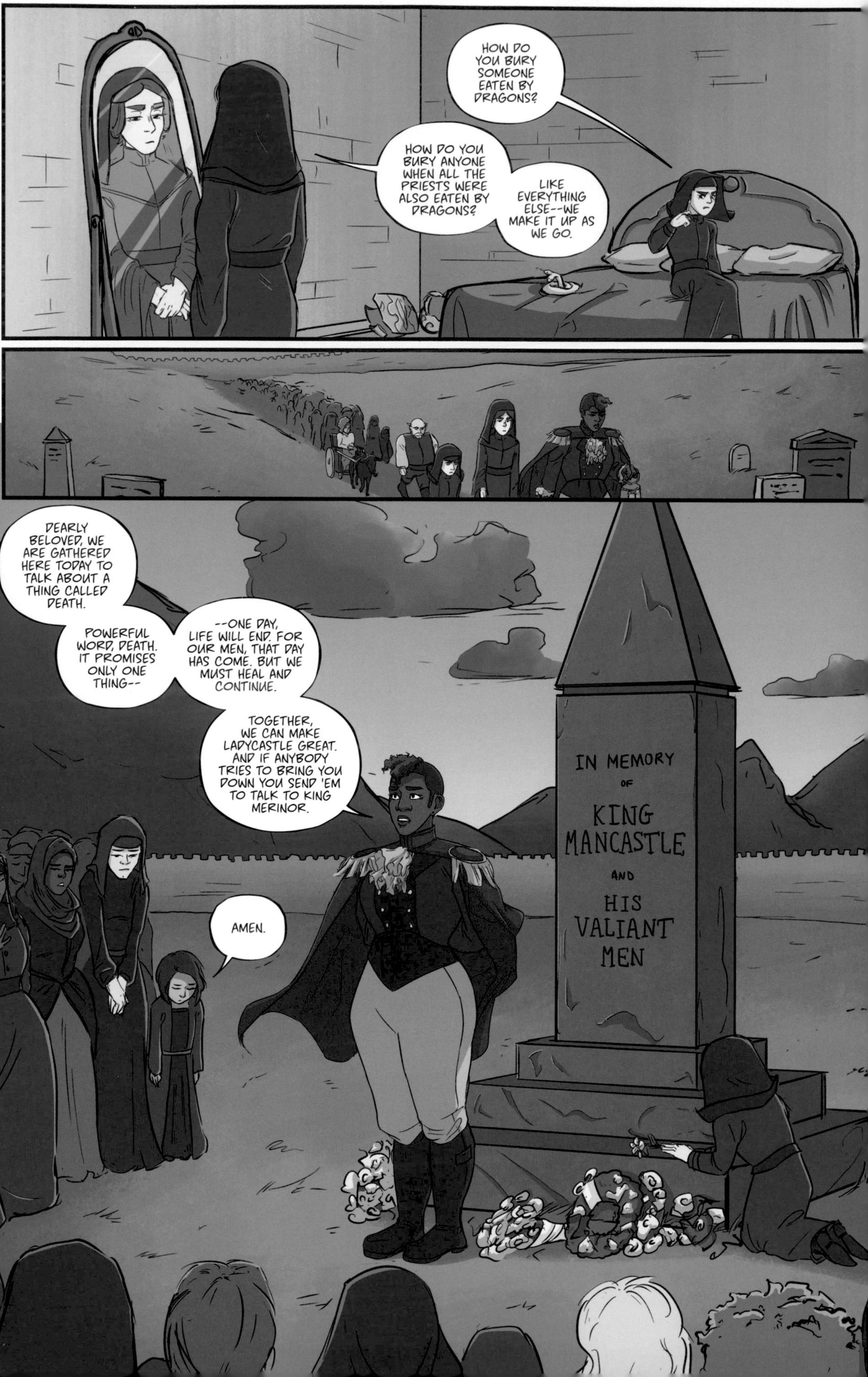
HOW DO YOU BURY SOMEONE EATEN BY DRAGONS?
HOW DO YOU BURY ANYONE WHEN ALL THE PRIESTS WERE ALSO EATEN BY DRAGONS?
LIKE EVERYTHING ELSE--WE MAKE IT UP AS WE GO.
DEARLY BELOVED, WE ARE GATHERED HERE TODAY TO TALK ABOUT A THING CALLED DEATH.
POWERFUL WORD, DEATH. IT PROMISES ONLY ONE THING--
--ONE DAY, LIFE WILL END. FOR OUR MEN, THAT DAY HAS COME. BUT WE MUST HEAL AND CONTINUE.
TOGETHER, WE CAN MAKE LADYCASTLE GREAT. AND IF ANYBODY TRIES TO BRING YOU DOWN YOU SEND 'EM TO TALK TO KING MERINOR.
IN MEMORY OF KING MANCASTLE AND HIS VALIANT MEN
AMEN.

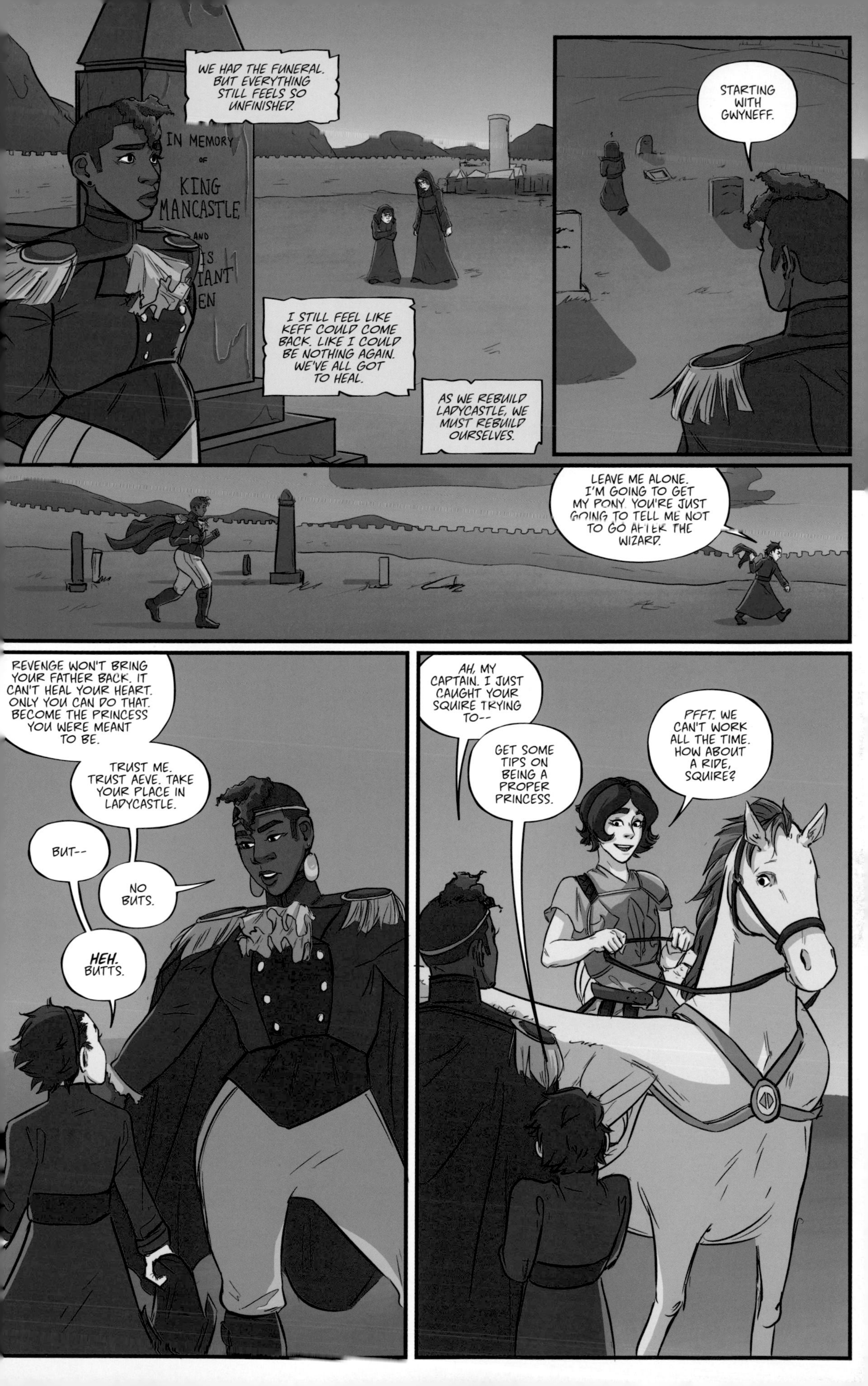
WE HAD THE FUNERAL. BUT EVERYTHING STILL FEELS SO UNFINISHED.
IN MEMORY OF KING MANCASTLE AND
I STILL FEEL LIKE KEFF COULD COME BACK. LIKE I COULD BE NOTHING AGAIN. WE'VE ALL GOT TO HEAL.
AS WE REBUILD LADYCASTLE, WE MUST REBUILD OURSELVES.
STARTING WITH GWYNEFF.
LEAVE ME ALONE. I'M GOING TO GET MY PONY. YOU'RE JUST GOING TO TELL ME NOT TO GO AFTER THE WIZARD.
REVENGE WON'T BRING YOUR FATHER BACK. IT CAN'T HEAL YOUR HEART. ONLY YOU CAN DO THAT. BECOME THE PRINCESS YOU WERE MEANT TO BE.
TRUST ME. TRUST AEVE. TAKE YOUR PLACE IN LADYCASTLE.
BUT--
NO BUTS.
HEH. BUTTS.
AH, MY CAPTAIN. I JUST CAUGHT YOUR SQUIRE TRYING TO--
GET SOME TIPS ON BEING A PROPER PRINCESS.
PFFT. WE CAN'T WORK ALL THE TIME. HOW ABOUT A RIDE, SQUIRE?

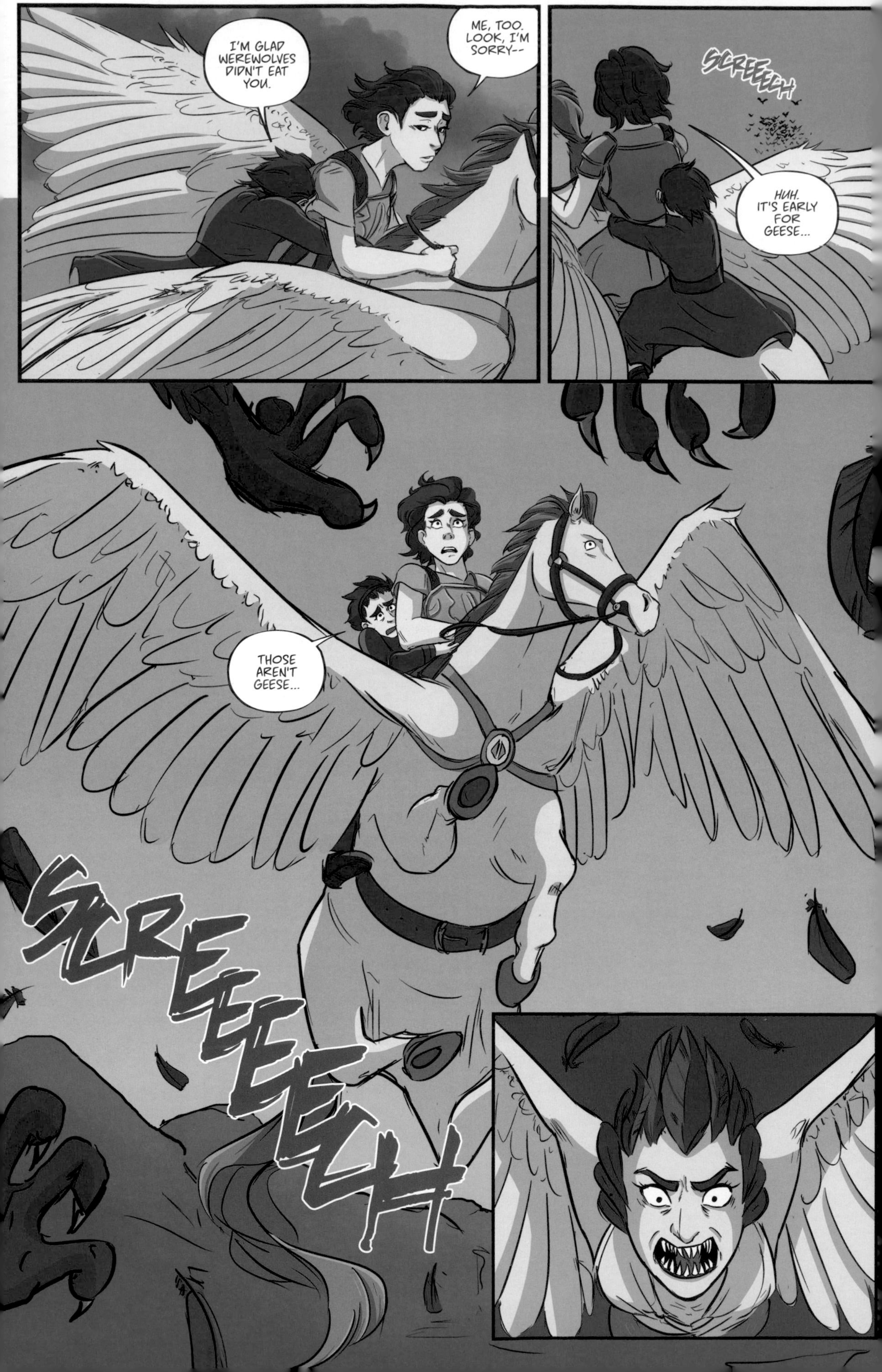
I'M GLAD WEREWOLVES DIDN'T EAT YOU.
ME, TOO. LOOK, I'M SORRY--
SCREEECH
HUH. IT'S EARLY FOR GEESE...
THOSE AREN'T GEESE...
SCREEEEECH

"IT'S NOT EASY
BEING **KING**."

CHAPTER THREE

WHEN HARPIES ATTACK

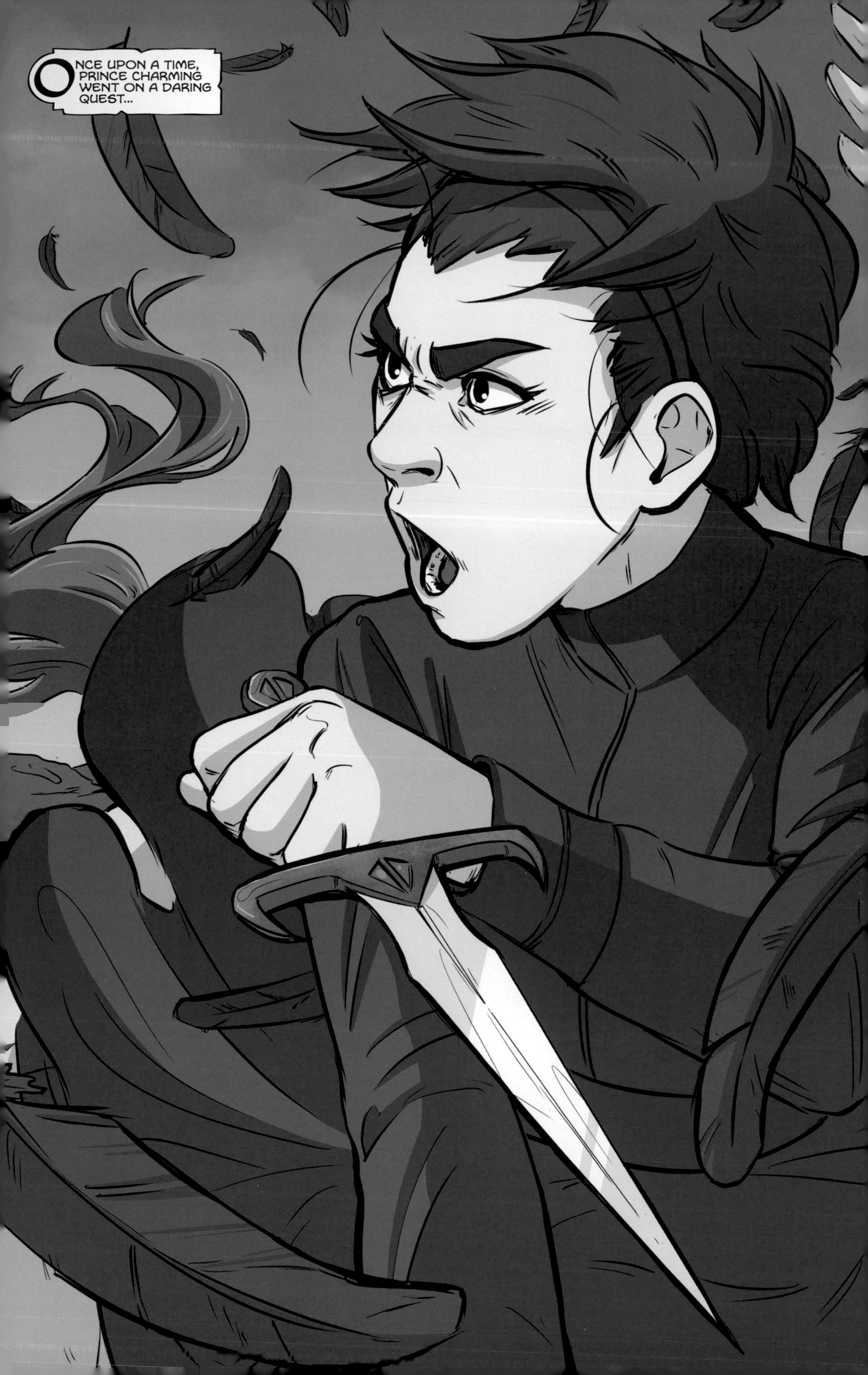
ONCE UPON A TIME, PRINCE CHARMING WENT ON A DARING QUEST...

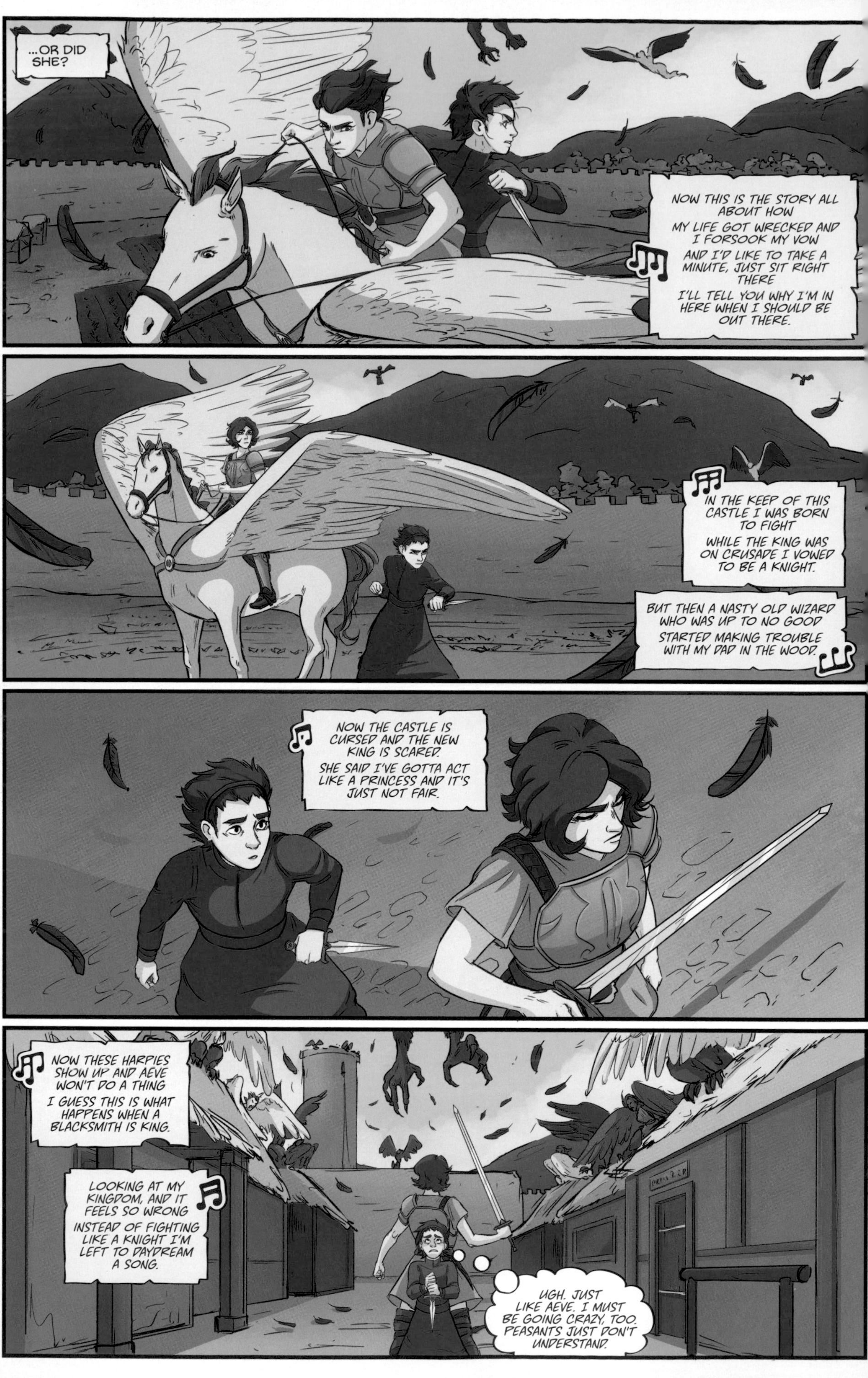
...OR DID SHE?
NOW THIS IS THE STORY ALL ABOUT HOW
MY LIFE GOT WRECKED AND I FORSOOK MY VOW
AND I'D LIKE TO TAKE A MINUTE, JUST SIT RIGHT THERE
I'LL TELL YOU WHY I'M IN HERE WHEN I SHOULD BE OUT THERE.
IN THE KEEP OF THIS CASTLE I WAS BORN TO FIGHT
WHILE THE KING WAS ON CRUSADE I VOWED TO BE A KNIGHT.
BUT THEN A NASTY OLD WIZARD WHO WAS UP TO NO GOOD
STARTED MAKING TROUBLE WITH MY DAD IN THE WOOD.
NOW THE CASTLE IS CURSED AND THE NEW KING IS SCARED.
SHE SAID I'VE GOTTA ACT LIKE A PRINCESS AND IT'S JUST NOT FAIR.
NOW THESE HARPIES SHOW UP AND AEVE WON'T DO A THING
I GUESS THIS IS WHAT HAPPENS WHEN A BLACKSMITH IS KING.
LOOKING AT MY KINGDOM, AND IT FEELS SO WRONG
INSTEAD OF FIGHTING LIKE A KNIGHT I'M LEFT TO DAYDREAM A SONG.
UGH. JUST LIKE AEVE. I MUST BE GOING CRAZY, TOO. PEASANTS JUST DON'T UNDERSTAND.

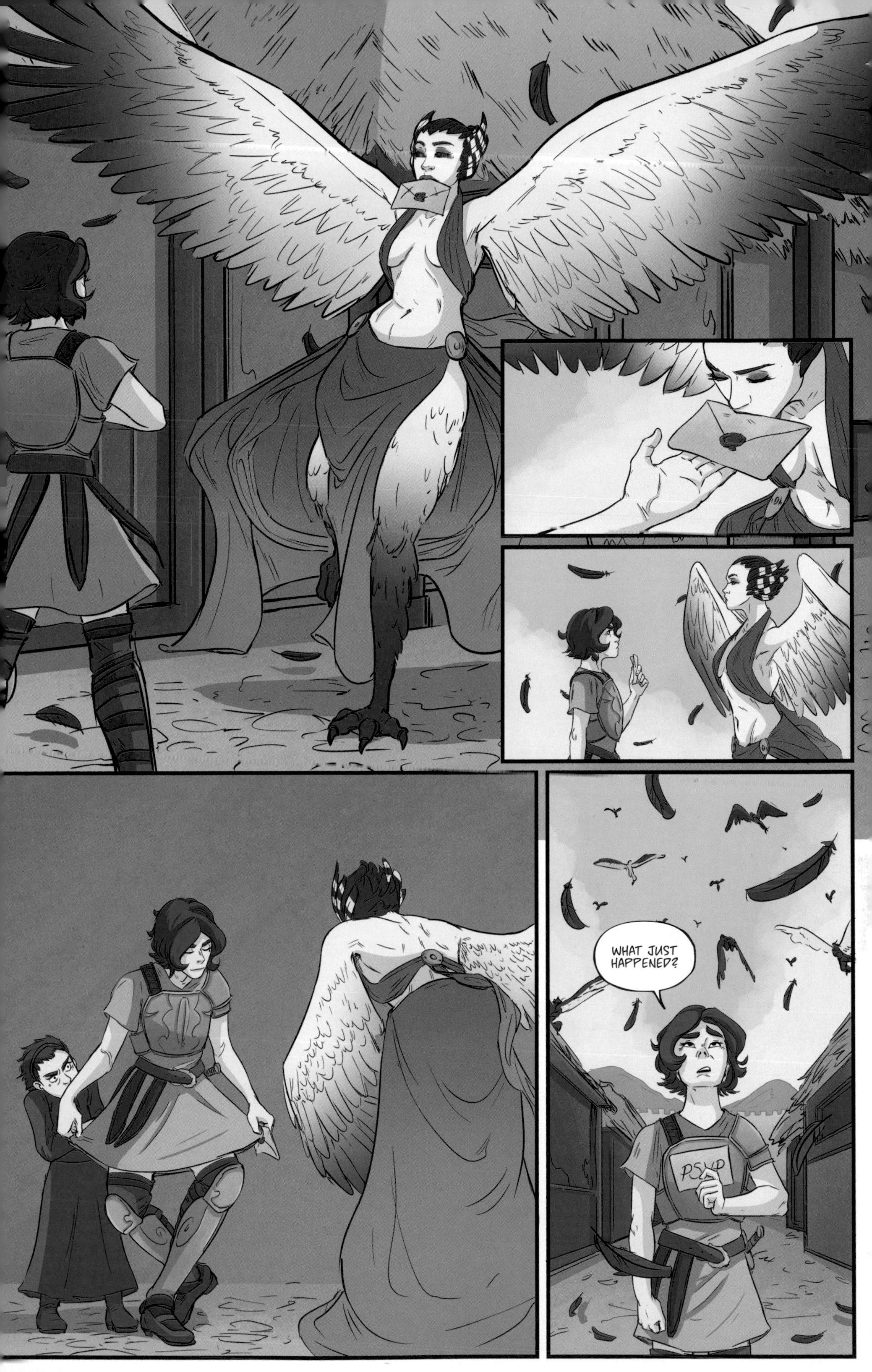
WHAT JUST HAPPENED?

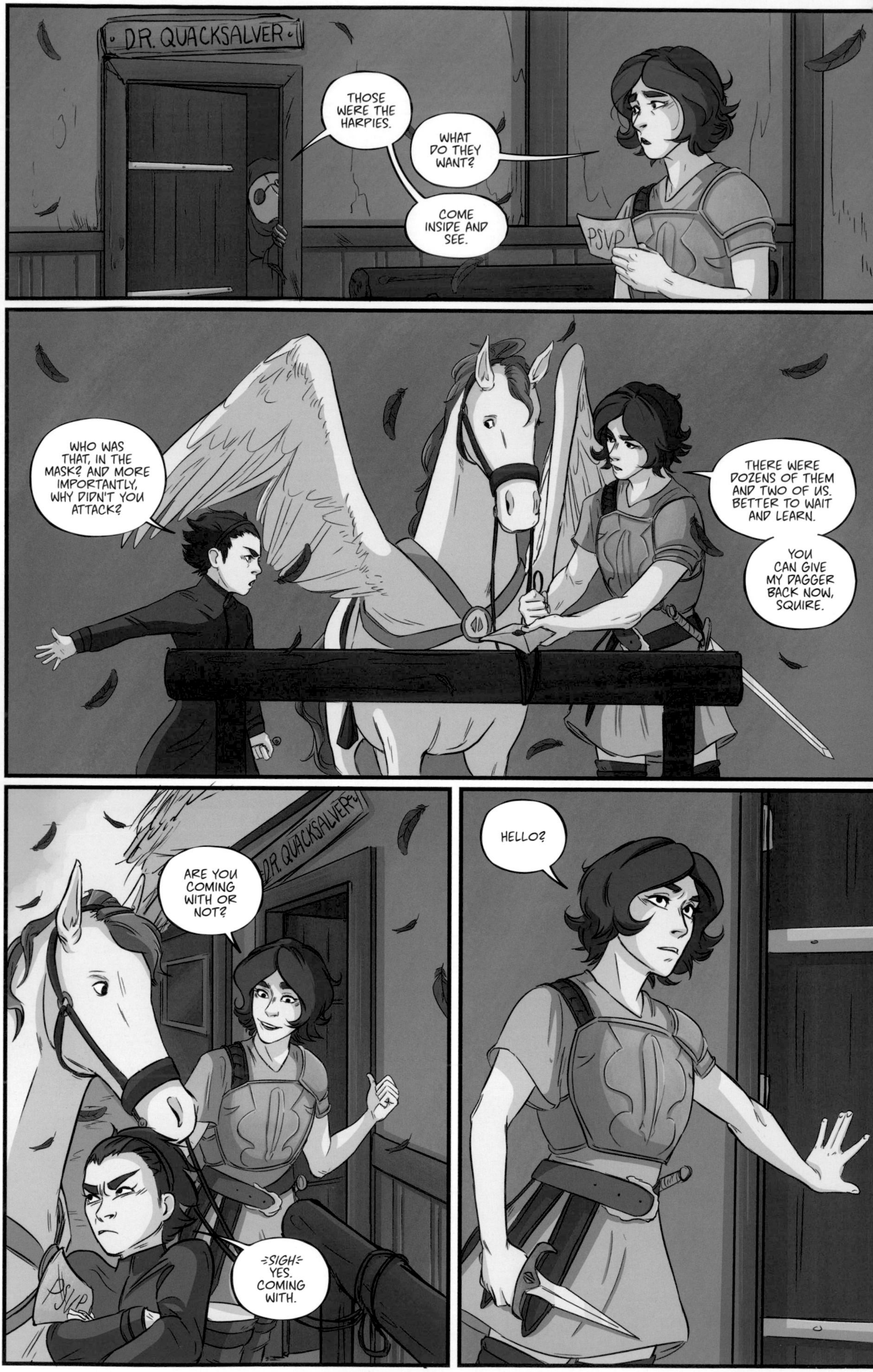
DR. QUACKSALVER
THOSE WERE THE HARPIES.
WHAT DO THEY WANT?
COME INSIDE AND SEE.
PSVP
WHO WAS THAT, IN THE MASK? AND MORE IMPORTANTLY, WHY DIDN'T YOU ATTACK?
THERE WERE DOZENS OF THEM AND TWO OF US. BETTER TO WAIT AND LEARN.
YOU CAN GIVE MY DAGGER BACK NOW, SQUIRE.
DR. QUACKSALVER
ARE YOU COMING WITH OR NOT?
SIGH YES. COMING WITH.
PSVP
HELLO?

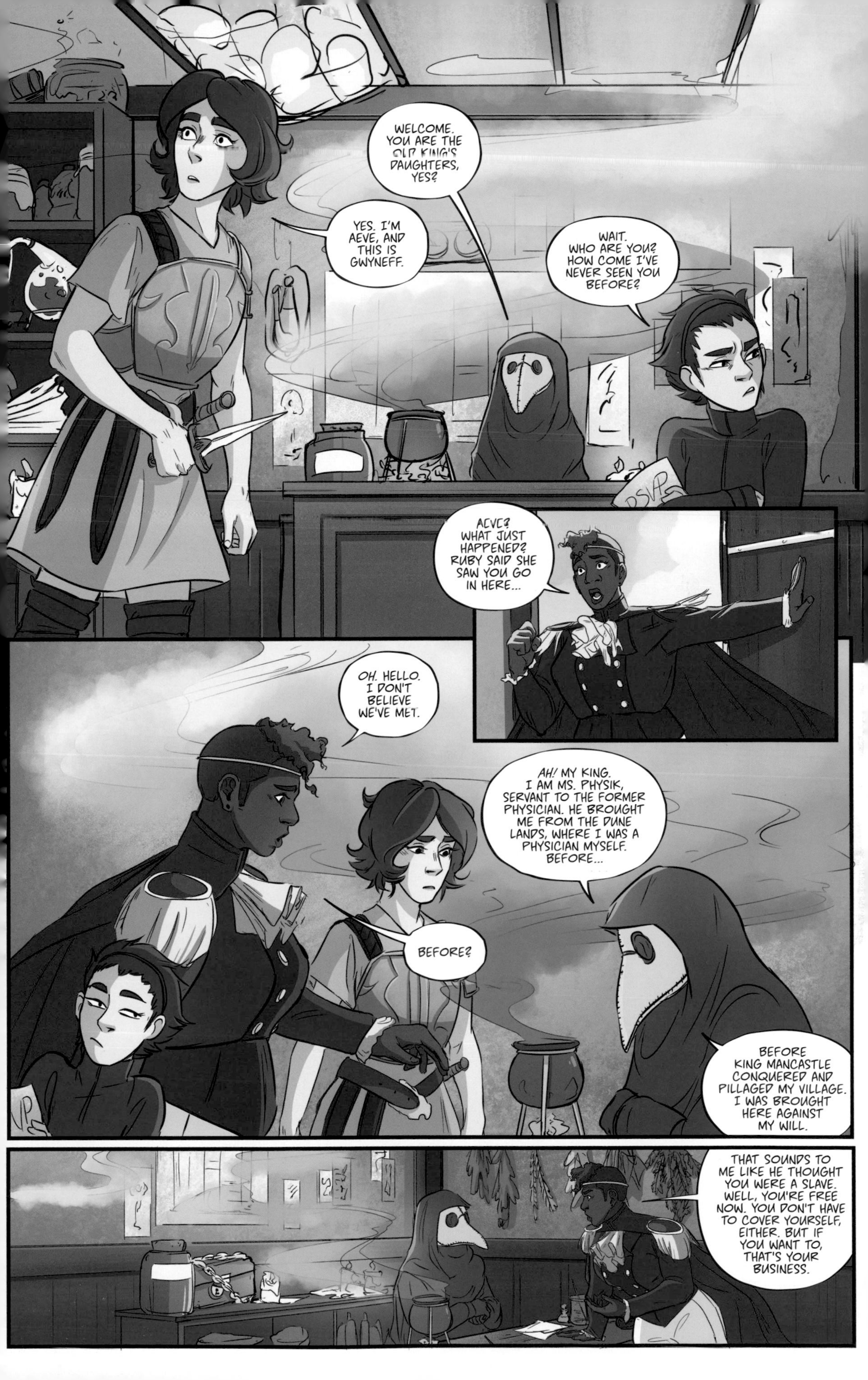
WELCOME. YOU ARE THE OLD KING'S DAUGHTERS, YES?
YES. I'M AEVE, AND THIS IS GWYNEFF.
WAIT. WHO ARE YOU? HOW COME I'VE NEVER SEEN YOU BEFORE?
AEVE? WHAT JUST HAPPENED? RUBY SAID SHE SAW YOU GO IN HERE...
OH. HELLO. I DON'T BELIEVE WE'VE MET.
AH! MY KING. I AM MS. PHYSIK, SERVANT TO THE FORMER PHYSICIAN. HE BROUGHT ME FROM THE DUNE LANDS, WHERE I WAS A PHYSICIAN MYSELF. BEFORE...
BEFORE?
BEFORE KING MANCASTLE CONQUERED AND PILLAGED MY VILLAGE. I WAS BROUGHT HERE AGAINST MY WILL.
THAT SOUNDS TO ME LIKE HE THOUGHT YOU WERE A SLAVE. WELL, YOU'RE FREE NOW. YOU DON'T HAVE TO COVER YOURSELF, EITHER. BUT IF YOU WANT TO, THAT'S YOUR BUSINESS.

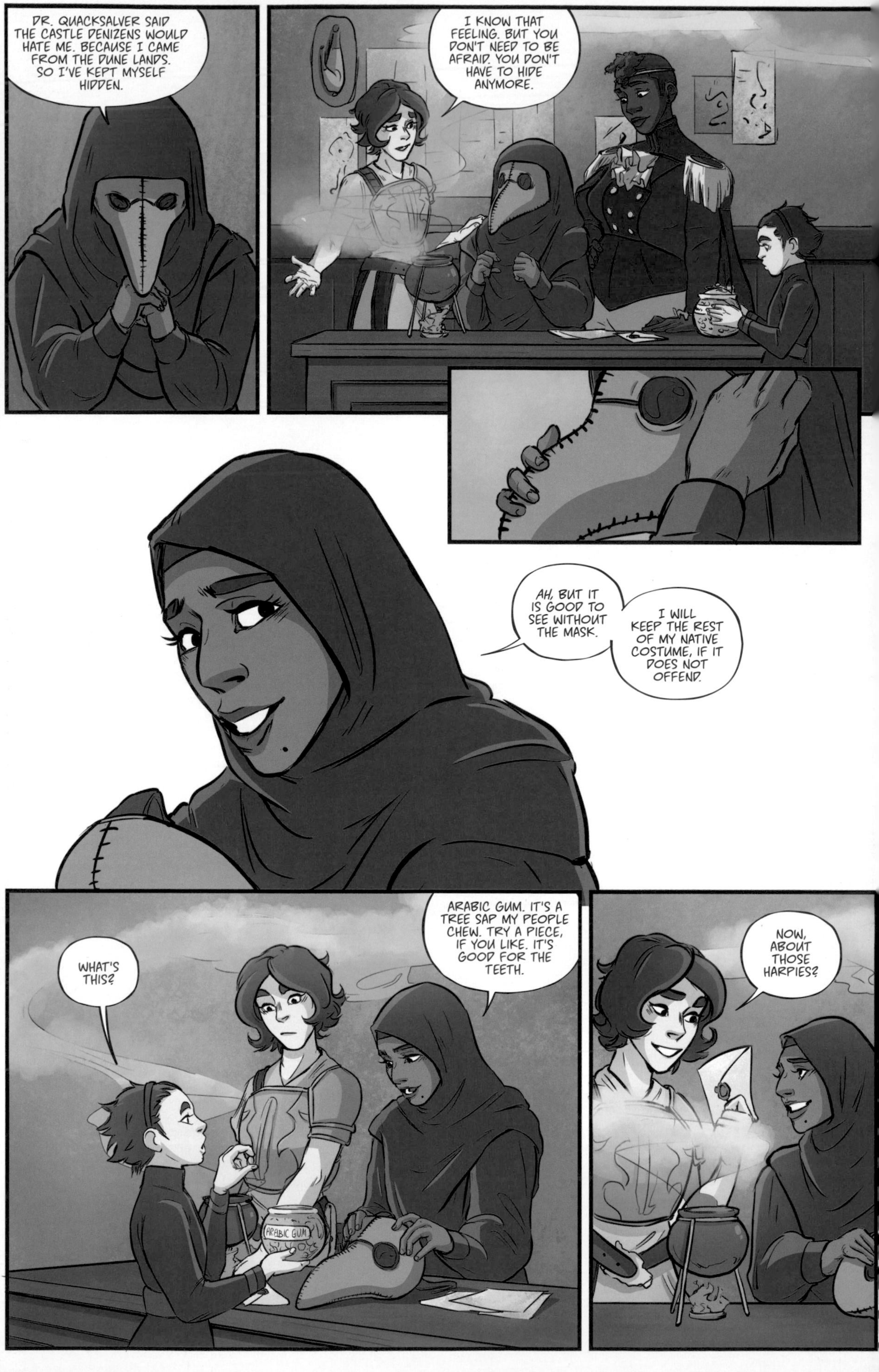
DR. QUACKSALVER SAID THE CASTLE DENIZENS WOULD HATE ME. BECAUSE I CAME FROM THE DUNE LANDS. SO I'VE KEPT MYSELF HIDDEN.
I KNOW THAT FEELING. BUT YOU DON'T NEED TO BE AFRAID. YOU DON'T HAVE TO HIDE ANYMORE.
AH, BUT IT IS GOOD TO SEE WITHOUT THE MASK.
I WILL KEEP THE REST OF MY NATIVE COSTUME, IF IT DOES NOT OFFEND.
WHAT'S THIS?
ARABIC GUM. IT'S A TREE SAP MY PEOPLE CHEW. TRY A PIECE, IF YOU LIKE. IT'S GOOD FOR THE TEETH.
ARABIC GUM
NOW, ABOUT THOSE HARPIES?

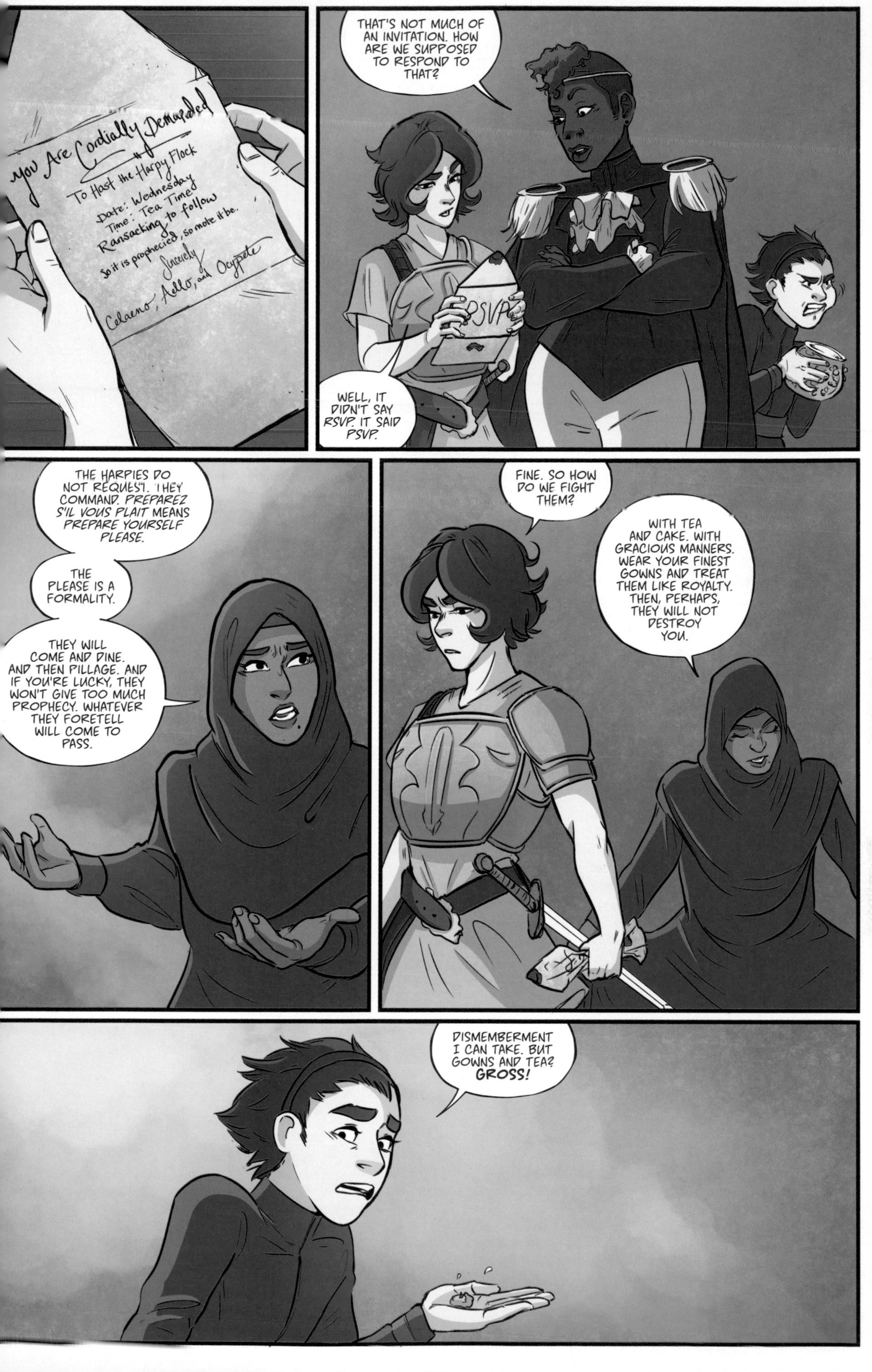
You Are Cordially Demanded
To Host the Harpy Flock
Date: Wednesday
Time: Tea Time
Ransacking to follow
So it is prophecied, so mote it be.
Sincerely
Celaeno, Aello, and Ocypete
THAT'S NOT MUCH OF AN INVITATION. HOW ARE WE SUPPOSED TO RESPOND TO THAT?
PSVP
WELL, IT DIDN'T SAY RSVP. IT SAID PSVP.
THE HARPIES DO NOT REQUEST. THEY COMMAND. PREPAREZ S'IL VOUS PLAIT MEANS PREPARE YOURSELF PLEASE.
THE PLEASE IS A FORMALITY.
THEY WILL COME AND DINE. AND THEN PILLAGE. AND IF YOU'RE LUCKY, THEY WON'T GIVE TOO MUCH PROPHECY. WHATEVER THEY FORETELL WILL COME TO PASS.
FINE. SO HOW DO WE FIGHT THEM?
WITH TEA AND CAKE. WITH GRACIOUS MANNERS. WEAR YOUR FINEST GOWNS AND TREAT THEM LIKE ROYALTY. THEN, PERHAPS, THEY WILL NOT DESTROY YOU.
DISMEMBERMENT I CAN TAKE. BUT GOWNS AND TEA? **GROSS!**

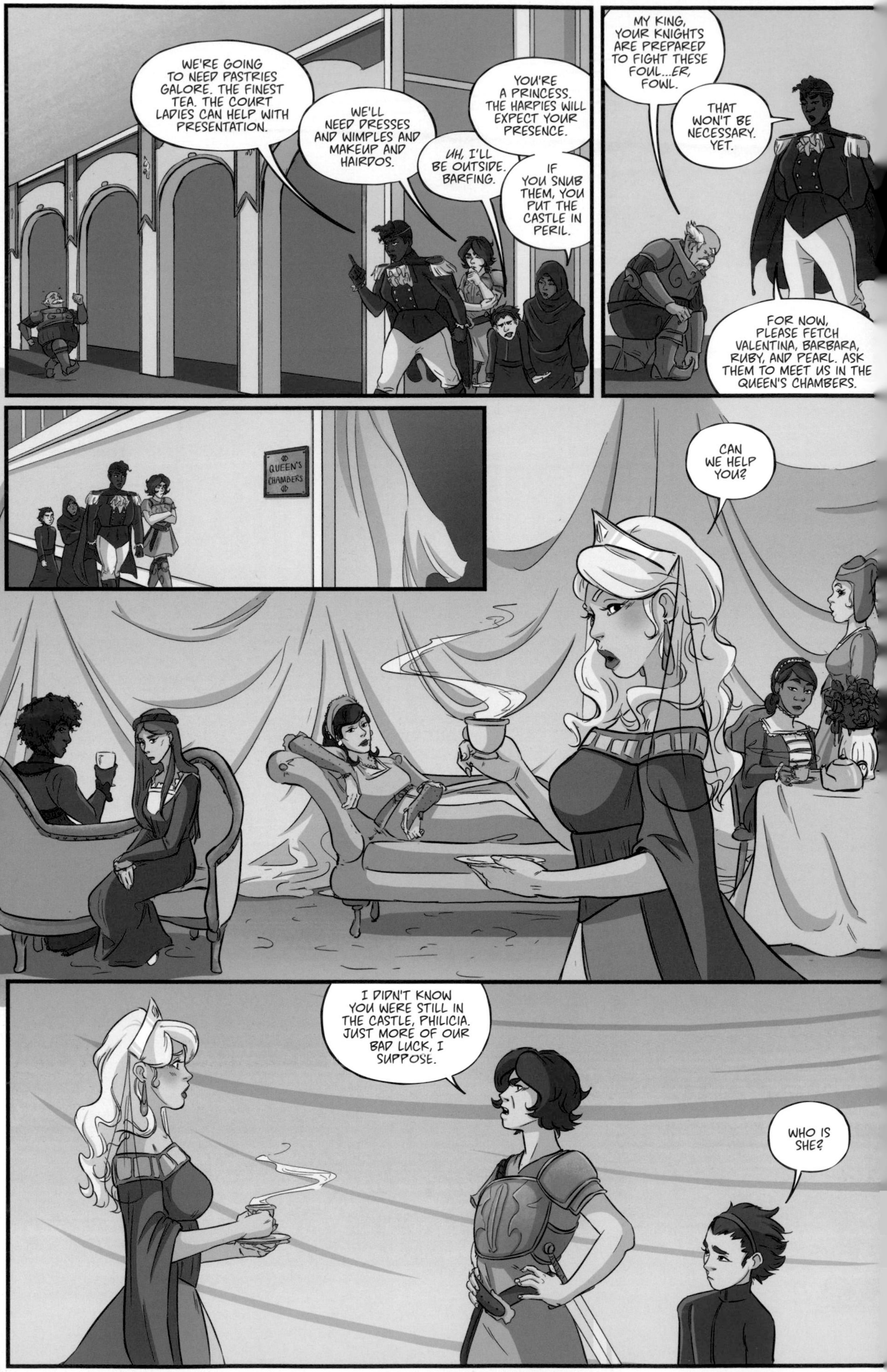
WE'RE GOING TO NEED PASTRIES GALORE. THE FINEST TEA. THE COURT LADIES CAN HELP WITH PRESENTATION.
WE'LL NEED DRESSES AND WIMPLES AND MAKEUP AND HAIRDOS.
UH, I'LL BE OUTSIDE. BARFING.
YOU'RE A PRINCESS. THE HARPIES WILL EXPECT YOUR PRESENCE.
IF YOU SNUB THEM, YOU PUT THE CASTLE IN PERIL.
MY KING, YOUR KNIGHTS ARE PREPARED TO FIGHT THESE FOUL...ER, FOWL.
THAT WON'T BE NECESSARY. YET.
FOR NOW, PLEASE FETCH VALENTINA, BARBARA, RUBY, AND PEARL. ASK THEM TO MEET US IN THE QUEEN'S CHAMBERS.
QUEEN'S CHAMBERS
CAN WE HELP YOU?
I DIDN'T KNOW YOU WERE STILL IN THE CASTLE, PHILICIA. JUST MORE OF OUR BAD LUCK, I SUPPOSE.
WHO IS SHE?

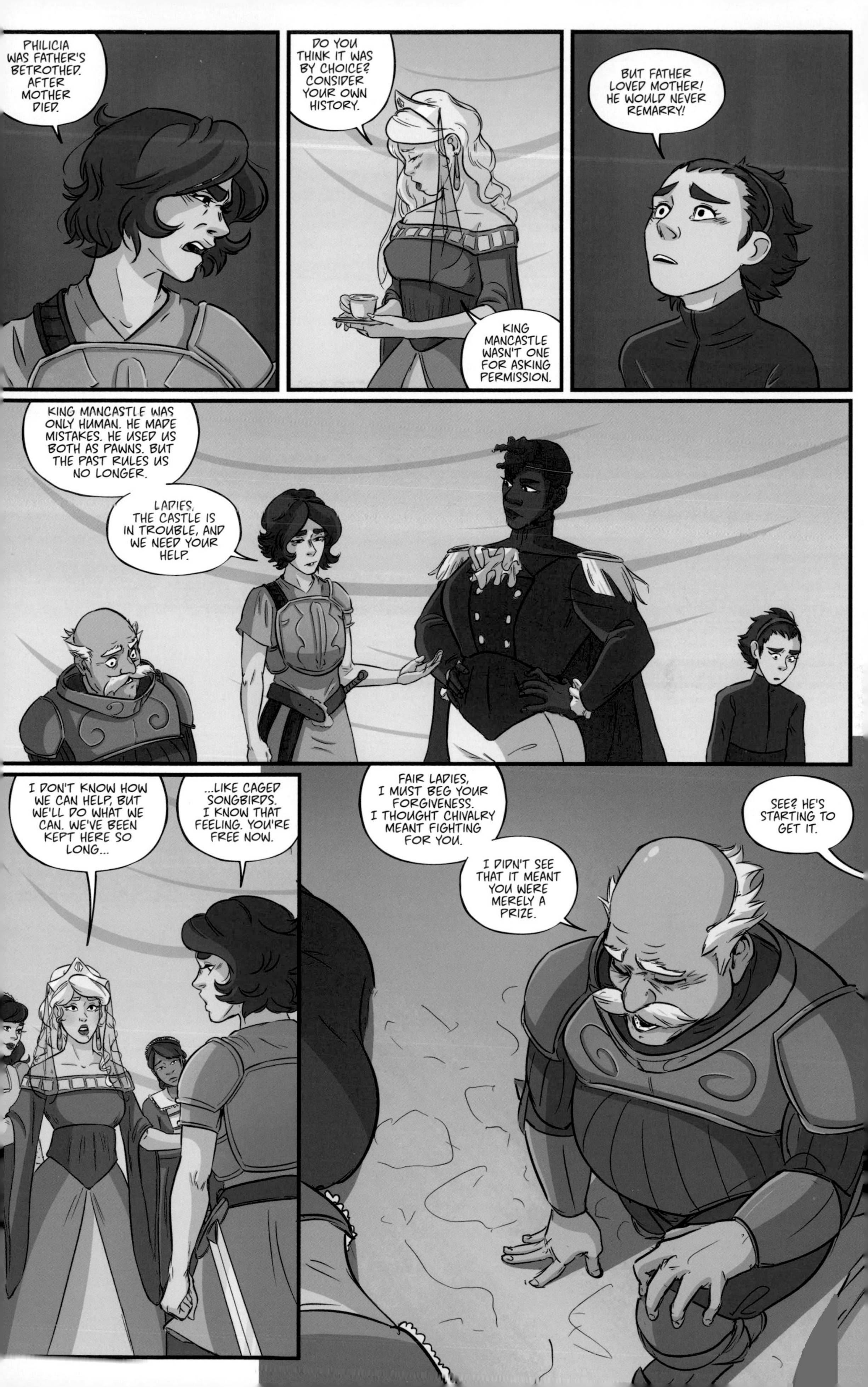
PHILICIA WAS FATHER'S BETROTHED. AFTER MOTHER DIED.
DO YOU THINK IT WAS BY CHOICE? CONSIDER YOUR OWN HISTORY.
KING MANCASTLE WASN'T ONE FOR ASKING PERMISSION.
BUT FATHER LOVED MOTHER! HE WOULD NEVER REMARRY!
KING MANCASTLE WAS ONLY HUMAN. HE MADE MISTAKES. HE USED US BOTH AS PAWNS. BUT THE PAST RULES US NO LONGER.
LADIES, THE CASTLE IS IN TROUBLE, AND WE NEED YOUR HELP.
I DON'T KNOW HOW WE CAN HELP, BUT WE'LL DO WHAT WE CAN. WE'VE BEEN KEPT HERE SO LONG...
...LIKE CAGED SONGBIRDS. I KNOW THAT FEELING. YOU'RE FREE NOW.
FAIR LADIES, I MUST BEG YOUR FORGIVENESS. I THOUGHT CHIVALRY MEANT FIGHTING FOR YOU.
I DIDN'T SEE THAT IT MEANT YOU WERE MERELY A PRIZE.
SEE? HE'S STARTING TO GET IT.

MIGHT I OFFER YOU SOME REFRESHMENT?

MMRPH MPRH YOURSELF!

GREEN IS YOUR COLOR.

I PREFER RED. THE COLOR OF THE ENEMY'S BLOOD.

SUCH THICK HAIR! SO LIKE YOUR MOTHER.

WELL, I HAVEN'T WASHED IT IN A YEAR, SO...WAIT, YOU KNEW MY MOTHER?

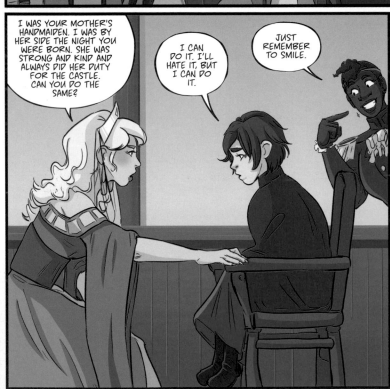

I WAS YOUR MOTHER'S HANDMAIDEN. I WAS BY HER SIDE THE NIGHT YOU WERE BORN. SHE WAS STRONG AND KIND AND ALWAYS DID HER DUTY FOR THE CASTLE. CAN YOU DO THE SAME?

I CAN DO IT. I'LL HATE IT, BUT I CAN DO IT.

JUST REMEMBER TO SMILE.

UH. SMILE LESS.

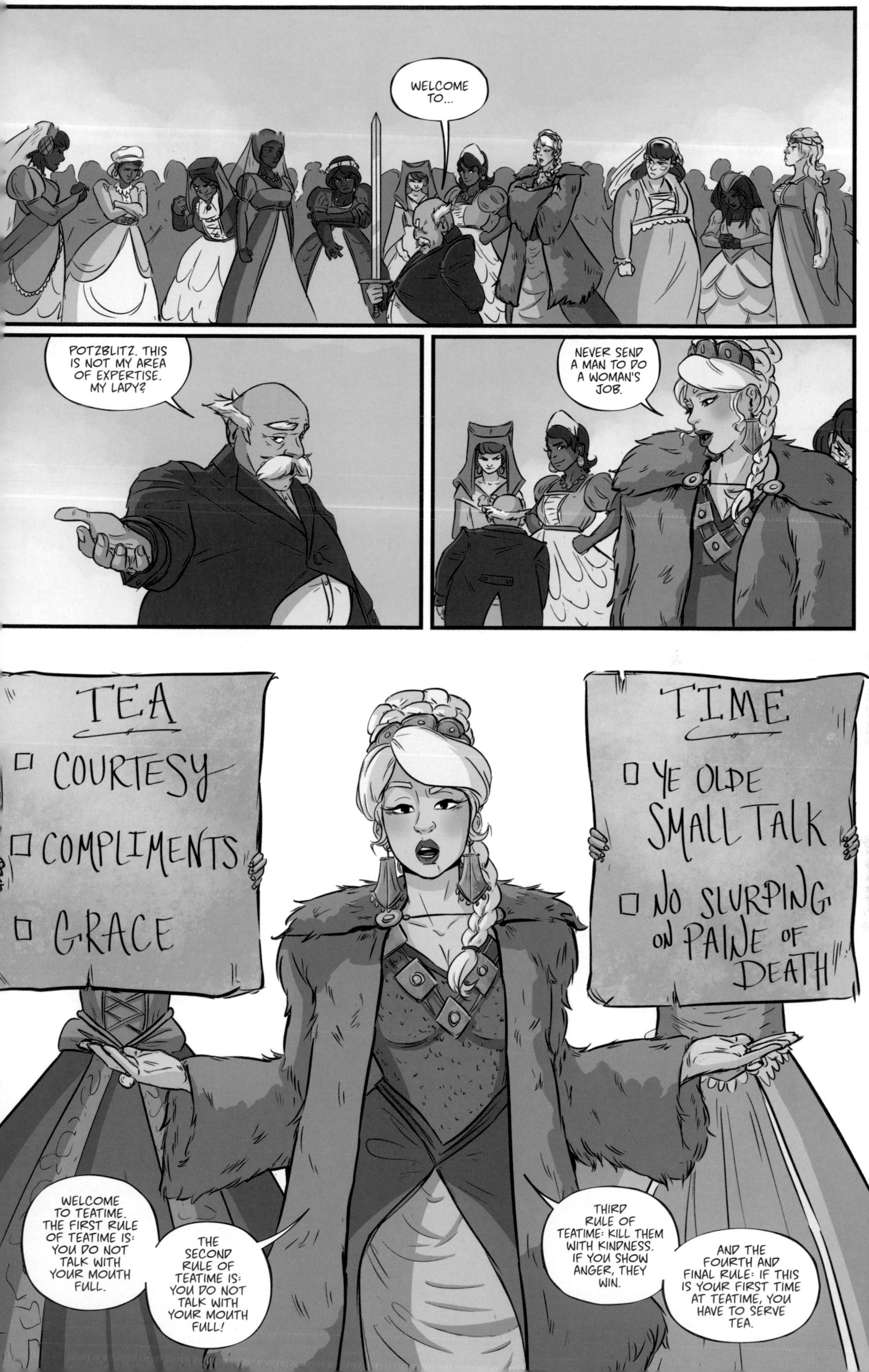
WELCOME TO...
POTZBLITZ. THIS IS NOT MY AREA OF EXPERTISE. MY LADY?
NEVER SEND A MAN TO DO A WOMAN'S JOB.
TEA
COURTESY
COMPLIMENTS
GRACE
TIME
YE OLDE SMALL TALK
NO SLURPING ON PAINE OF DEATH
WELCOME TO TEATIME. THE FIRST RULE OF TEATIME IS: YOU DO NOT TALK WITH YOUR MOUTH FULL.
THE SECOND RULE OF TEATIME IS: YOU DO NOT TALK WITH YOUR MOUTH FULL!
THIRD RULE OF TEATIME: KILL THEM WITH KINDNESS. IF YOU SHOW ANGER, THEY WIN.
AND THE FOURTH AND FINAL RULE: IF THIS IS YOUR FIRST TIME AT TEATIME, YOU HAVE TO SERVE TEA.

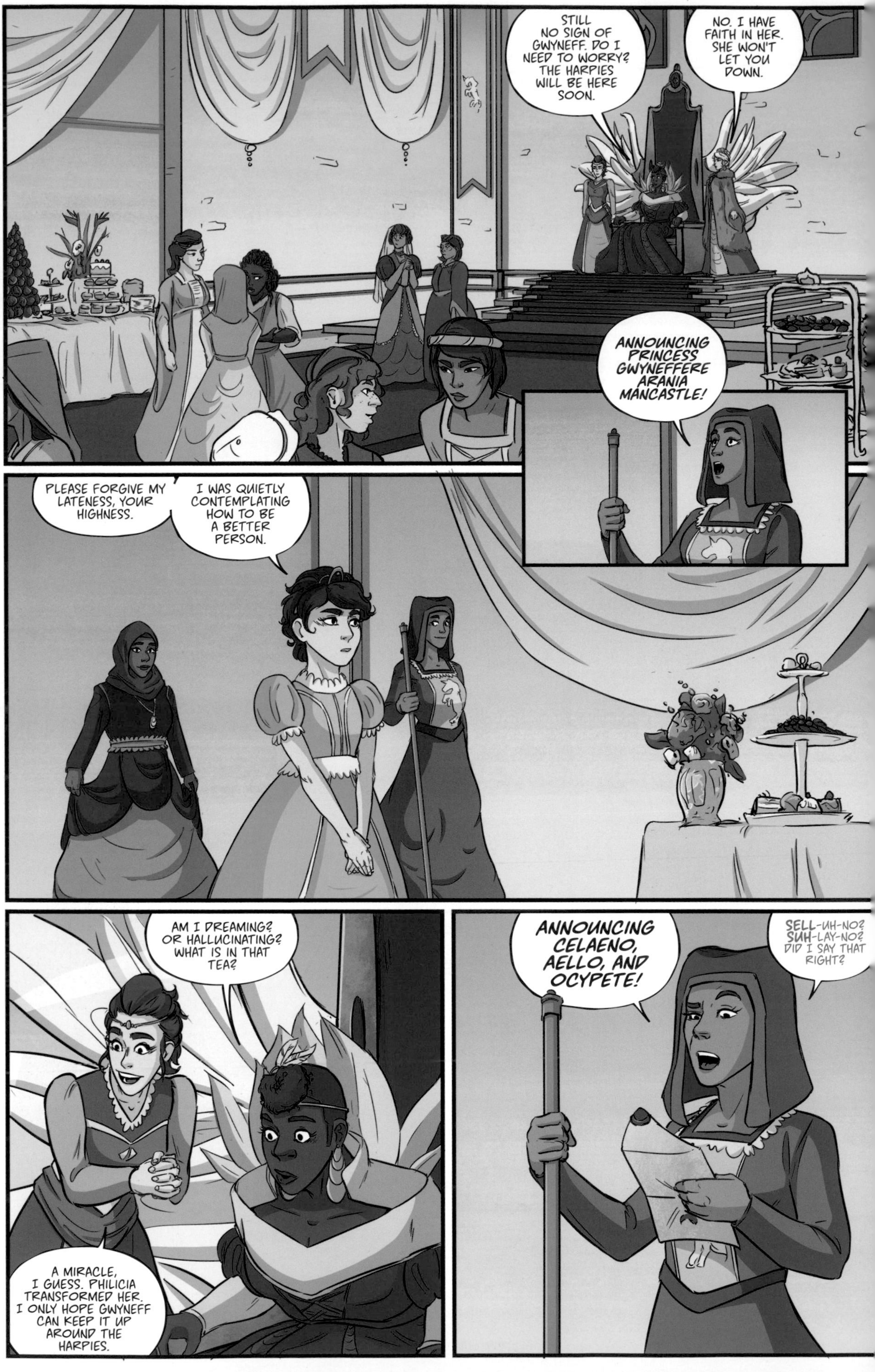
STILL NO SIGN OF GWYNEFF. DO I NEED TO WORRY? THE HARPIES WILL BE HERE SOON.
NO. I HAVE FAITH IN HER. SHE WON'T LET YOU DOWN.
ANNOUNCING PRINCESS GWYNEFFERE ARANIA MANCASTLE!
PLEASE FORGIVE MY LATENESS, YOUR HIGHNESS.
I WAS QUIETLY CONTEMPLATING HOW TO BE A BETTER PERSON.
AM I DREAMING? OR HALLUCINATING? WHAT IS IN THAT TEA?
A MIRACLE, I GUESS. PHILICIA TRANSFORMED HER. I ONLY HOPE GWYNEFF CAN KEEP IT UP AROUND THE HARPIES.
ANNOUNCING CELAENO, AELLO, AND OCYPETE!
SELL-UH-NO? SUH-LAY-NO? DID I SAY THAT RIGHT?

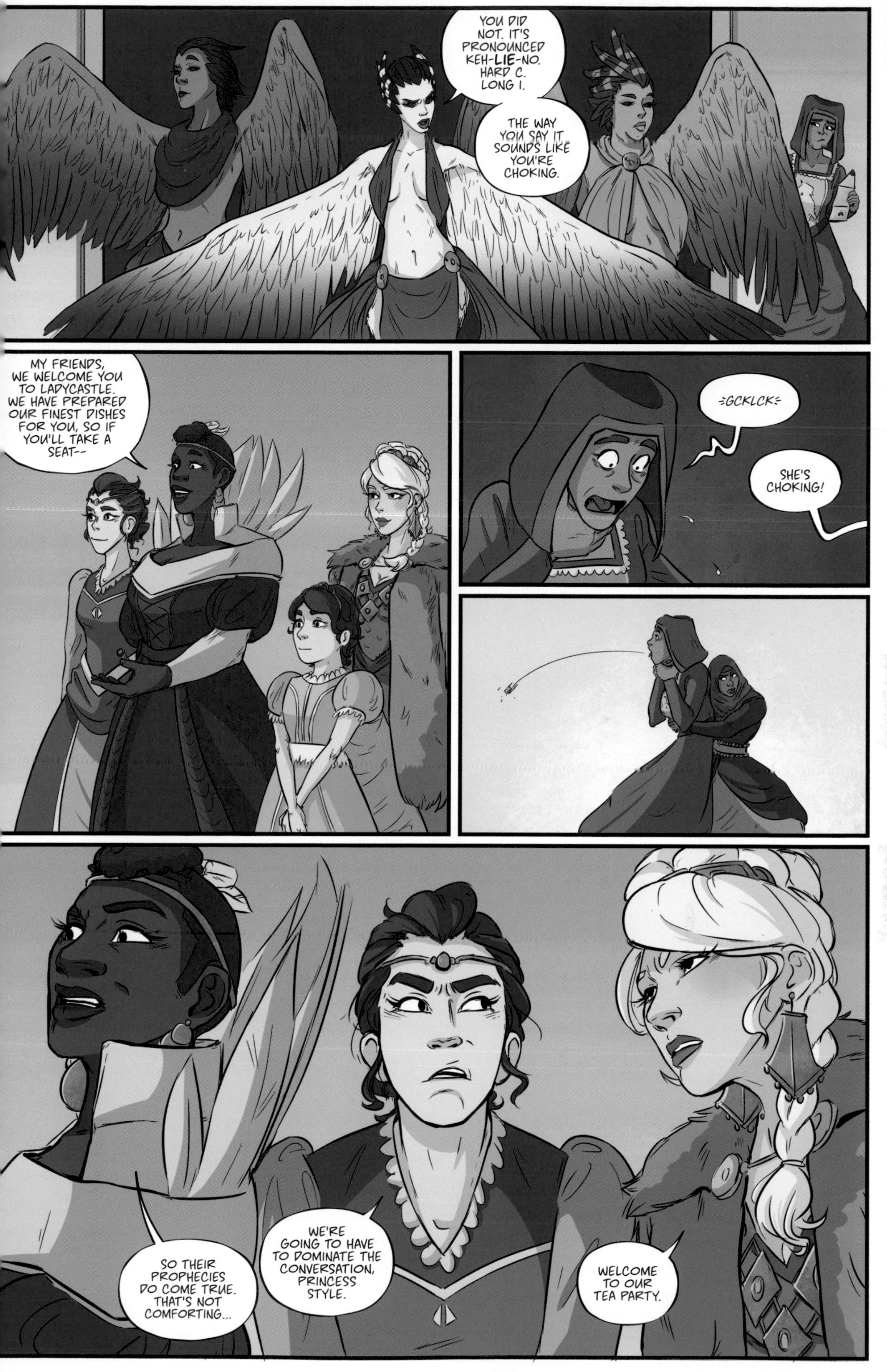
YOU DID NOT. IT'S PRONOUNCED KEH-LIE-NO. HARD C. LONG I.
THE WAY YOU SAY IT SOUNDS LIKE YOU'RE CHOKING.
MY FRIENDS, WE WELCOME YOU TO LADYCASTLE. WE HAVE PREPARED OUR FINEST DISHES FOR YOU, SO IF YOU'LL TAKE A SEAT--
GCKLCK
SHE'S CHOKING!
SO THEIR PROPHECIES DO COME TRUE. THAT'S NOT COMFORTING...
WE'RE GOING TO HAVE TO DOMINATE THE CONVERSATION, PRINCESS STYLE.
WELCOME TO OUR TEA PARTY.

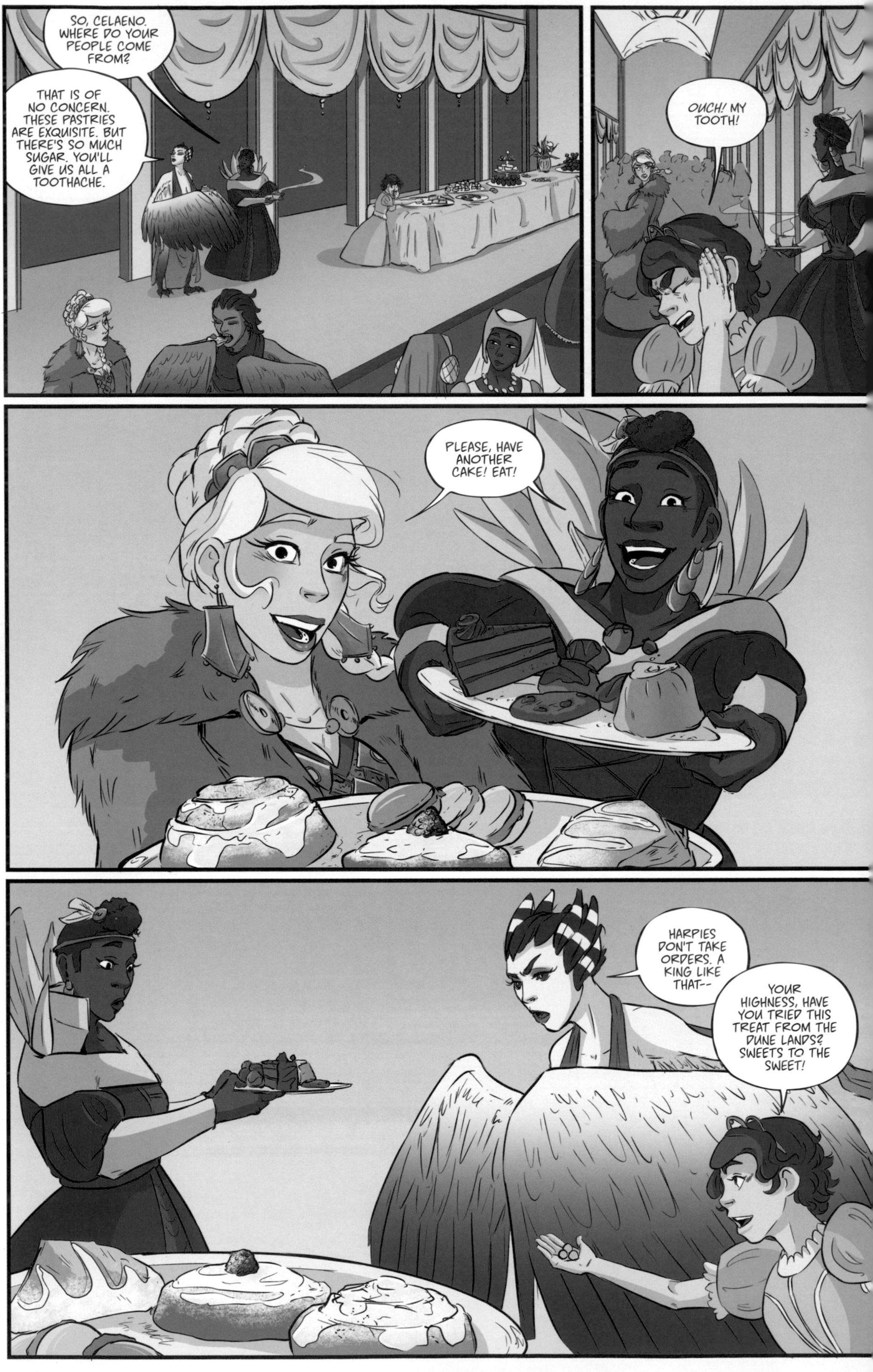
SO, CELAENO. WHERE DO YOUR PEOPLE COME FROM?
THAT IS OF NO CONCERN. THESE PASTRIES ARE EXQUISITE. BUT THERE'S SO MUCH SUGAR. YOU'LL GIVE US ALL A TOOTHACHE.
OUCH! MY TOOTH!
PLEASE, HAVE ANOTHER CAKE! EAT!
HARPIES DON'T TAKE ORDERS. A KING LIKE THAT--
YOUR HIGHNESS, HAVE YOU TRIED THIS TREAT FROM THE DUNE LANDS? SWEETS TO THE SWEET!

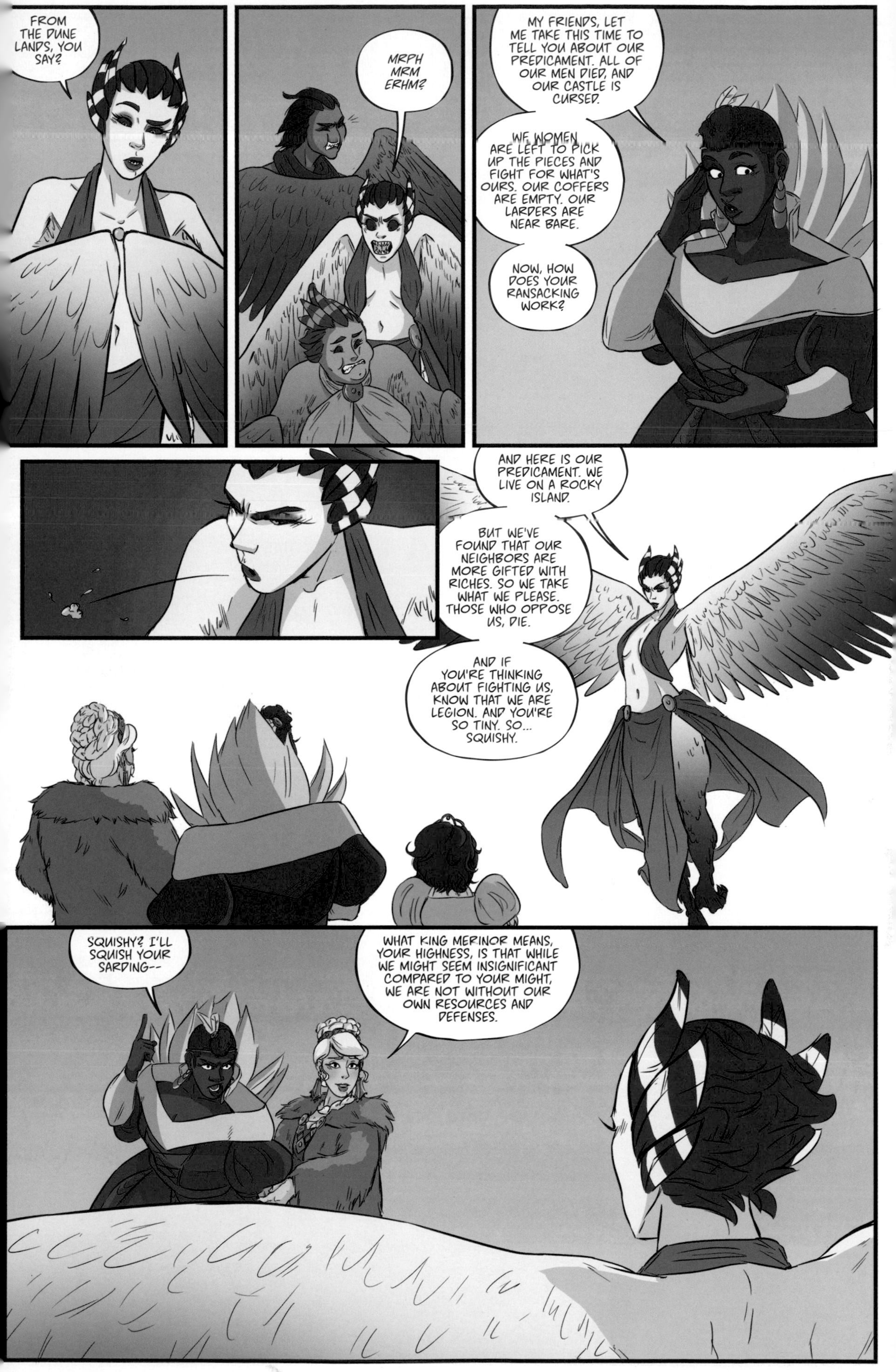
FROM THE DUNE LANDS, YOU SAY?
MRPH MRM ERHM?
MY FRIENDS, LET ME TAKE THIS TIME TO TELL YOU ABOUT OUR PREDICAMENT. ALL OF OUR MEN DIED, AND OUR CASTLE IS CURSED.
WE WOMEN ARE LEFT TO PICK UP THE PIECES AND FIGHT FOR WHAT'S OURS. OUR COFFERS ARE EMPTY. OUR LARDERS ARE NEAR BARE.
NOW, HOW DOES YOUR RANSACKING WORK?
AND HERE IS OUR PREDICAMENT. WE LIVE ON A ROCKY ISLAND.
BUT WE'VE FOUND THAT OUR NEIGHBORS ARE MORE GIFTED WITH RICHES. SO WE TAKE WHAT WE PLEASE. THOSE WHO OPPOSE US, DIE.
AND IF YOU'RE THINKING ABOUT FIGHTING US, KNOW THAT WE ARE LEGION. AND YOU'RE SO TINY. SO... SQUISHY.
SQUISHY? I'LL SQUISH YOUR SARDING--
WHAT KING MERINOR MEANS, YOUR HIGHNESS, IS THAT WHILE WE MIGHT SEEM INSIGNIFICANT COMPARED TO YOUR MIGHT, WE ARE NOT WITHOUT OUR OWN RESOURCES AND DEFENSES.

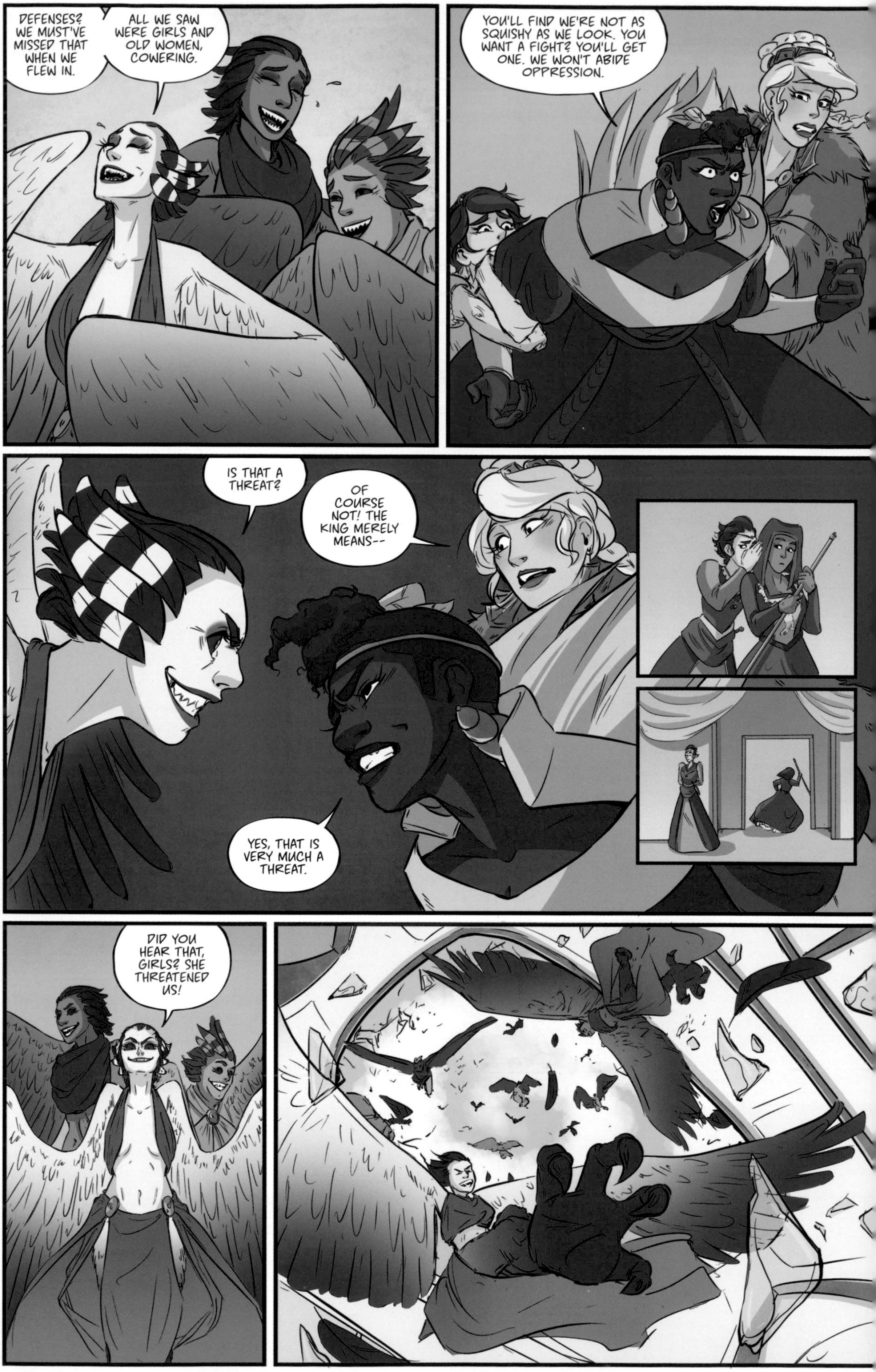
DEFENSES? WE MUST'VE MISSED THAT WHEN WE FLEW IN.
ALL WE SAW WERE GIRLS AND OLD WOMEN, COWERING.
YOU'LL FIND WE'RE NOT AS SQUISHY AS WE LOOK. YOU WANT A FIGHT? YOU'LL GET ONE. WE WON'T ABIDE OPPRESSION.
IS THAT A THREAT?
OF COURSE NOT! THE KING MERELY MEANS--
YES, THAT IS VERY MUCH A THREAT.
DID YOU HEAR THAT, GIRLS? SHE THREATENED US!

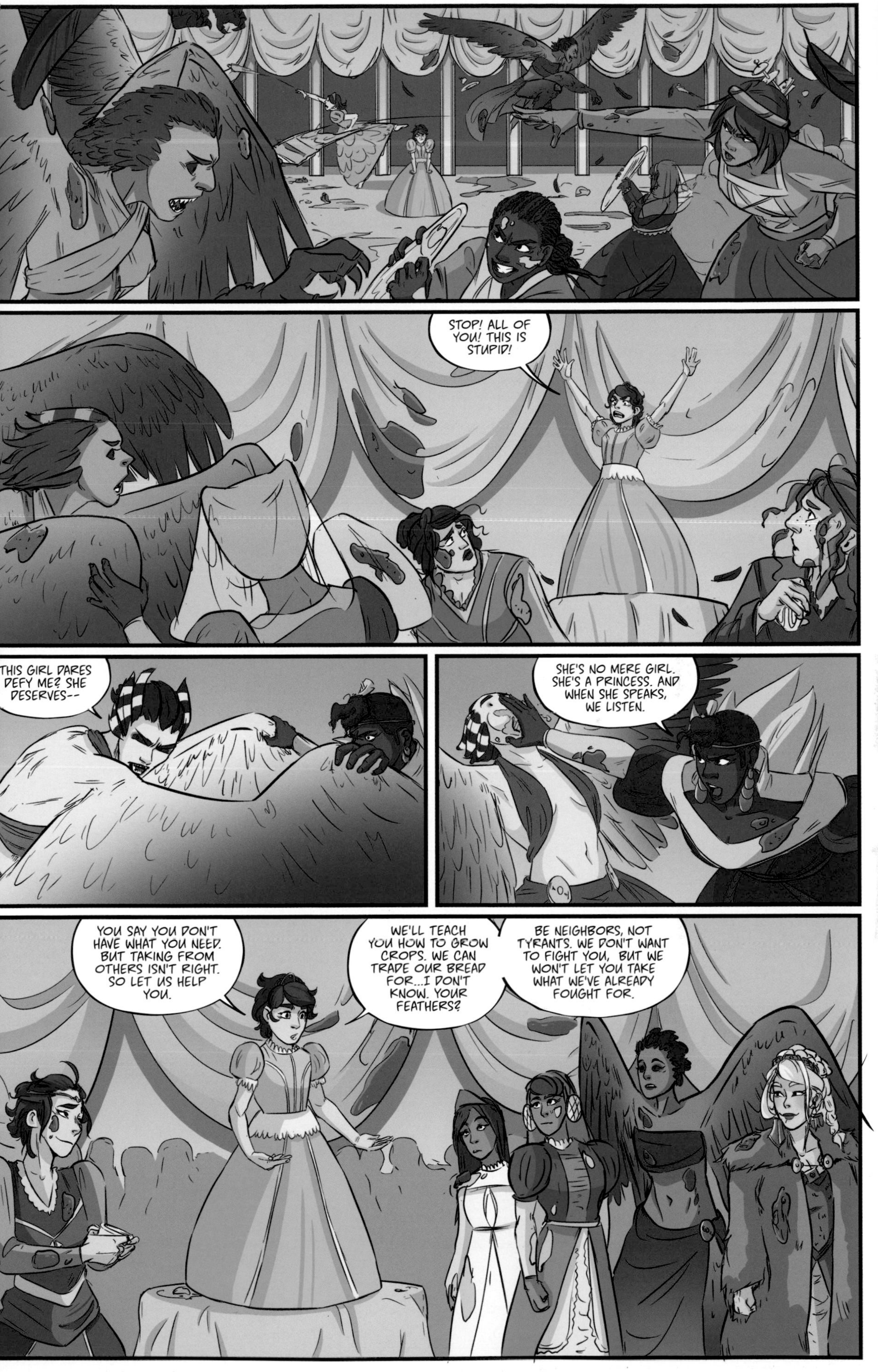

STOP! ALL OF YOU! THIS IS STUPID!
THIS GIRL DARES DEFY ME? SHE DESERVES--
SHE'S NO MERE GIRL. SHE'S A PRINCESS. AND WHEN SHE SPEAKS, WE LISTEN.
YOU SAY YOU DON'T HAVE WHAT YOU NEED. BUT TAKING FROM OTHERS ISN'T RIGHT. SO LET US HELP YOU.
WE'LL TEACH YOU HOW TO GROW CROPS. WE CAN TRADE OUR BREAD FOR...I DON'T KNOW. YOUR FEATHERS?
BE NEIGHBORS, NOT TYRANTS. WE DON'T WANT TO FIGHT YOU, BUT WE WON'T LET YOU TAKE WHAT WE'VE ALREADY FOUGHT FOR.

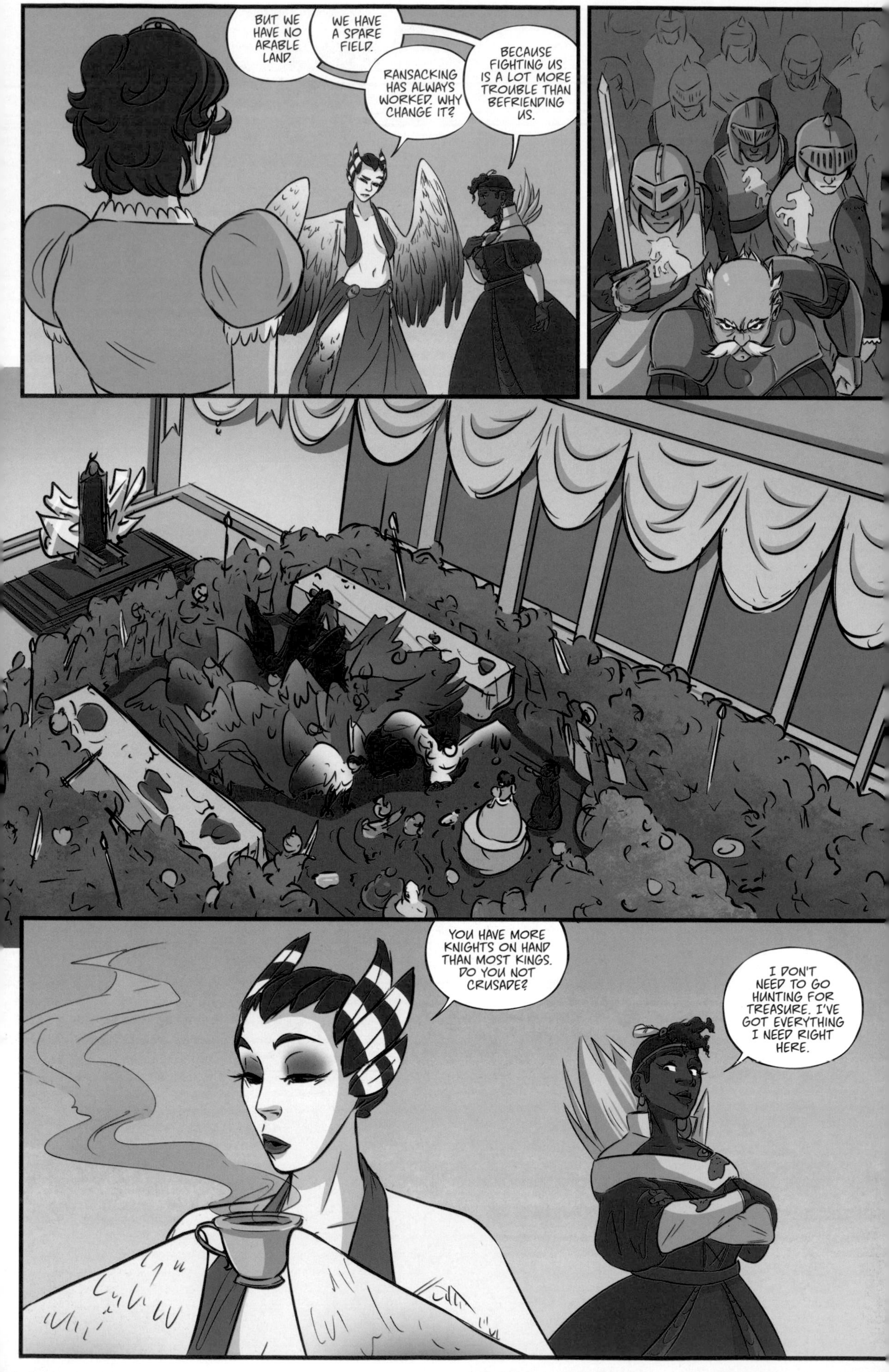
BUT WE HAVE NO ARABLE LAND.
WE HAVE A SPARE FIELD.
RANSACKING HAS ALWAYS WORKED. WHY CHANGE IT?
BECAUSE FIGHTING US IS A LOT MORE TROUBLE THAN BEFRIENDING US.
YOU HAVE MORE KNIGHTS ON HAND THAN MOST KINGS. DO YOU NOT CRUSADE?
I DON'T NEED TO GO HUNTING FOR TREASURE. I'VE GOT EVERYTHING I NEED RIGHT HERE.

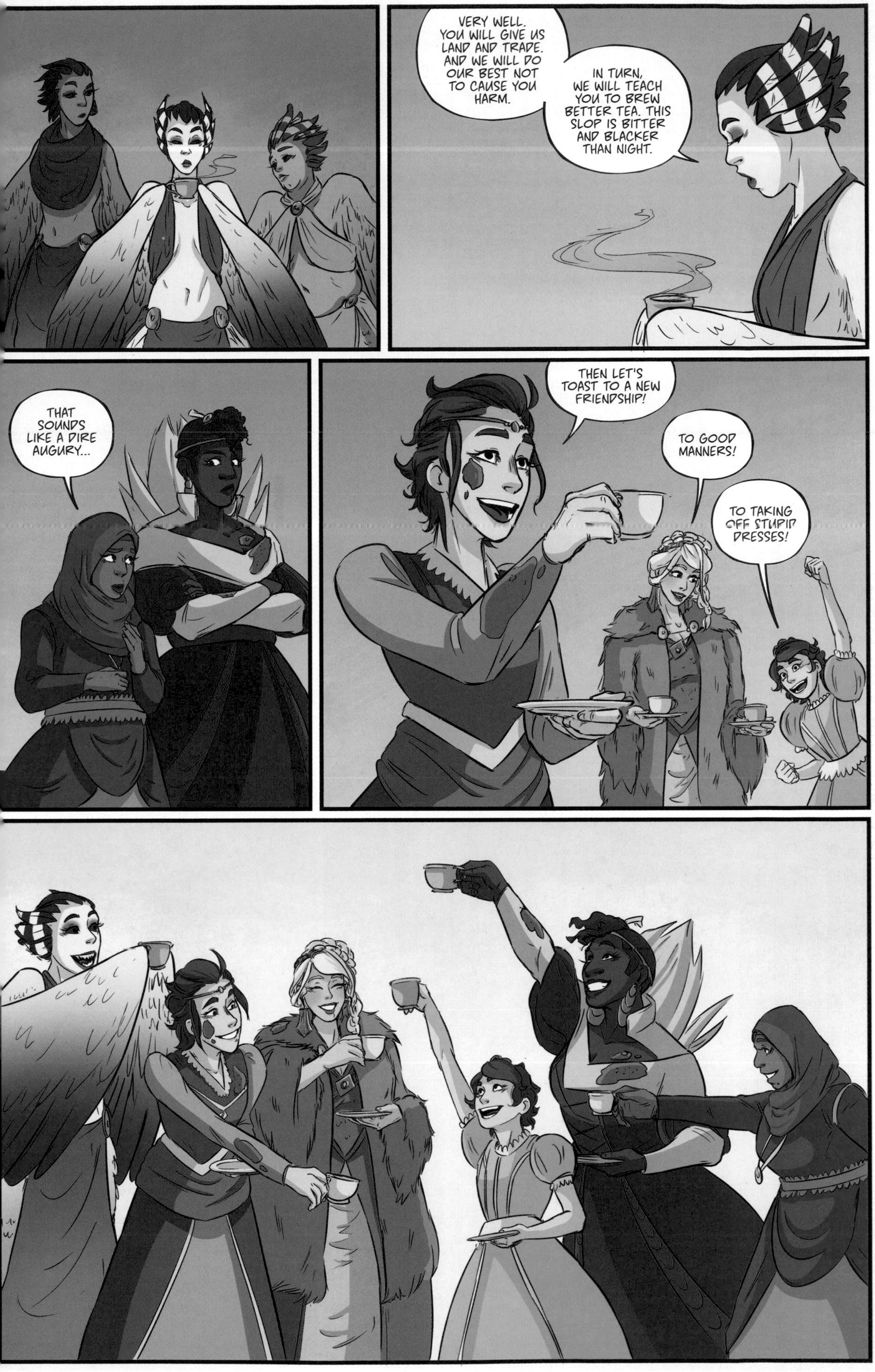
VERY WELL. YOU WILL GIVE US LAND AND TRADE. AND WE WILL DO OUR BEST NOT TO CAUSE YOU HARM.
IN TURN, WE WILL TEACH YOU TO BREW BETTER TEA. THIS SLOP IS BITTER AND BLACKER THAN NIGHT.
THAT SOUNDS LIKE A DIRE AUGURY...
THEN LET'S TOAST TO A NEW FRIENDSHIP!
TO GOOD MANNERS!
TO TAKING OFF STUPID DRESSES!

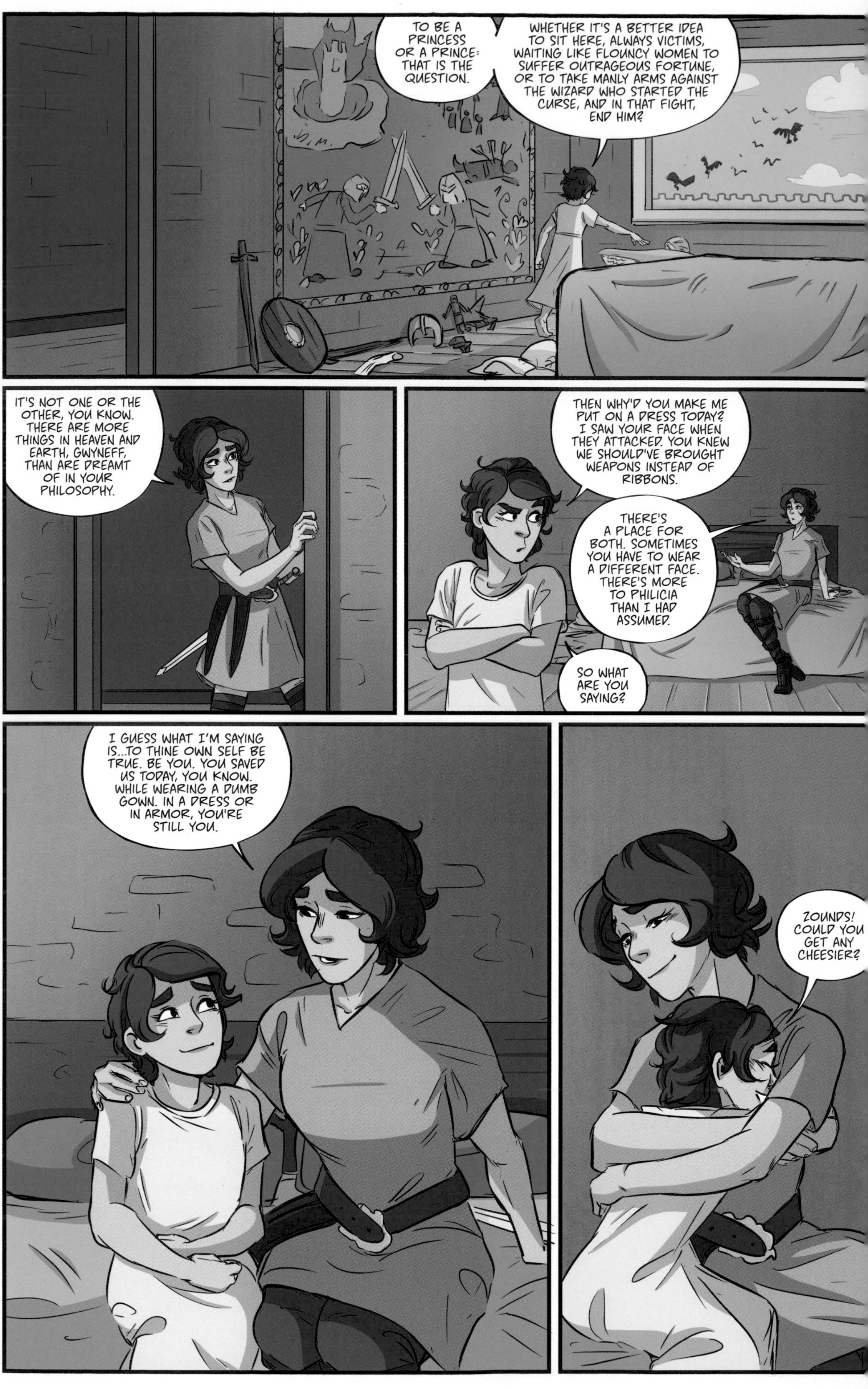
TO BE A PRINCESS OR A PRINCE: THAT IS THE QUESTION.
WHETHER IT'S A BETTER IDEA TO SIT HERE, ALWAYS VICTIMS, WAITING LIKE FLOUNCY WOMEN TO SUFFER OUTRAGEOUS FORTUNE, OR TO TAKE MANLY ARMS AGAINST THE WIZARD WHO STARTED THE CURSE, AND IN THAT FIGHT, END HIM?
IT'S NOT ONE OR THE OTHER, YOU KNOW. THERE ARE MORE THINGS IN HEAVEN AND EARTH, GWYNEFF, THAN ARE DREAMT OF IN YOUR PHILOSOPHY.
THEN WHY'D YOU MAKE ME PUT ON A DRESS TODAY? I SAW YOUR FACE WHEN THEY ATTACKED. YOU KNEW WE SHOULD'VE BROUGHT WEAPONS INSTEAD OF RIBBONS.
THERE'S A PLACE FOR BOTH. SOMETIMES YOU HAVE TO WEAR A DIFFERENT FACE. THERE'S MORE TO PHILICIA THAN I HAD ASSUMED.
SO WHAT ARE YOU SAYING?
I GUESS WHAT I'M SAYING IS...TO THINE OWN SELF BE TRUE. BE YOU. YOU SAVED US TODAY, YOU KNOW. WHILE WEARING A DUMB GOWN. IN A DRESS OR IN ARMOR, YOU'RE STILL YOU.
ZOUNDS! COULD YOU GET ANY CHEESIER?

THIS CURSE. IT'S CRAZY, RIGHT?

HISS!

RIGHT. BECAUSE YOU GUYS SHOWED UP, AND NOW WE'RE PALS.

THEN THE WEREWOLVES SHOWED UP, AND THEY DIDN'T EVEN WANT A FIGHT. NOW WE'RE LEASING LAND TO HARPIES, WORKING TOGETHER.

GUESS WE'LL NEVER RUN OUT OF FEATHER PILLOWS AND FISH FOR DINNER.

IT'S ALMOST LIKE THE CURSE... WAS GOOD FOR US.

WELL, ME AND KEFF, WE COULDN'T HAVE KIDS. WANTED 'EM, THOUGH. NOW HE'S GONE, AND I GOT A WHOLE CASTLE TO LOOK AFTER.

AT LEAST GWYNEFF IS GETTING BACK ON TRACK. WHY ARE PRINCESSES SO MELANCHOLY?

HISS?

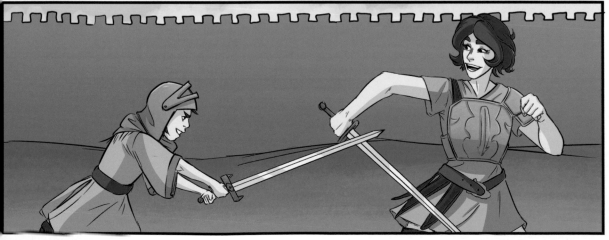

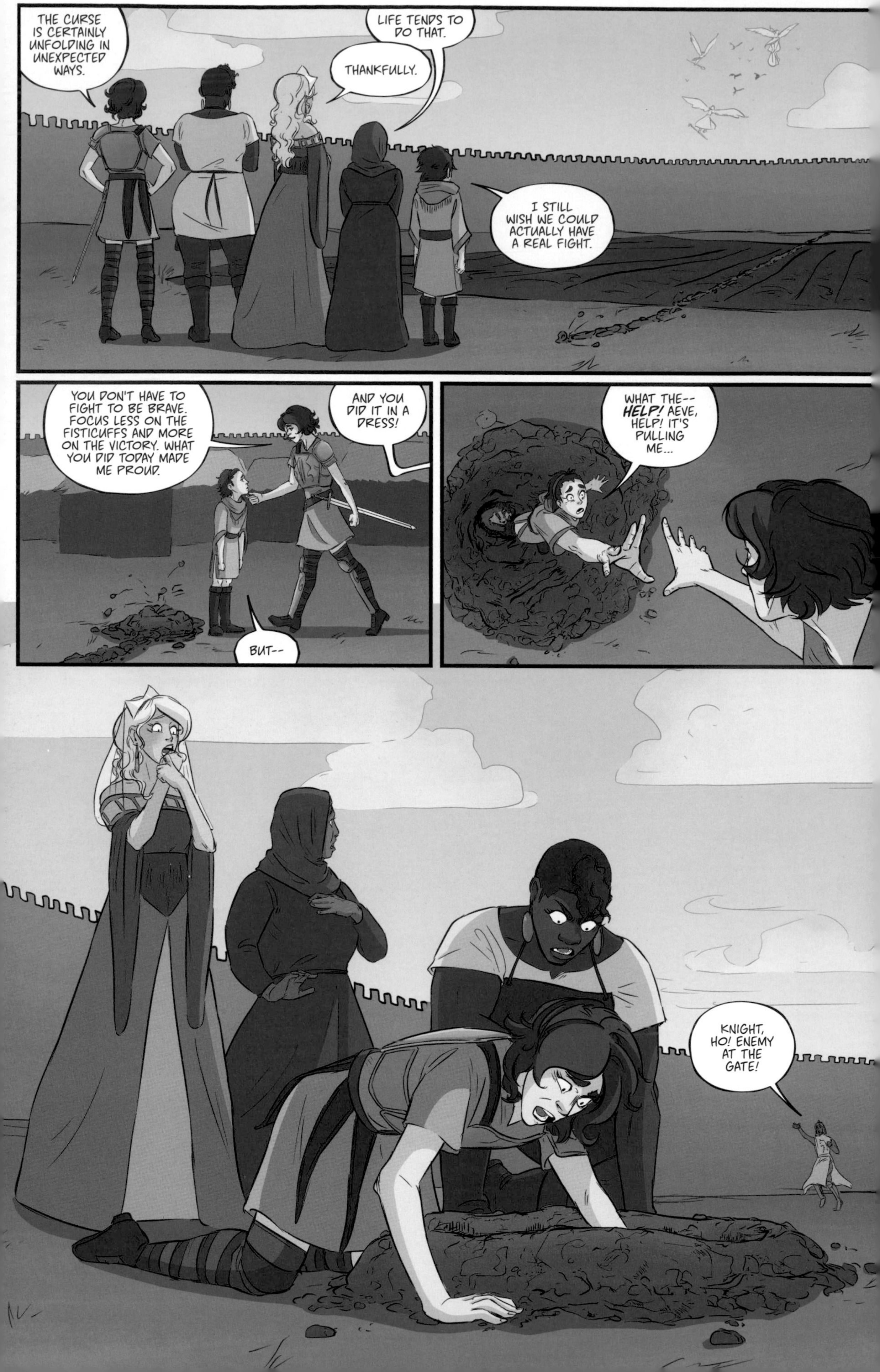
THE CURSE IS CERTAINLY UNFOLDING IN UNEXPECTED WAYS.
LIFE TENDS TO DO THAT.
THANKFULLY.
I STILL WISH WE COULD ACTUALLY HAVE A REAL FIGHT.
YOU DON'T HAVE TO FIGHT TO BE BRAVE. FOCUS LESS ON THE FISTICUFFS AND MORE ON THE VICTORY. WHAT YOU DID TODAY MADE ME PROUD.
AND YOU DID IT IN A DRESS!
BUT--
WHAT THE-- HELP! AEVE, HELP! IT'S PULLING ME...
KNIGHT, HO! ENEMY AT THE GATE!

"READY, AIM,
SQUIRE!"

CHAPTER FOUR

THE BLACK KNIGHT RISES

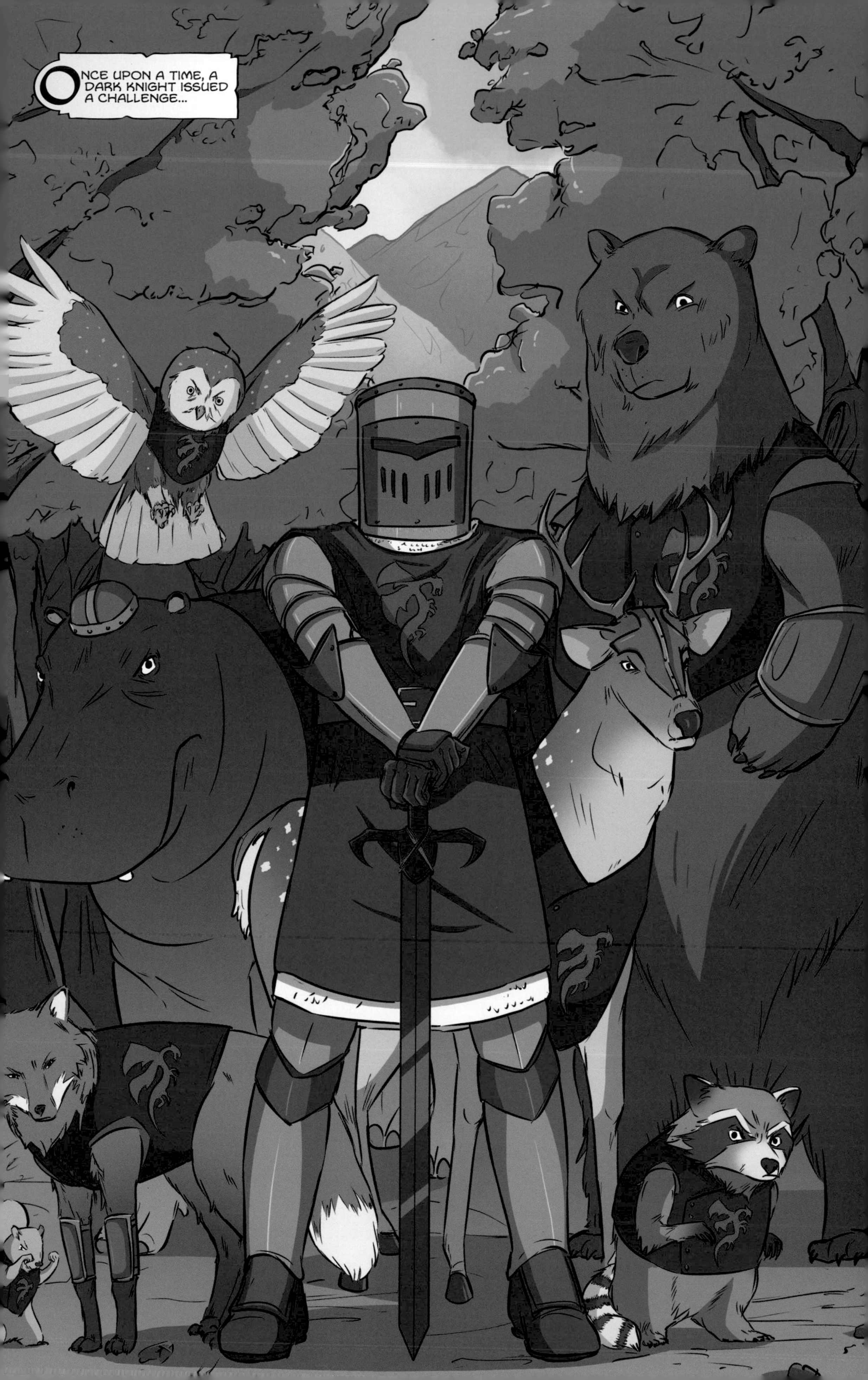
ONCE UPON A TIME, A DARK KNIGHT ISSUED A CHALLENGE...

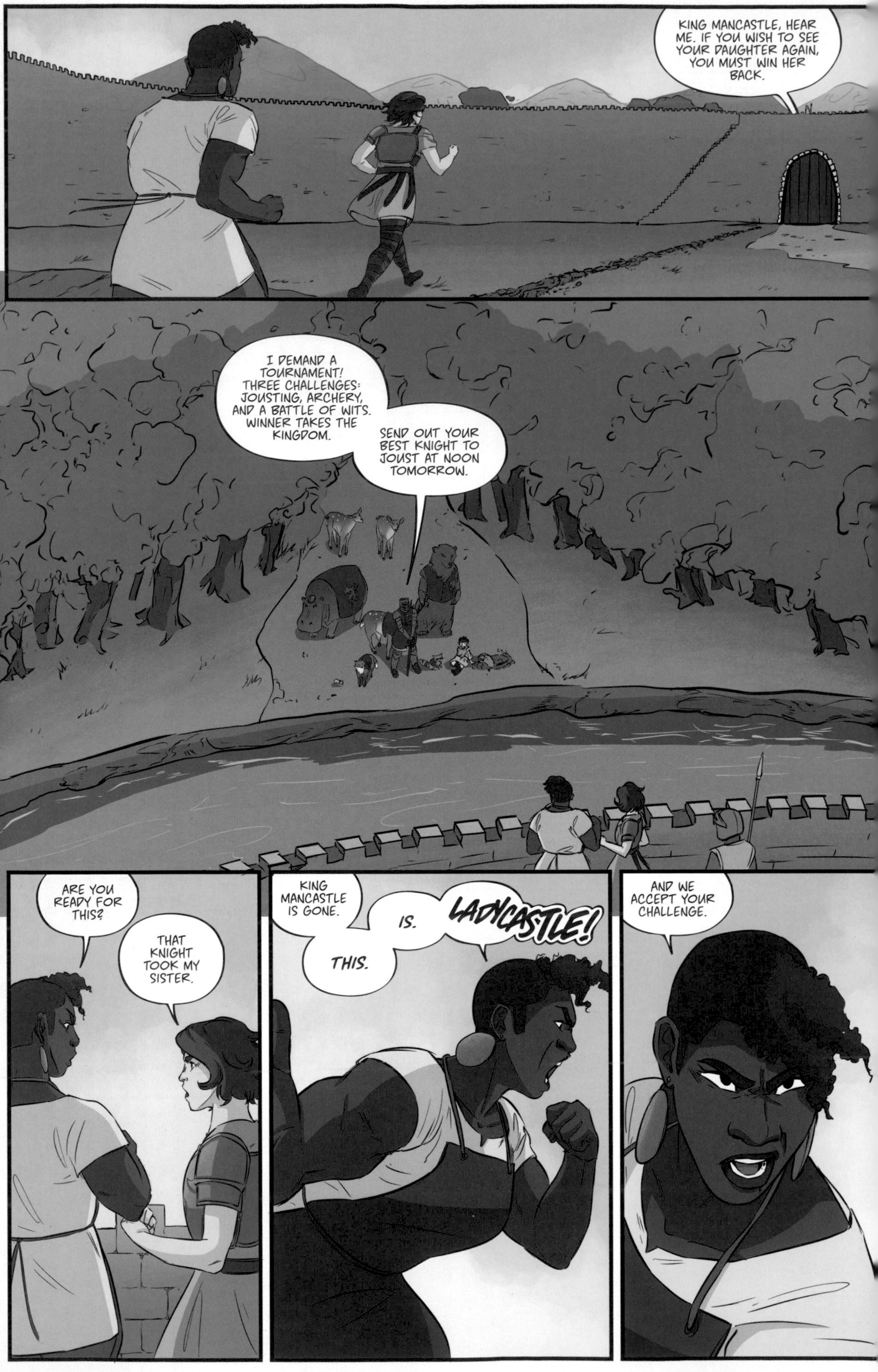
KING MANCASTLE, HEAR ME. IF YOU WISH TO SEE YOUR DAUGHTER AGAIN, YOU MUST WIN HER BACK.
I DEMAND A TOURNAMENT! THREE CHALLENGES: JOUSTING, ARCHERY, AND A BATTLE OF WITS. WINNER TAKES THE KINGDOM.
SEND OUT YOUR BEST KNIGHT TO JOUST AT NOON TOMORROW.
ARE YOU READY FOR THIS?
THAT KNIGHT TOOK MY SISTER.
KING MANCASTLE IS GONE.
THIS.
IS.
LADYCASTLE!
AND WE ACCEPT YOUR CHALLENGE.

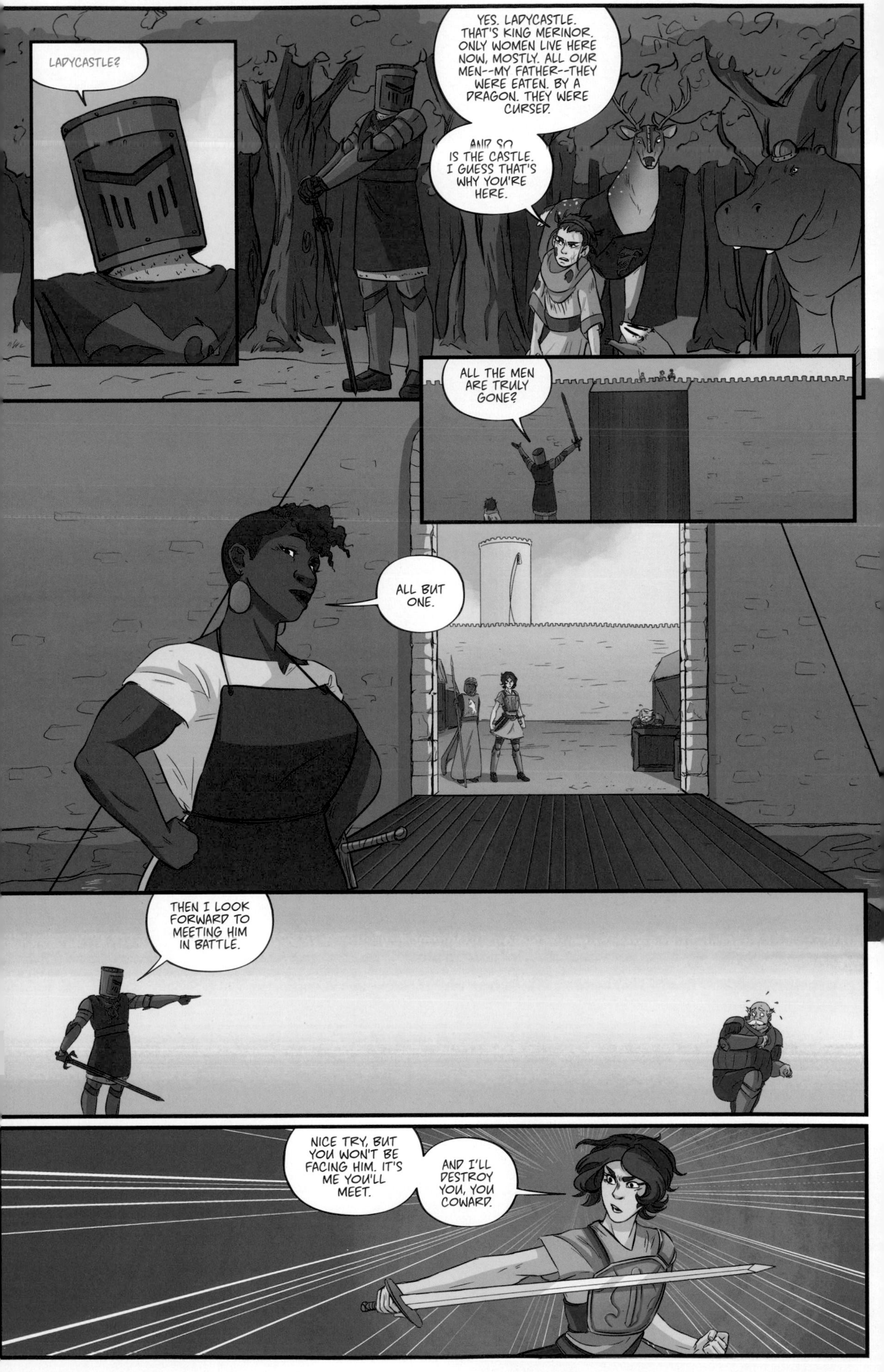
LADYCASTLE?
YES. LADYCASTLE. THAT'S KING MERINOR. ONLY WOMEN LIVE HERE NOW, MOSTLY. ALL OUR MEN--MY FATHER--THEY WERE EATEN. BY A DRAGON. THEY WERE CURSED.
AND SO IS THE CASTLE. I GUESS THAT'S WHY YOU'RE HERE.
ALL THE MEN ARE TRULY GONE?
ALL BUT ONE.
THEN I LOOK FORWARD TO MEETING HIM IN BATTLE.
NICE TRY, BUT YOU WON'T BE FACING HIM. IT'S ME YOU'LL MEET.
AND I'LL DESTROY YOU, YOU COWARD.

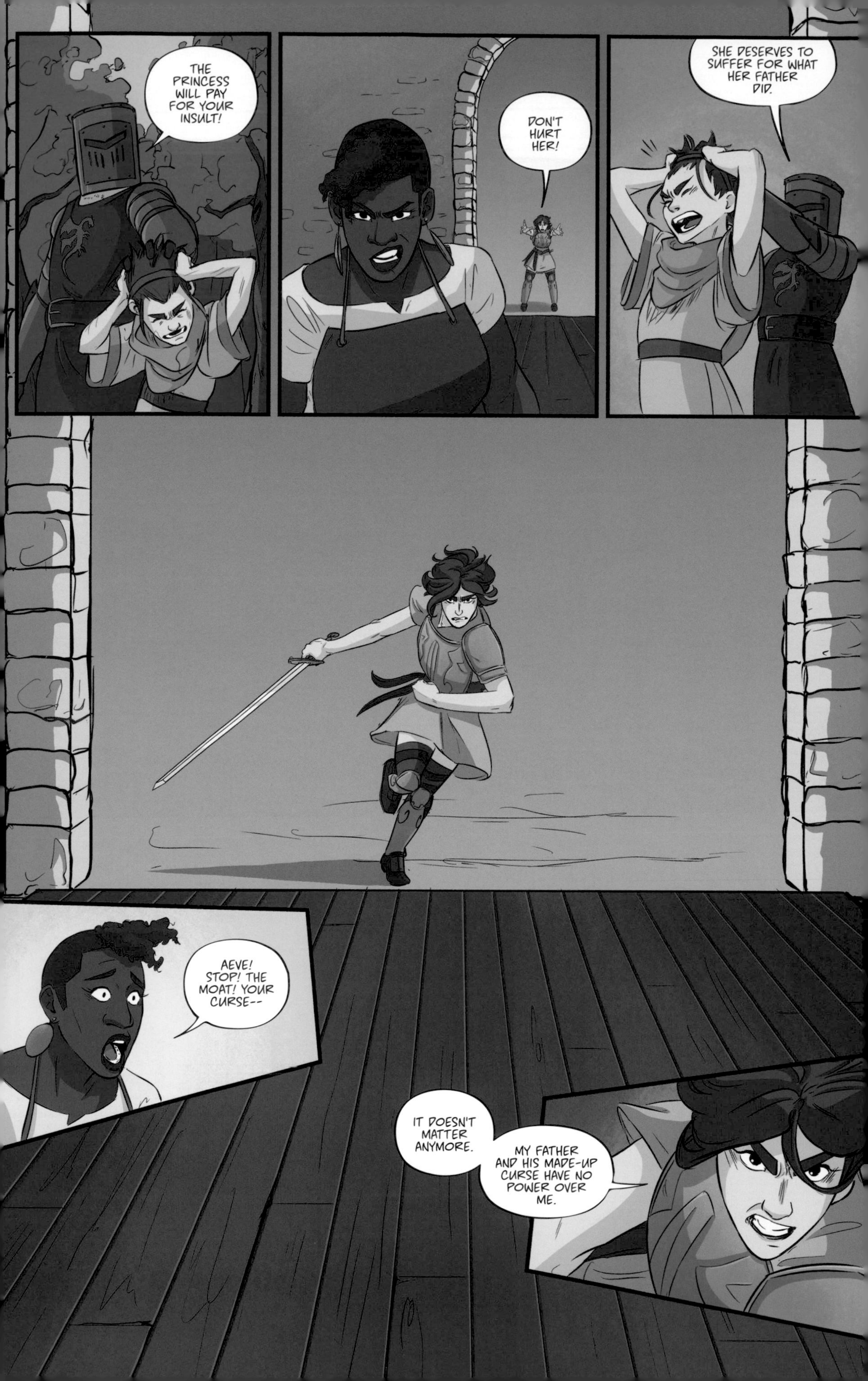
THE PRINCESS WILL PAY FOR YOUR INSULT!
DON'T HURT HER!
SHE DESERVES TO SUFFER FOR WHAT HER FATHER DID.
AEVE! STOP! THE MOAT! YOUR CURSE--
IT DOESN'T MATTER ANYMORE.
MY FATHER AND HIS MADE-UP CURSE HAVE NO POWER OVER ME.

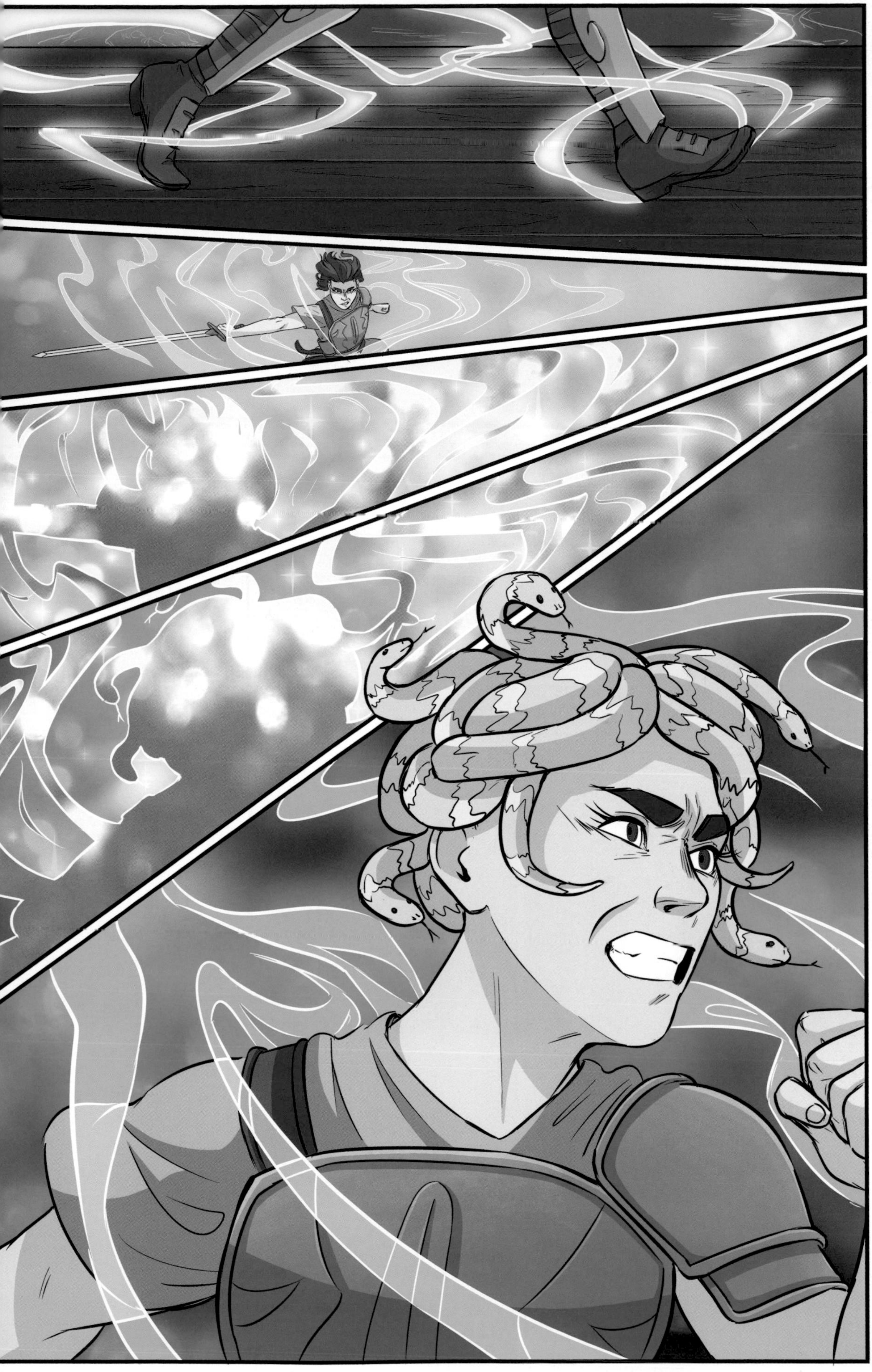

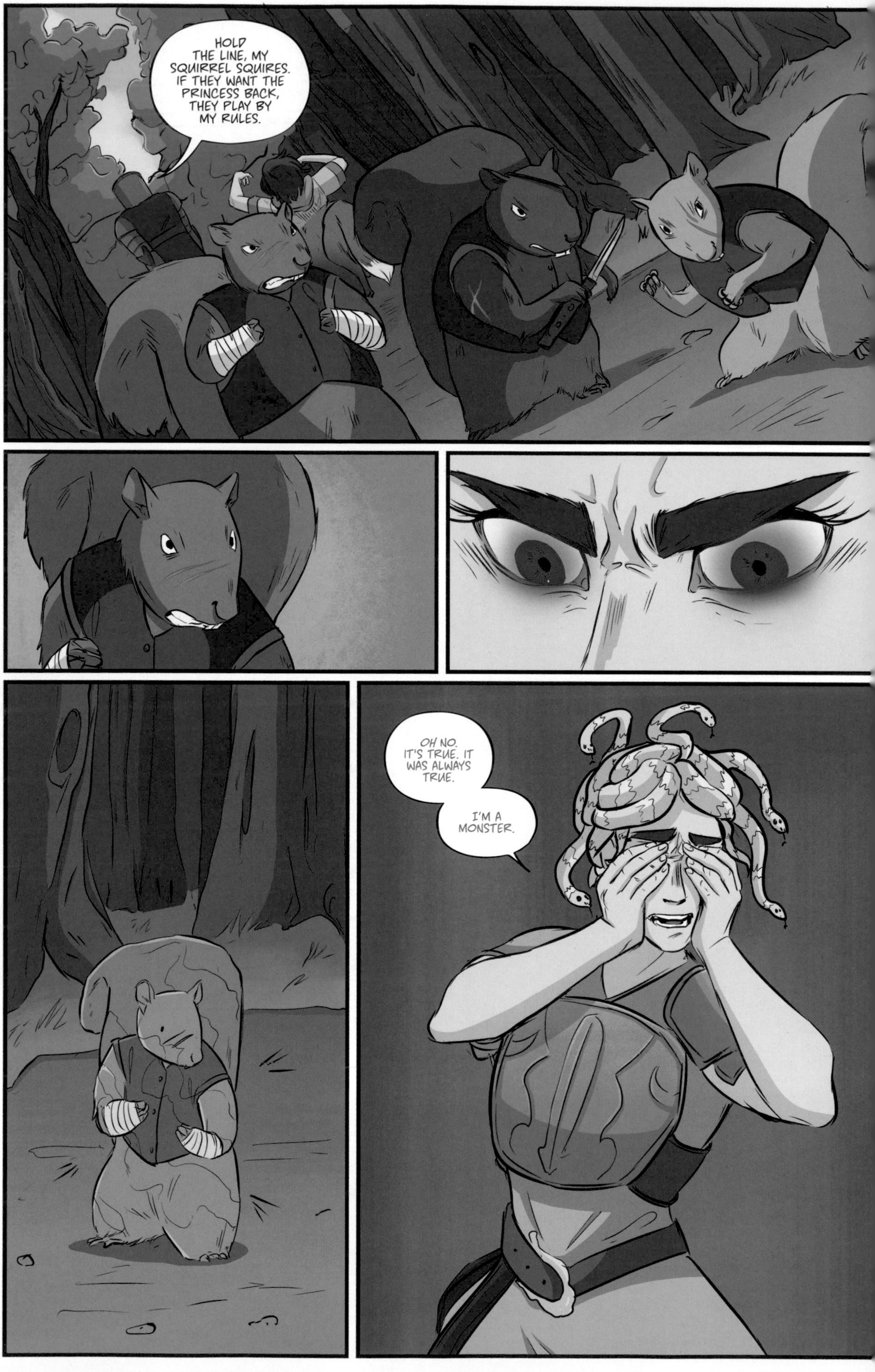
HOLD THE LINE, MY SQUIRREL SQUIRES. IF THEY WANT THE PRINCESS BACK, THEY PLAY BY MY RULES.
OH NO. IT'S TRUE. IT WAS ALWAYS TRUE.
I'M A MONSTER.

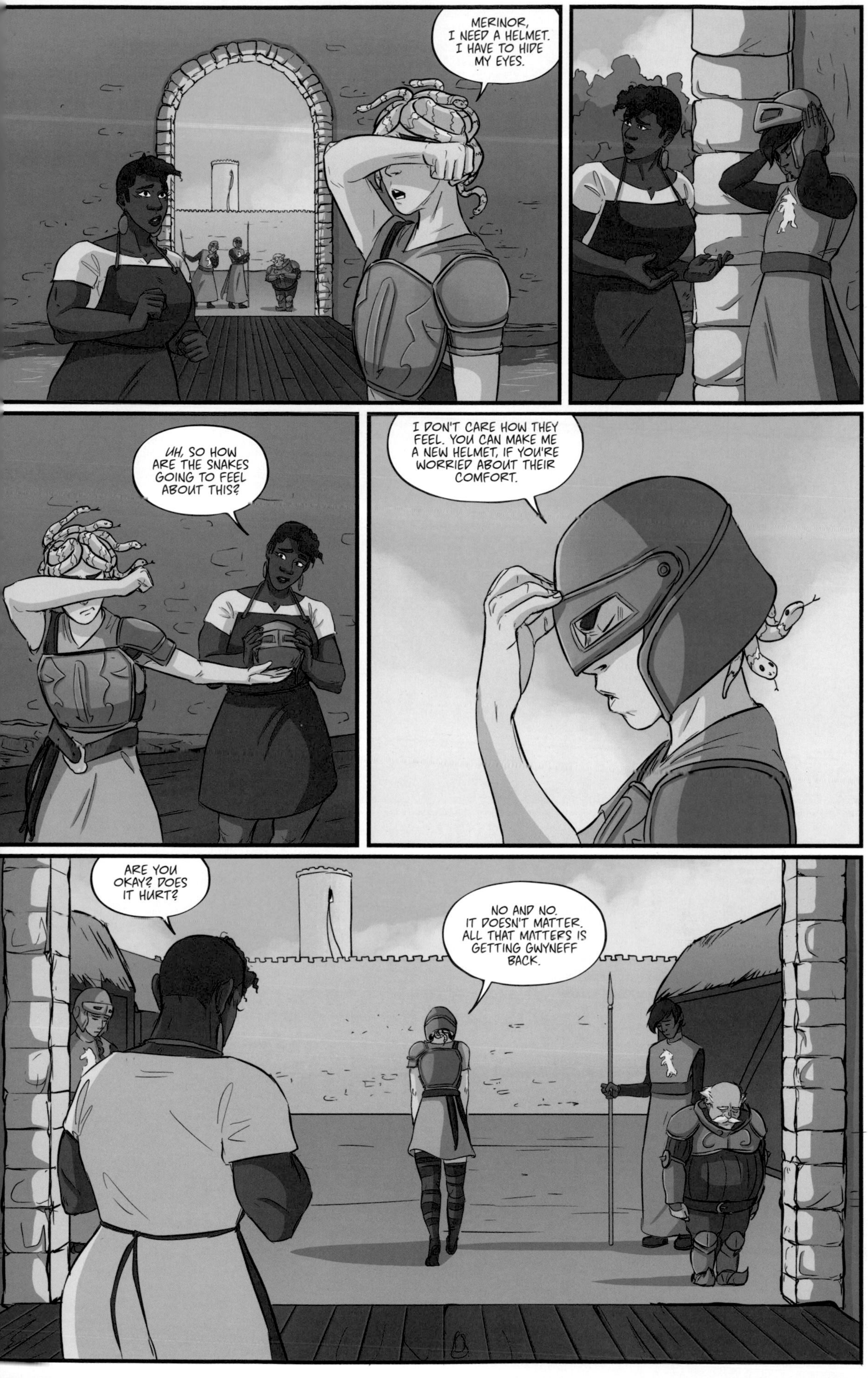
MERINOR, I NEED A HELMET. I HAVE TO HIDE MY EYES.
UH, SO HOW ARE THE SNAKES GOING TO FEEL ABOUT THIS?
I DON'T CARE HOW THEY FEEL. YOU CAN MAKE ME A NEW HELMET, IF YOU'RE WORRIED ABOUT THEIR COMFORT.
ARE YOU OKAY? DOES IT HURT?
NO AND NO. IT DOESN'T MATTER. ALL THAT MATTERS IS GETTING GWYNEFF BACK.

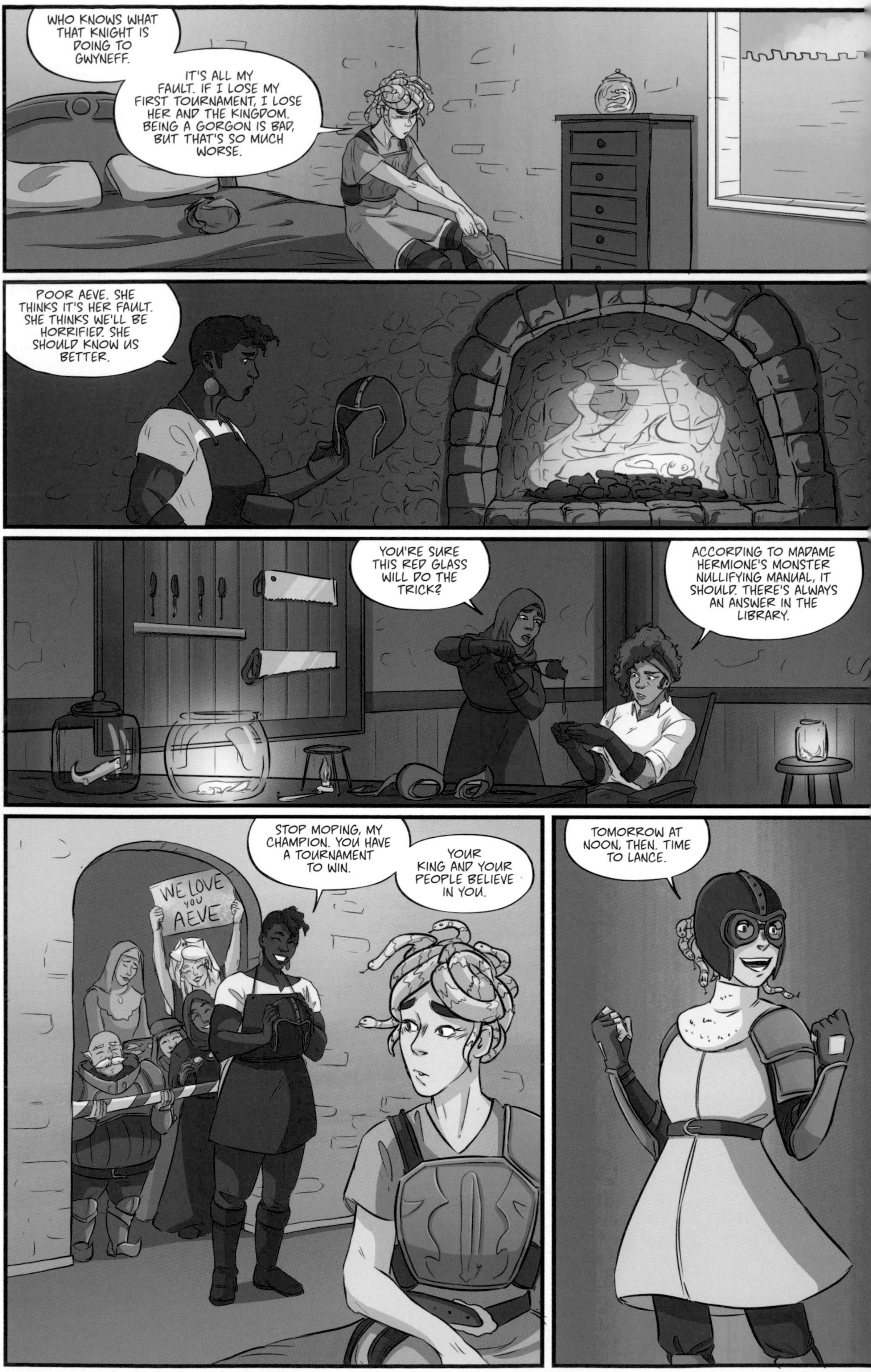

WHO KNOWS WHAT THAT KNIGHT IS DOING TO GWYNEFF.
IT'S ALL MY FAULT. IF I LOSE MY FIRST TOURNAMENT, I LOSE HER AND THE KINGDOM. BEING A GORGON IS BAD, BUT THAT'S SO MUCH WORSE.
POOR AEVE. SHE THINKS IT'S HER FAULT. SHE THINKS WE'LL BE HORRIFIED. SHE SHOULD KNOW US BETTER.
YOU'RE SURE THIS RED GLASS WILL DO THE TRICK?
ACCORDING TO MADAME HERMIONE'S MONSTER NULLIFYING MANUAL, IT SHOULD. THERE'S ALWAYS AN ANSWER IN THE LIBRARY.
WE LOVE YOU AEVE
STOP MOPING, MY CHAMPION. YOU HAVE A TOURNAMENT TO WIN.
YOUR KING AND YOUR PEOPLE BELIEVE IN YOU.
TOMORROW AT NOON, THEN. TIME TO LANCE.

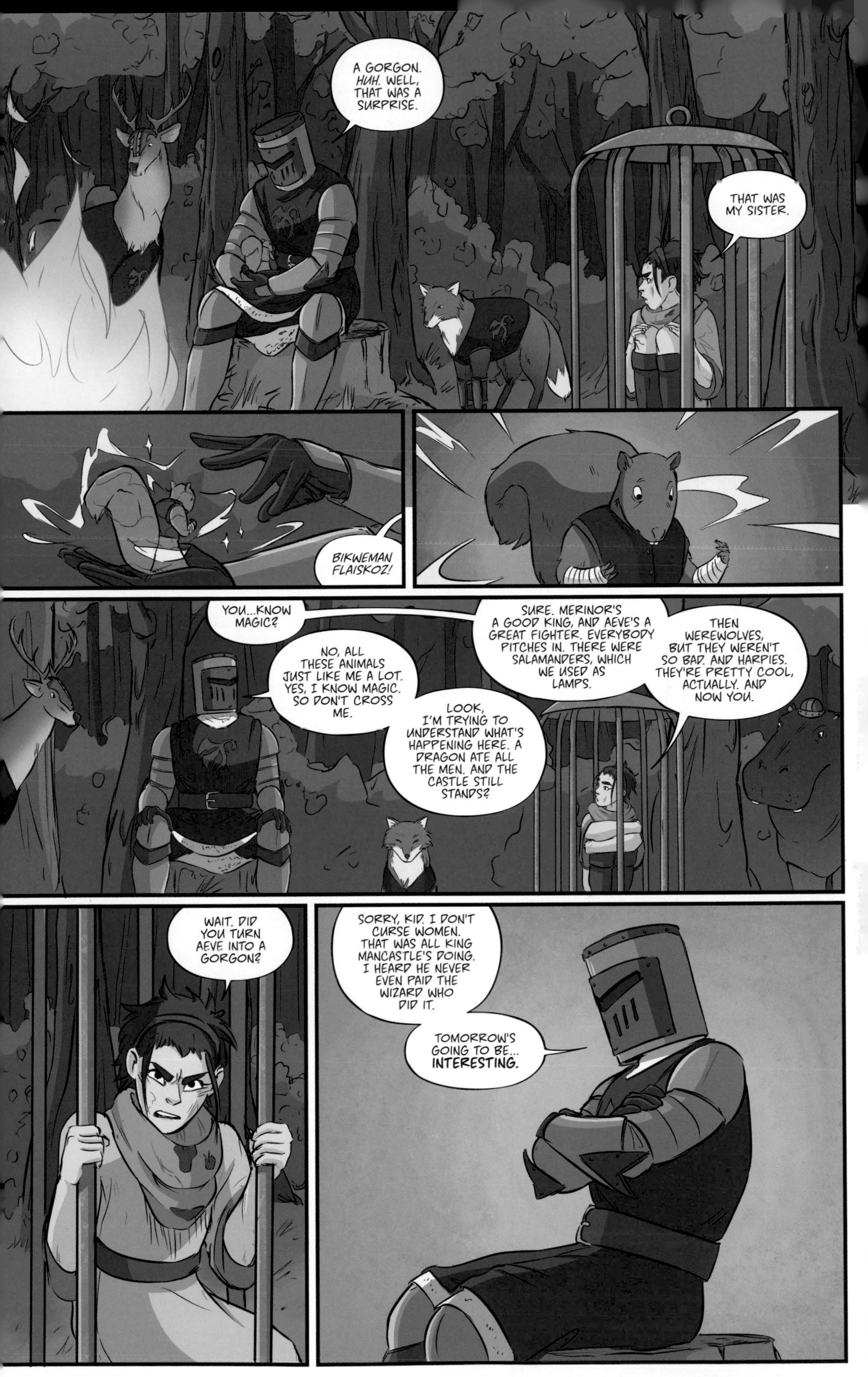
A GORGON. *HUH.* WELL, THAT WAS A SURPRISE.
THAT WAS MY SISTER.
BIKWEMAN FLAISKOZ!
YOU...KNOW MAGIC?
NO, ALL THESE ANIMALS JUST LIKE ME A LOT. YES, I KNOW MAGIC. SO DON'T CROSS ME.
LOOK, I'M TRYING TO UNDERSTAND WHAT'S HAPPENING HERE. A DRAGON ATE ALL THE MEN. AND THE CASTLE STILL STANDS?
SURE. MERINOR'S A GOOD KING, AND AEVE'S A GREAT FIGHTER. EVERYBODY PITCHES IN. THERE WERE SALAMANDERS, WHICH WE USED AS LAMPS.
THEN WEREWOLVES, BUT THEY WEREN'T SO BAD. AND HARPIES. THEY'RE PRETTY COOL, ACTUALLY. AND NOW YOU.
WAIT. DID YOU TURN AEVE INTO A GORGON?
SORRY, KID. I DON'T CURSE WOMEN. THAT WAS ALL KING MANCASTLE'S DOING. I HEARD HE NEVER EVEN PAID THE WIZARD WHO DID IT.
TOMORROW'S GOING TO BE... **INTERESTING.**

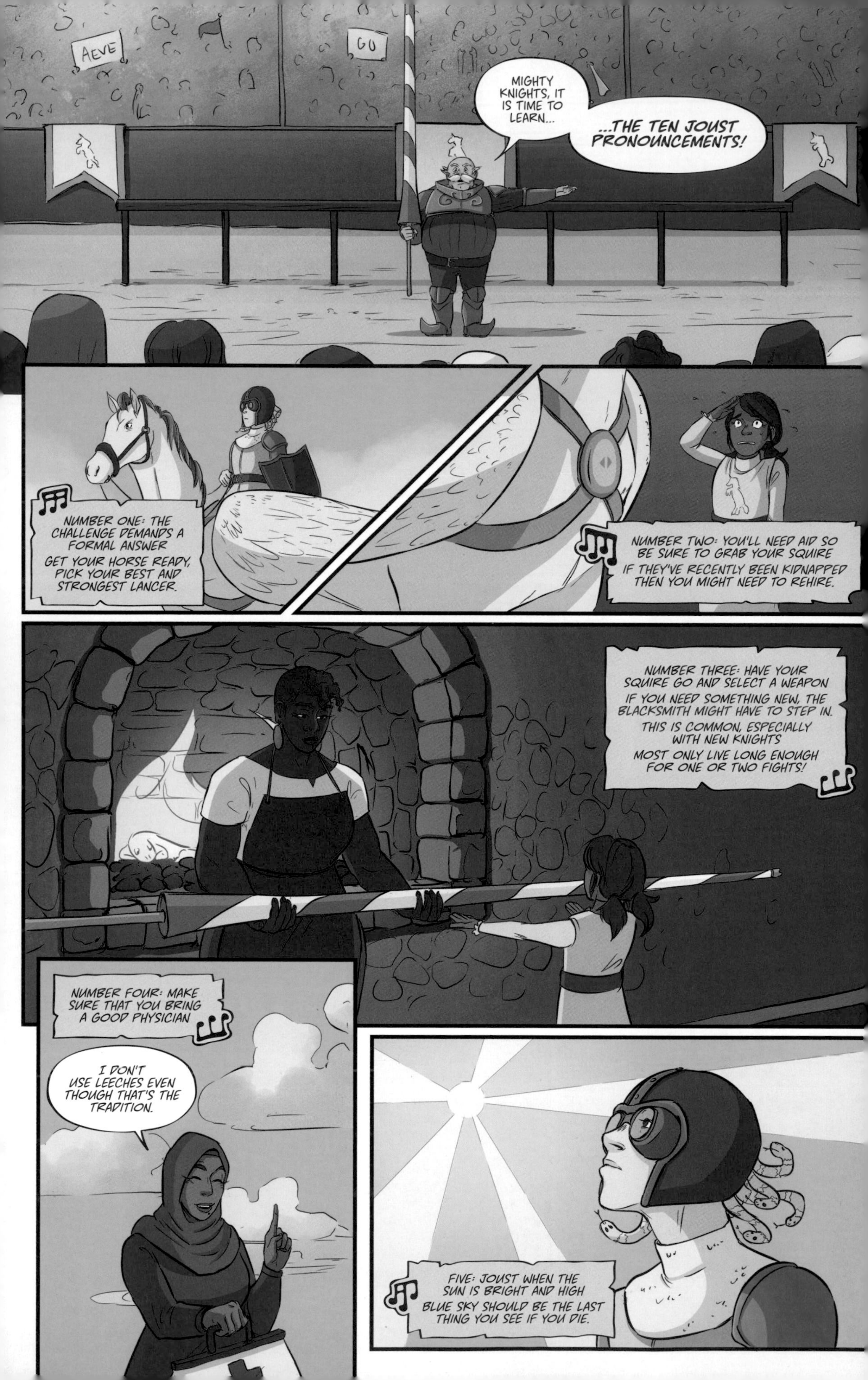
AEVE
GO
MIGHTY KNIGHTS, IT IS TIME TO LEARN...
...THE TEN JOUST PRONOUNCEMENTS!
NUMBER ONE: THE CHALLENGE DEMANDS A FORMAL ANSWER
GET YOUR HORSE READY, PICK YOUR BEST AND STRONGEST LANCER.
NUMBER TWO: YOU'LL NEED AID SO BE SURE TO GRAB YOUR SQUIRE
IF THEY'VE RECENTLY BEEN KIDNAPPED THEN YOU MIGHT NEED TO REHIRE.
NUMBER THREE: HAVE YOUR SQUIRE GO AND SELECT A WEAPON
IF YOU NEED SOMETHING NEW, THE BLACKSMITH MIGHT HAVE TO STEP IN.
THIS IS COMMON, ESPECIALLY WITH NEW KNIGHTS
MOST ONLY LIVE LONG ENOUGH FOR ONE OR TWO FIGHTS!
NUMBER FOUR: MAKE SURE THAT YOU BRING A GOOD PHYSICIAN
I DON'T USE LEECHES EVEN THOUGH THAT'S THE TRADITION.
FIVE: JOUST WHEN THE SUN IS BRIGHT AND HIGH
BLUE SKY SHOULD BE THE LAST THING YOU SEE IF YOU DIE.

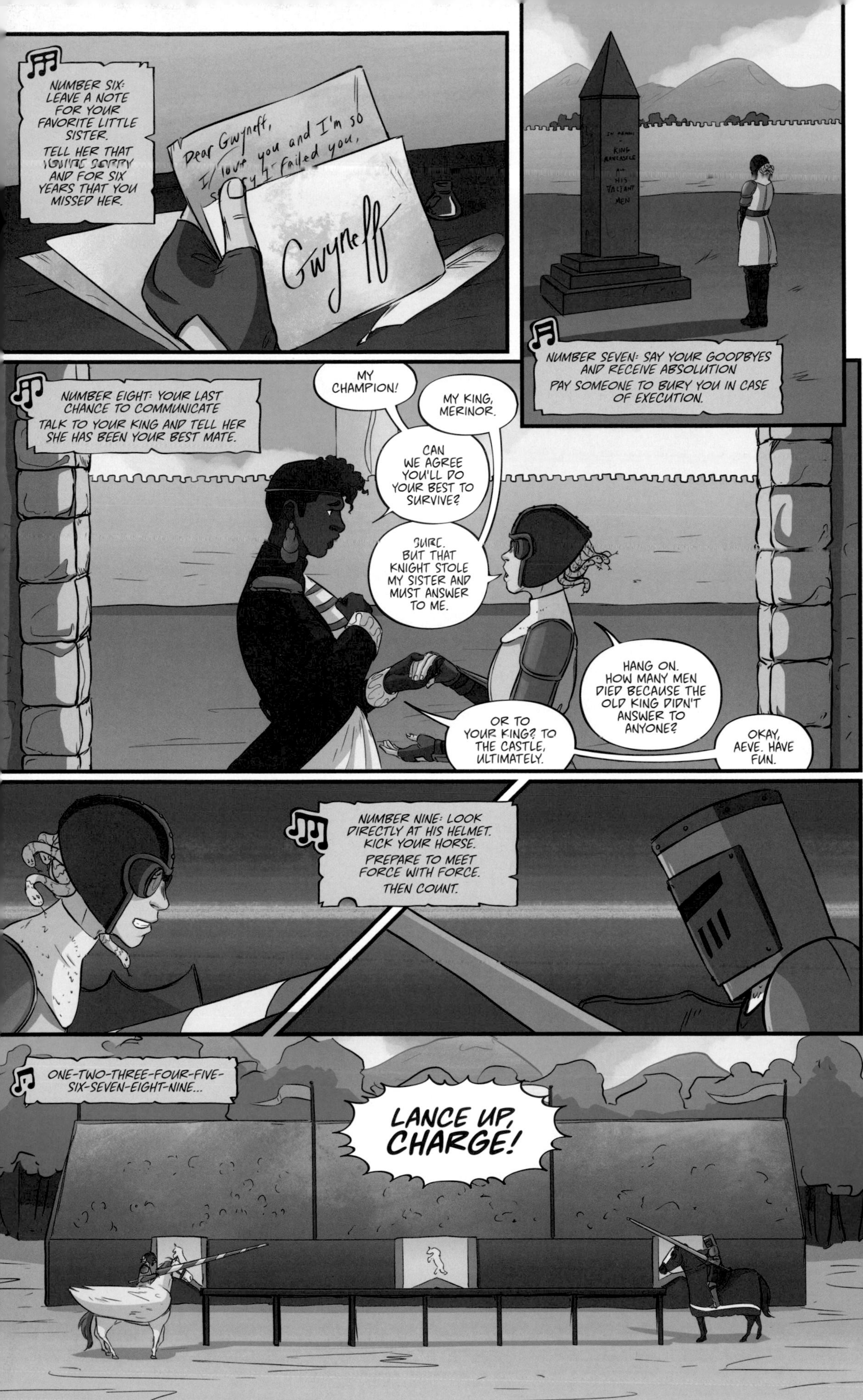
NUMBER SIX: LEAVE A NOTE FOR YOUR FAVORITE LITTLE SISTER.
TELL HER THAT YOU'RE SORRY AND FOR SIX YEARS THAT YOU MISSED HER.
Dear Gwyneff, I love you and I'm so sorry I failed you,
Gwyneff
NUMBER SEVEN: SAY YOUR GOODBYES AND RECEIVE ABSOLUTION
PAY SOMEONE TO BURY YOU IN CASE OF EXECUTION.
NUMBER EIGHT: YOUR LAST CHANCE TO COMMUNICATE
TALK TO YOUR KING AND TELL HER SHE HAS BEEN YOUR BEST MATE.
MY CHAMPION!
MY KING, MERINOR.
CAN WE AGREE YOU'LL DO YOUR BEST TO SURVIVE?
SURE. BUT THAT KNIGHT STOLE MY SISTER AND MUST ANSWER TO ME.
OR TO YOUR KING? TO THE CASTLE, ULTIMATELY.
HANG ON. HOW MANY MEN DIED BECAUSE THE OLD KING DIDN'T ANSWER TO ANYONE?
OKAY, AEVE. HAVE FUN.
NUMBER NINE: LOOK DIRECTLY AT HIS HELMET. KICK YOUR HORSE.
PREPARE TO MEET FORCE WITH FORCE.
THEN COUNT.
ONE-TWO-THREE-FOUR-FIVE-SIX-SEVEN-EIGHT-NINE...
LANCE UP, CHARGE!

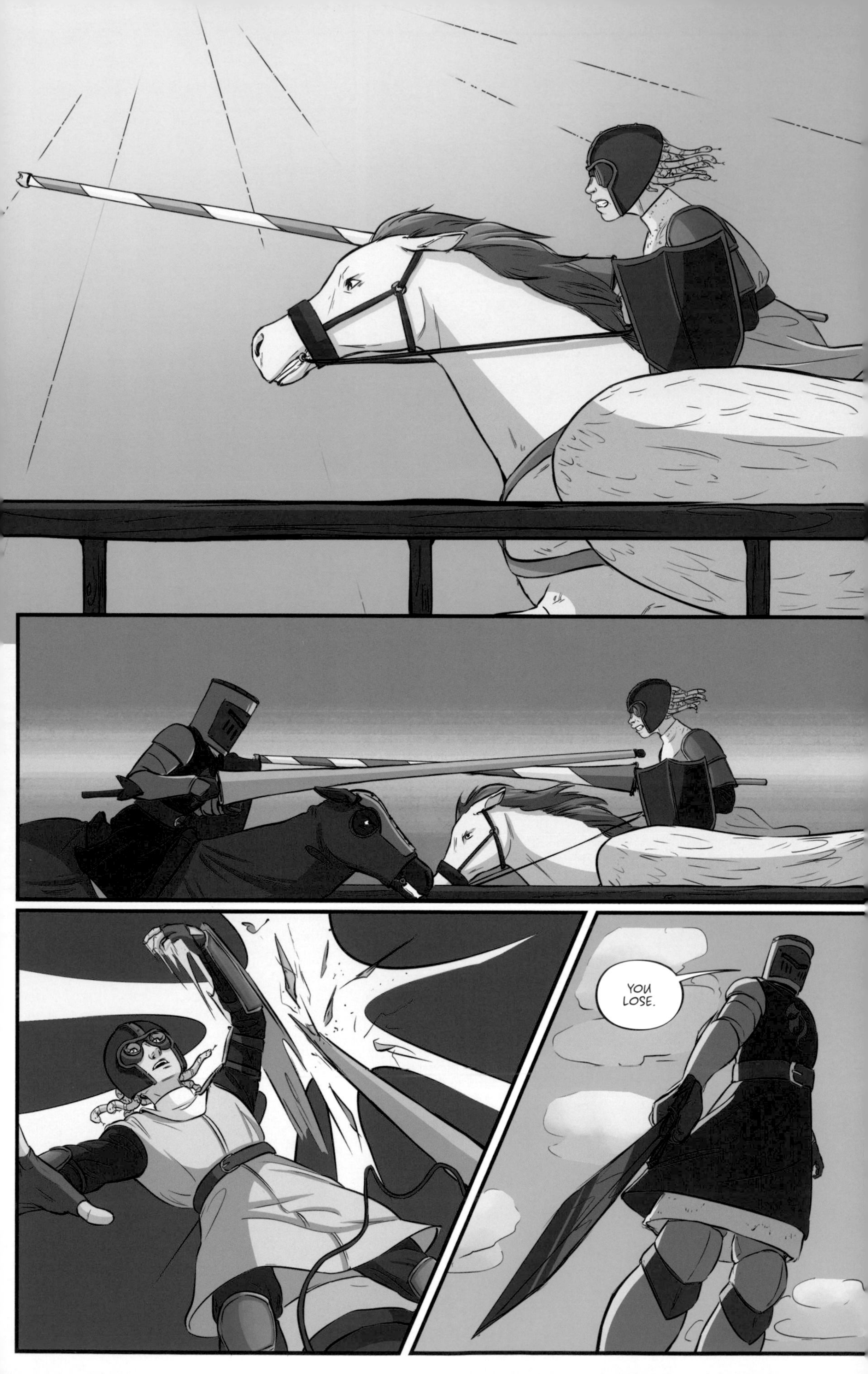
YOU LOSE.

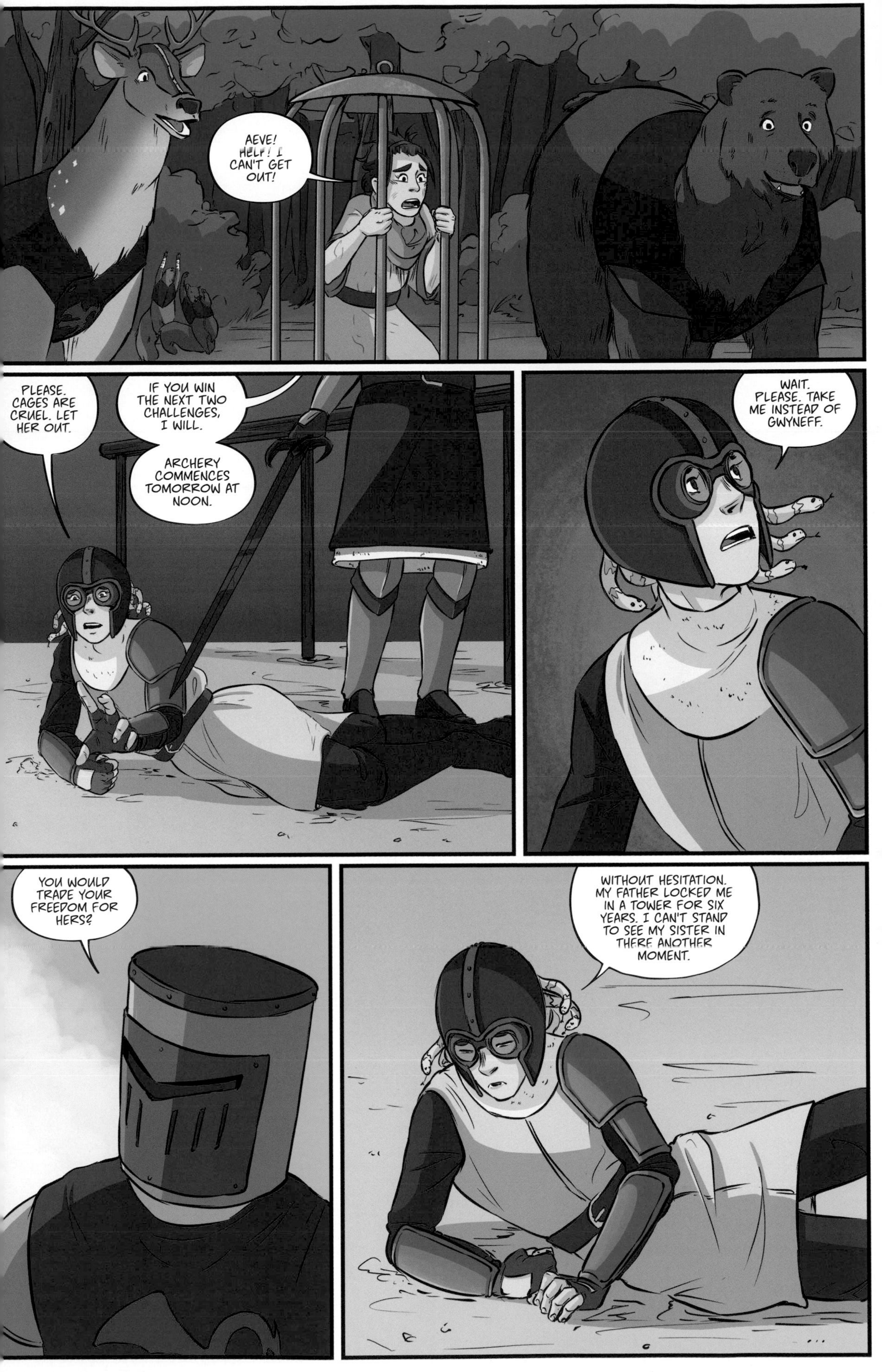
AEVE! HELP! I CAN'T GET OUT!
PLEASE. CAGES ARE CRUEL. LET HER OUT.
IF YOU WIN THE NEXT TWO CHALLENGES, I WILL.
ARCHERY COMMENCES TOMORROW AT NOON.
WAIT. PLEASE. TAKE ME INSTEAD OF GWYNEFF.
YOU WOULD TRADE YOUR FREEDOM FOR HERS?
WITHOUT HESITATION. MY FATHER LOCKED ME IN A TOWER FOR SIX YEARS. I CAN'T STAND TO SEE MY SISTER IN THERE ANOTHER MOMENT.

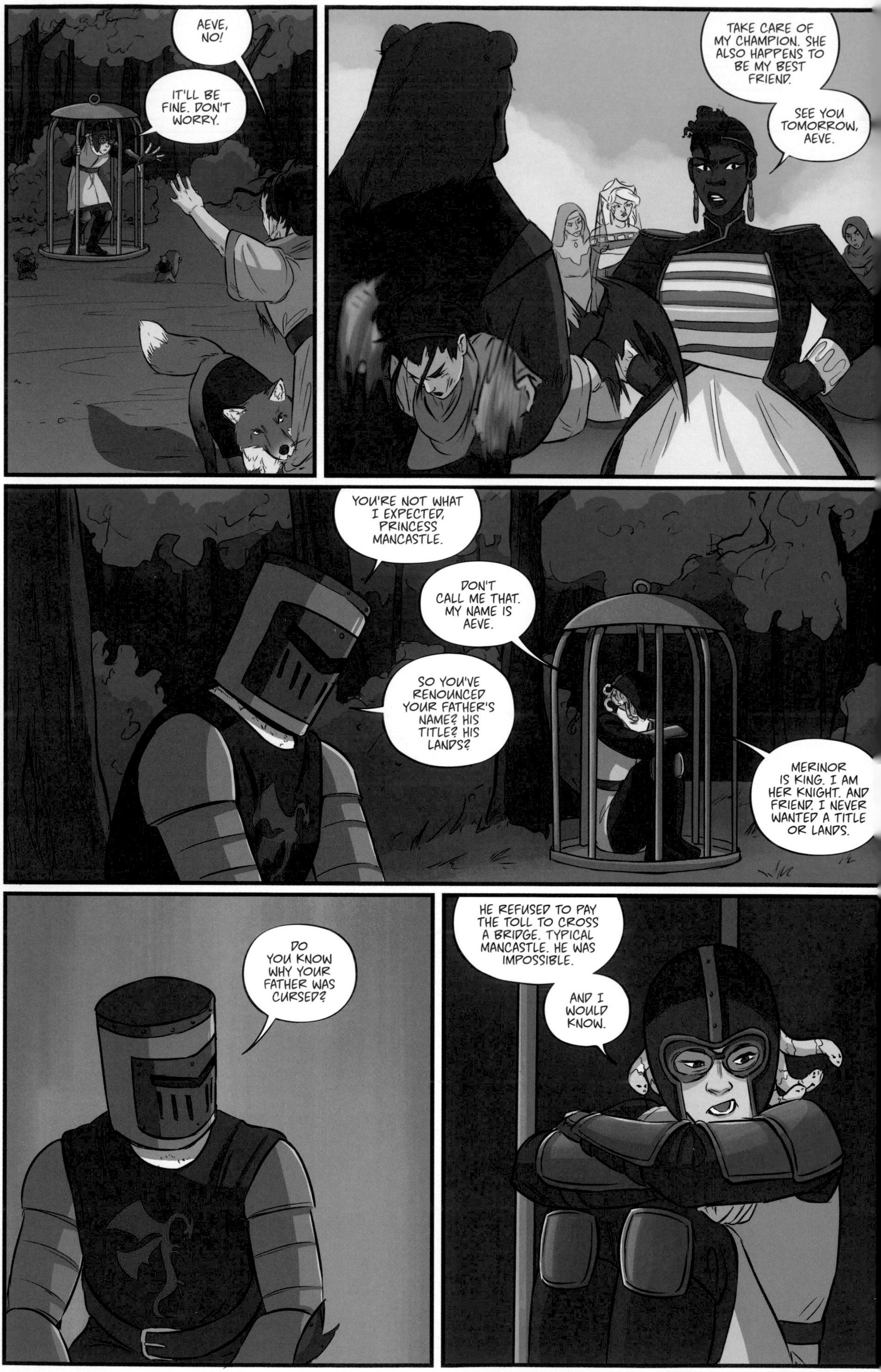
AEVE, NO!
IT'LL BE FINE. DON'T WORRY.
TAKE CARE OF MY CHAMPION. SHE ALSO HAPPENS TO BE MY BEST FRIEND.
SEE YOU TOMORROW, AEVE.
YOU'RE NOT WHAT I EXPECTED, PRINCESS MANCASTLE.
DON'T CALL ME THAT. MY NAME IS AEVE.
SO YOU'VE RENOUNCED YOUR FATHER'S NAME? HIS TITLE? HIS LANDS?
MERINOR IS KING. I AM HER KNIGHT. AND FRIEND. I NEVER WANTED A TITLE OR LANDS.
DO YOU KNOW WHY YOUR FATHER WAS CURSED?
HE REFUSED TO PAY THE TOLL TO CROSS A BRIDGE. TYPICAL MANCASTLE. HE WAS IMPOSSIBLE.
AND I WOULD KNOW.

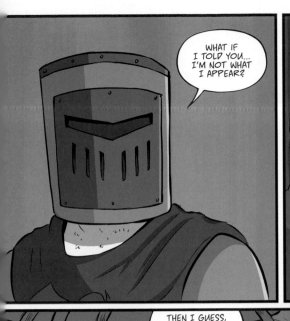

WHAT IF I TOLD YOU... I'M NOT WHAT I APPEAR?

I'D SAY AS LONG AS I'M IN THIS CAGE AND YOU'RE THREATENING MY FRIENDS, IT DOESN'T REALLY MATTER WHAT YOU ARE.

THEN I GUESS, TOMORROW, WE LEARN WHO'S THE BETTER ARCHER.

SLAEPANAN!

CURSES ARE FUNNY THINGS.

FROM BOTH SIDES.

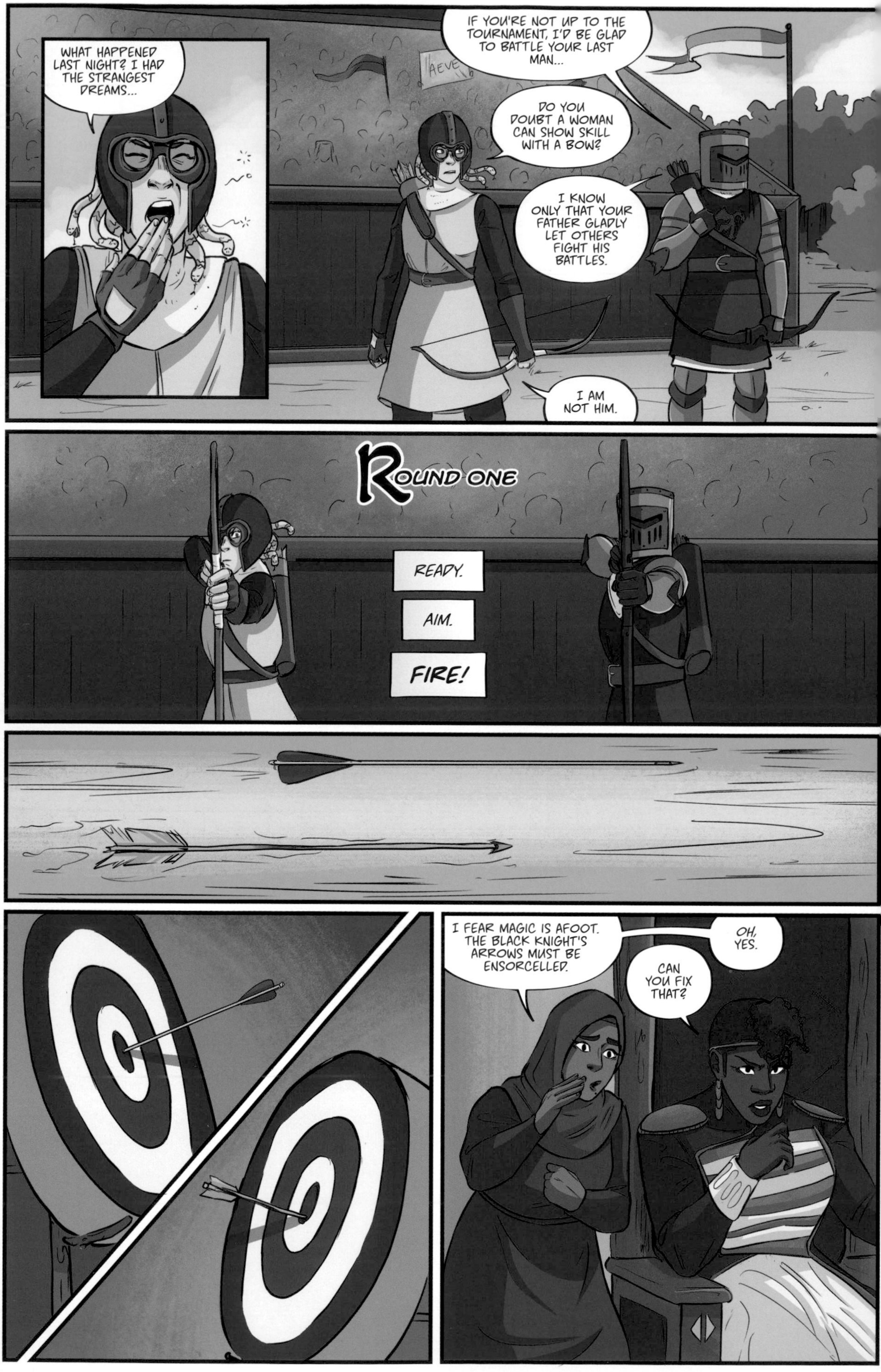

WHAT HAPPENED LAST NIGHT? I HAD THE STRANGEST DREAMS...
AEVE
IF YOU'RE NOT UP TO THE TOURNAMENT, I'D BE GLAD TO BATTLE YOUR LAST MAN...
DO YOU DOUBT A WOMAN CAN SHOW SKILL WITH A BOW?
I KNOW ONLY THAT YOUR FATHER GLADLY LET OTHERS FIGHT HIS BATTLES.
I AM NOT HIM.
ROUND ONE
READY.
AIM.
FIRE!
I FEAR MAGIC IS AFOOT. THE BLACK KNIGHT'S ARROWS MUST BE ENSORCELLED.
OH, YES.
CAN YOU FIX THAT?

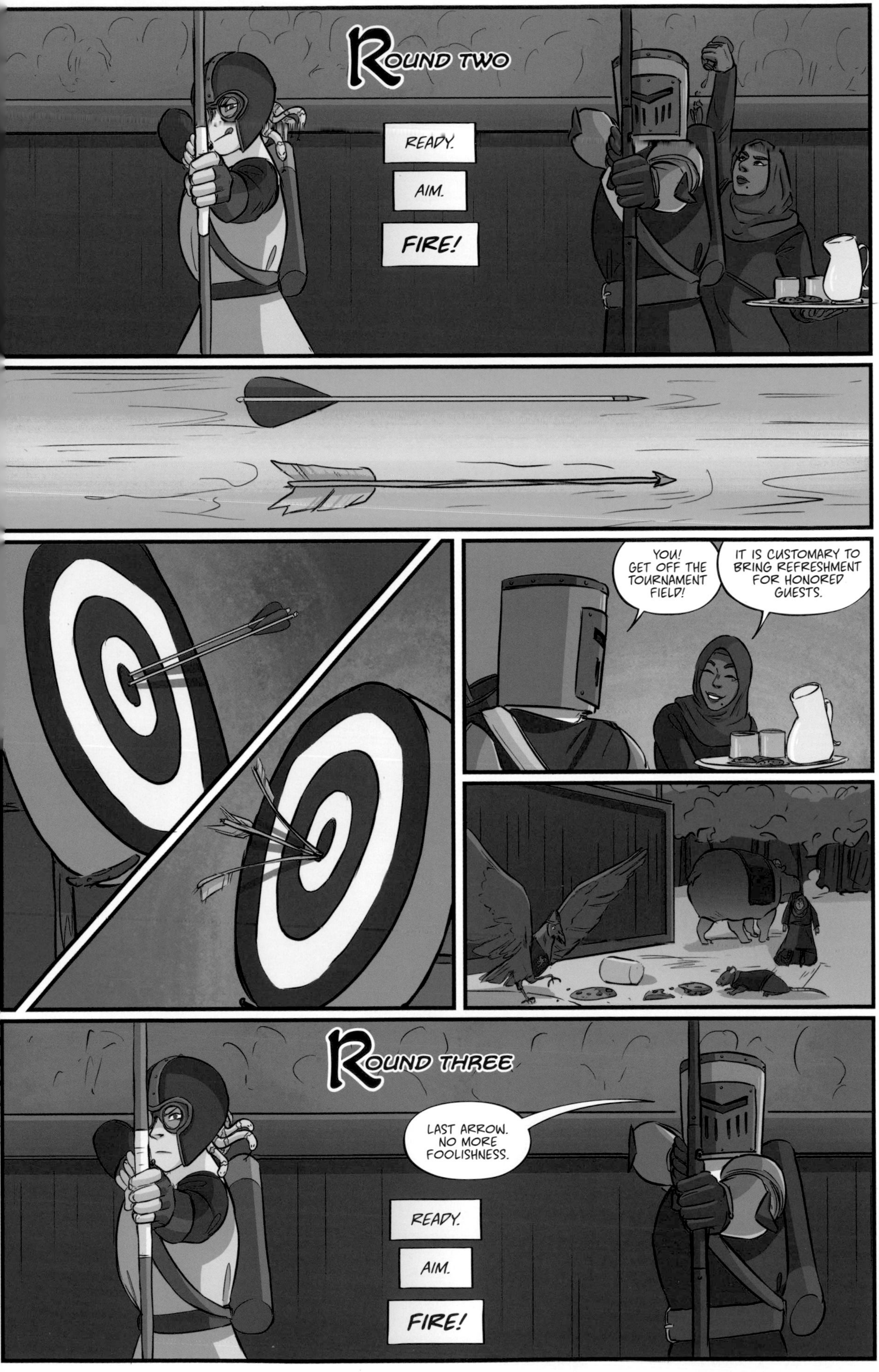
ROUND TWO
READY.
AIM.
FIRE!
YOU! GET OFF THE TOURNAMENT FIELD!
IT IS CUSTOMARY TO BRING REFRESHMENT FOR HONORED GUESTS.
ROUND THREE
LAST ARROW. NO MORE FOOLISHNESS.
READY.
AIM.
FIRE!

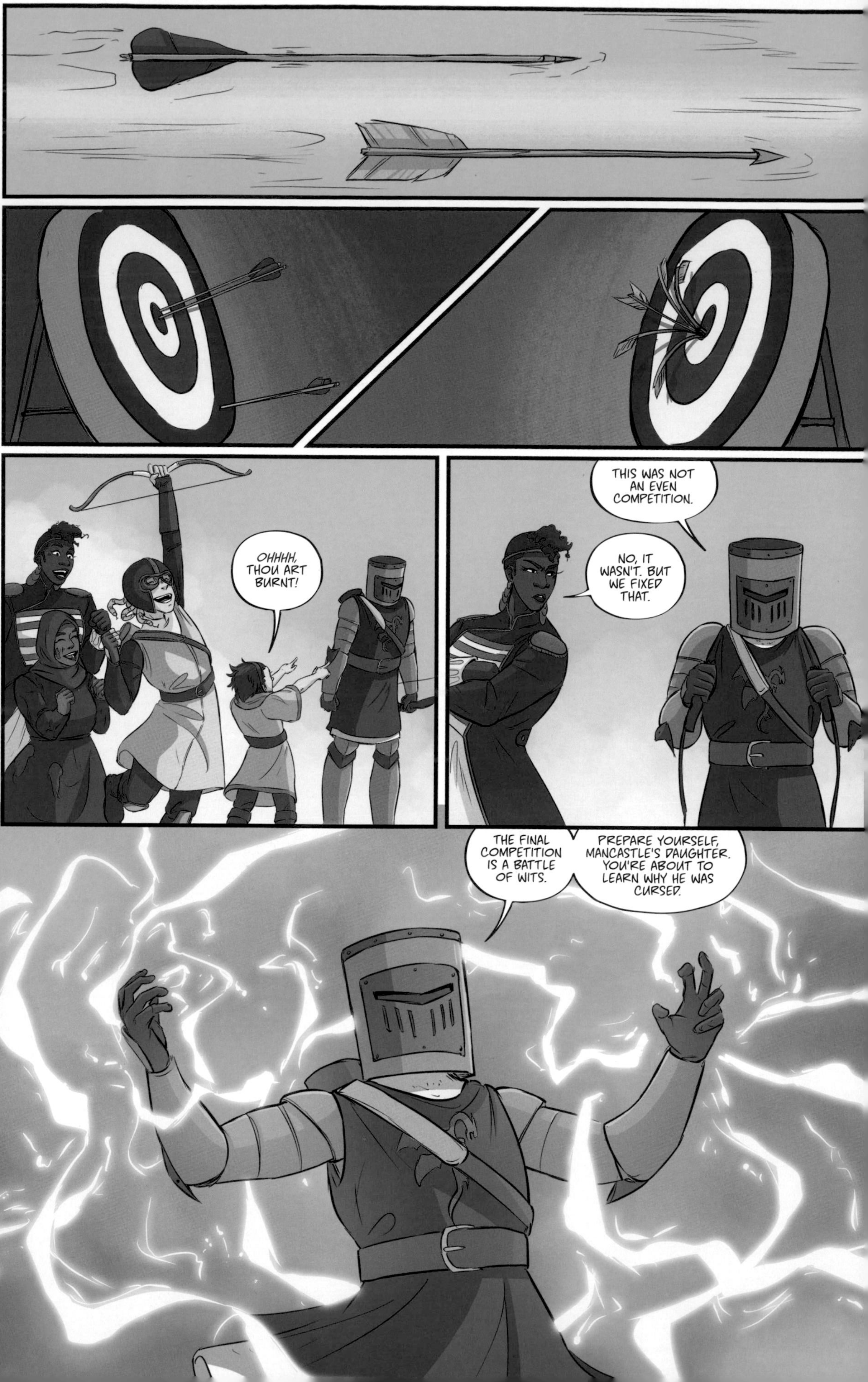
OHHHH, THOU ART BURNT!
THIS WAS NOT AN EVEN COMPETITION.
NO, IT WASN'T. BUT WE FIXED THAT.
THE FINAL COMPETITION IS A BATTLE OF WITS.
PREPARE YOURSELF, MANCASTLE'S DAUGHTER. YOU'RE ABOUT TO LEARN WHY HE WAS CURSED.

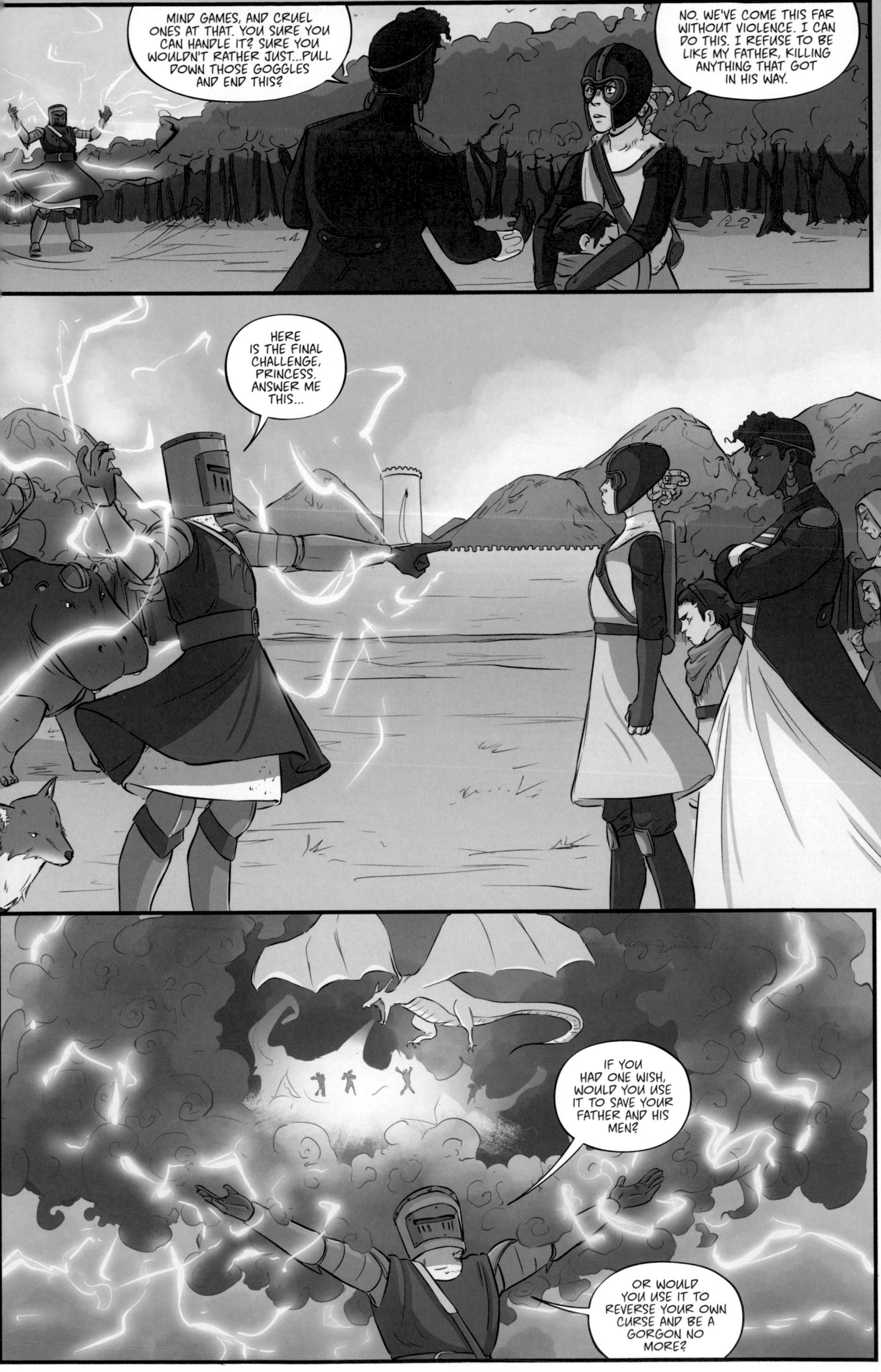
MIND GAMES, AND CRUEL ONES AT THAT. YOU SURE YOU CAN HANDLE IT? SURE YOU WOULDN'T RATHER JUST...PULL DOWN THOSE GOGGLES AND END THIS?
NO. WE'VE COME THIS FAR WITHOUT VIOLENCE. I CAN DO THIS. I REFUSE TO BE LIKE MY FATHER, KILLING ANYTHING THAT GOT IN HIS WAY.
HERE IS THE FINAL CHALLENGE, PRINCESS. ANSWER ME THIS...
IF YOU HAD ONE WISH, WOULD YOU USE IT TO SAVE YOUR FATHER AND HIS MEN?
OR WOULD YOU USE IT TO REVERSE YOUR OWN CURSE AND BE A GORGON NO MORE?

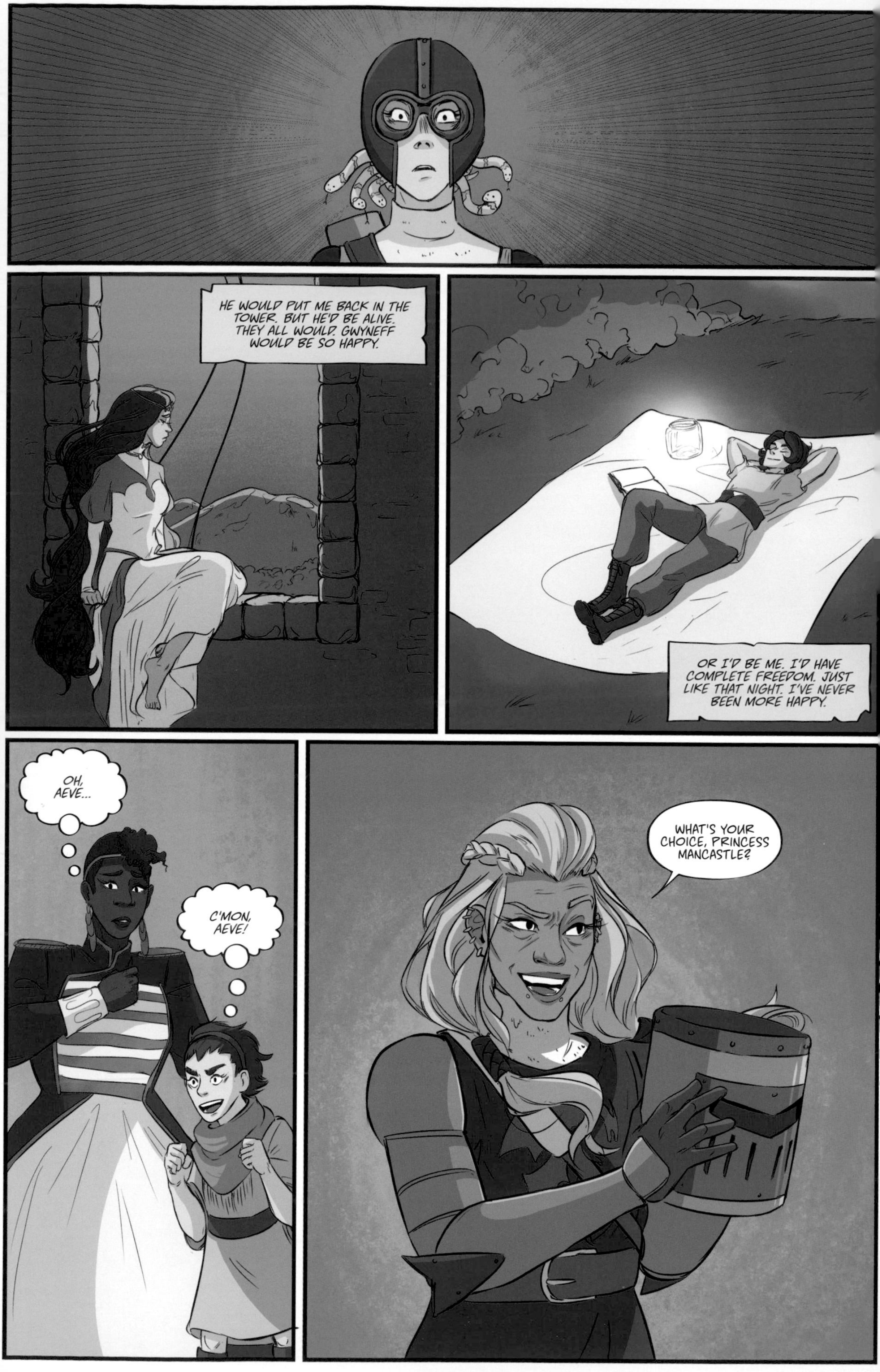
HE WOULD PUT ME BACK IN THE TOWER. BUT HE'D BE ALIVE. THEY ALL WOULD. GWYNEFF WOULD BE SO HAPPY.
OR I'D BE ME. I'D HAVE COMPLETE FREEDOM. JUST LIKE THAT NIGHT. I'VE NEVER BEEN MORE HAPPY.
OH, AEVE...
C'MON, AEVE!
WHAT'S YOUR CHOICE, PRINCESS MANCASTLE?

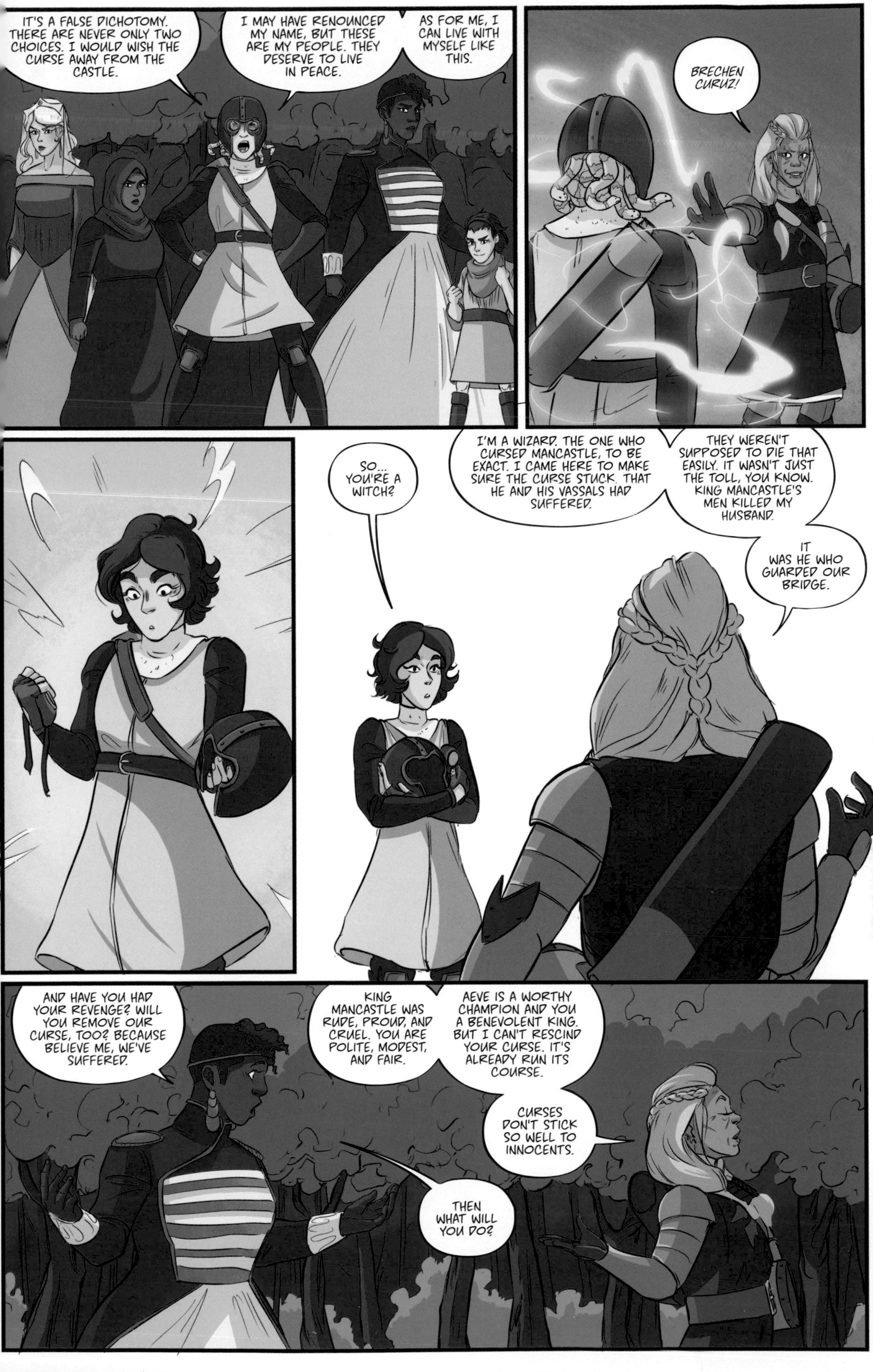
IT'S A FALSE DICHOTOMY. THERE ARE NEVER ONLY TWO CHOICES. I WOULD WISH THE CURSE AWAY FROM THE CASTLE.
I MAY HAVE RENOUNCED MY NAME, BUT THESE ARE MY PEOPLE. THEY DESERVE TO LIVE IN PEACE.
AS FOR ME, I CAN LIVE WITH MYSELF LIKE THIS.
BRECHEN CURUZ!
SO... YOU'RE A WITCH?
I'M A WIZARD. THE ONE WHO CURSED MANCASTLE, TO BE EXACT. I CAME HERE TO MAKE SURE THE CURSE STUCK. THAT HE AND HIS VASSALS HAD SUFFERED.
THEY WEREN'T SUPPOSED TO DIE THAT EASILY. IT WASN'T JUST THE TOLL, YOU KNOW. KING MANCASTLE'S MEN KILLED MY HUSBAND.
IT WAS HE WHO GUARDED OUR BRIDGE.
AND HAVE YOU HAD YOUR REVENGE? WILL YOU REMOVE OUR CURSE, TOO? BECAUSE BELIEVE ME, WE'VE SUFFERED.
KING MANCASTLE WAS RUDE, PROUD, AND CRUEL. YOU ARE POLITE, MODEST, AND FAIR.
AEVE IS A WORTHY CHAMPION AND YOU A BENEVOLENT KING. BUT I CAN'T RESCIND YOUR CURSE. IT'S ALREADY RUN ITS COURSE.
CURSES DON'T STICK SO WELL TO INNOCENTS.
THEN WHAT WILL YOU DO?

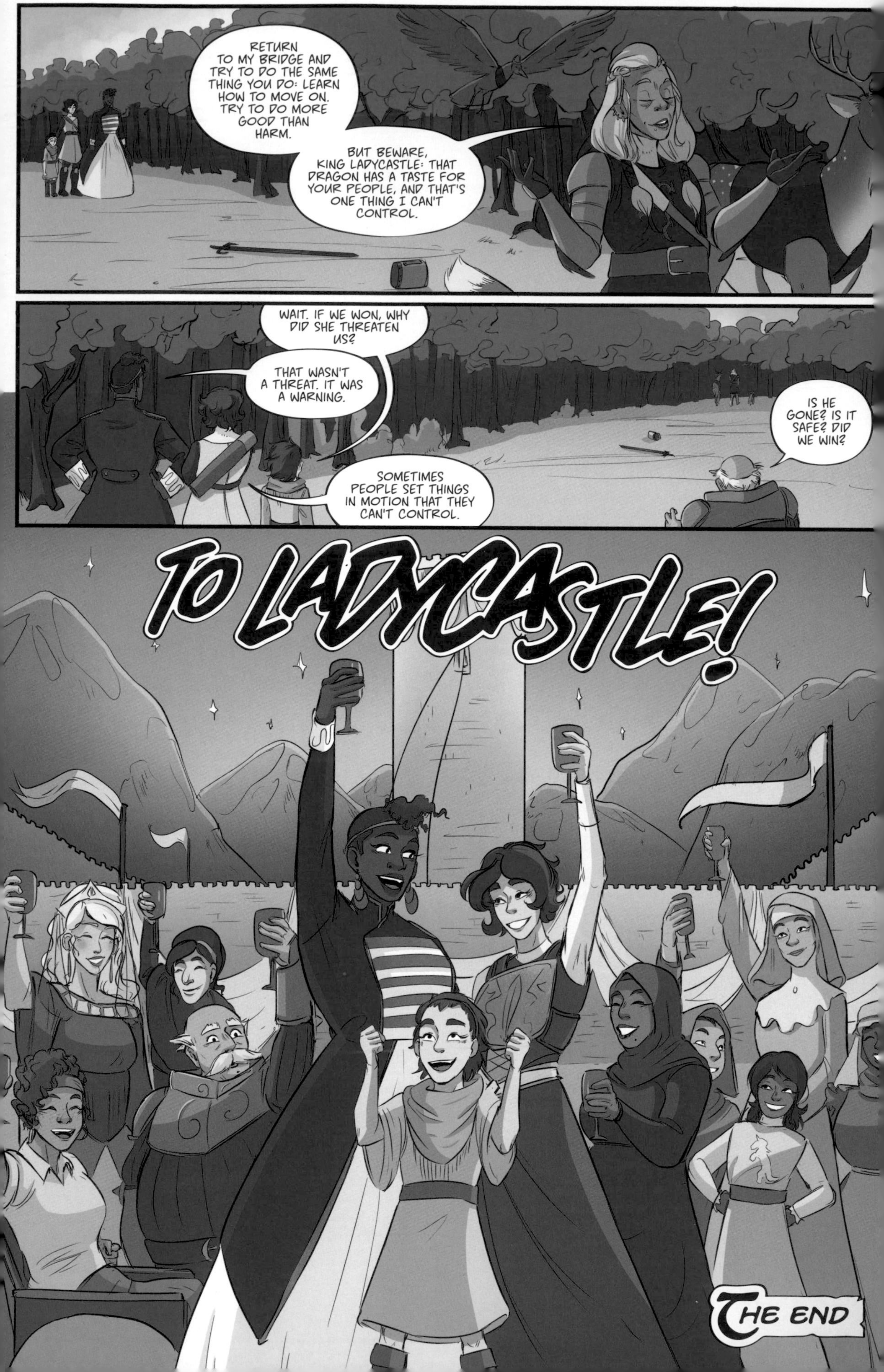
RETURN TO MY BRIDGE AND TRY TO DO THE SAME THING YOU DO: LEARN HOW TO MOVE ON. TRY TO DO MORE GOOD THAN HARM.
BUT BEWARE, KING LADYCASTLE: THAT DRAGON HAS A TASTE FOR YOUR PEOPLE, AND THAT'S ONE THING I CAN'T CONTROL.
WAIT. IF WE WON, WHY DID SHE THREATEN US?
THAT WASN'T A THREAT. IT WAS A WARNING.
SOMETIMES PEOPLE SET THINGS IN MOTION THAT THEY CAN'T CONTROL.
IS HE GONE? IS IT SAFE? DID WE WIN?
TO LADYCASTLE!
THE END

"A **KNIGHT** TO DISMEMBER."

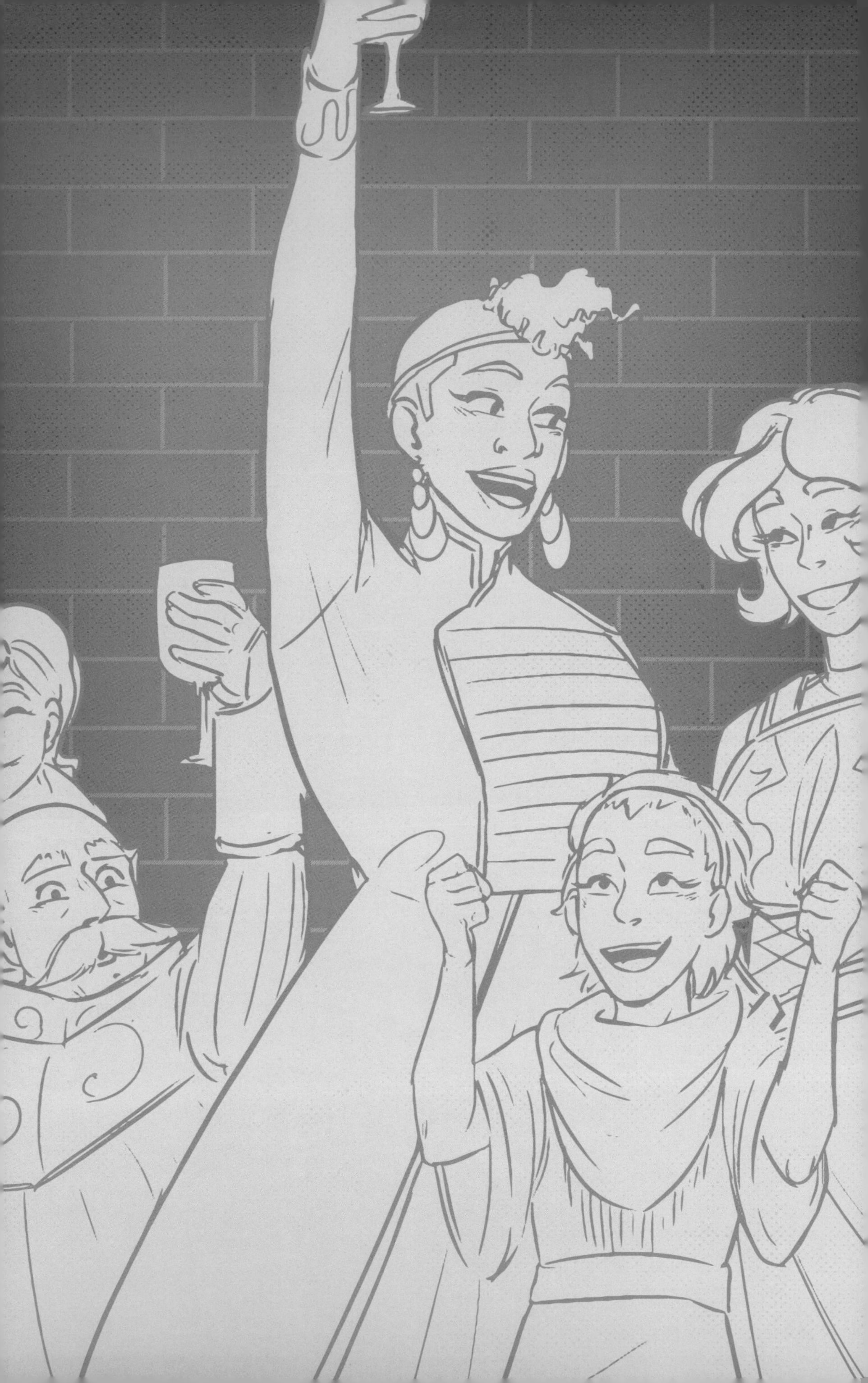

COVER GALLERY

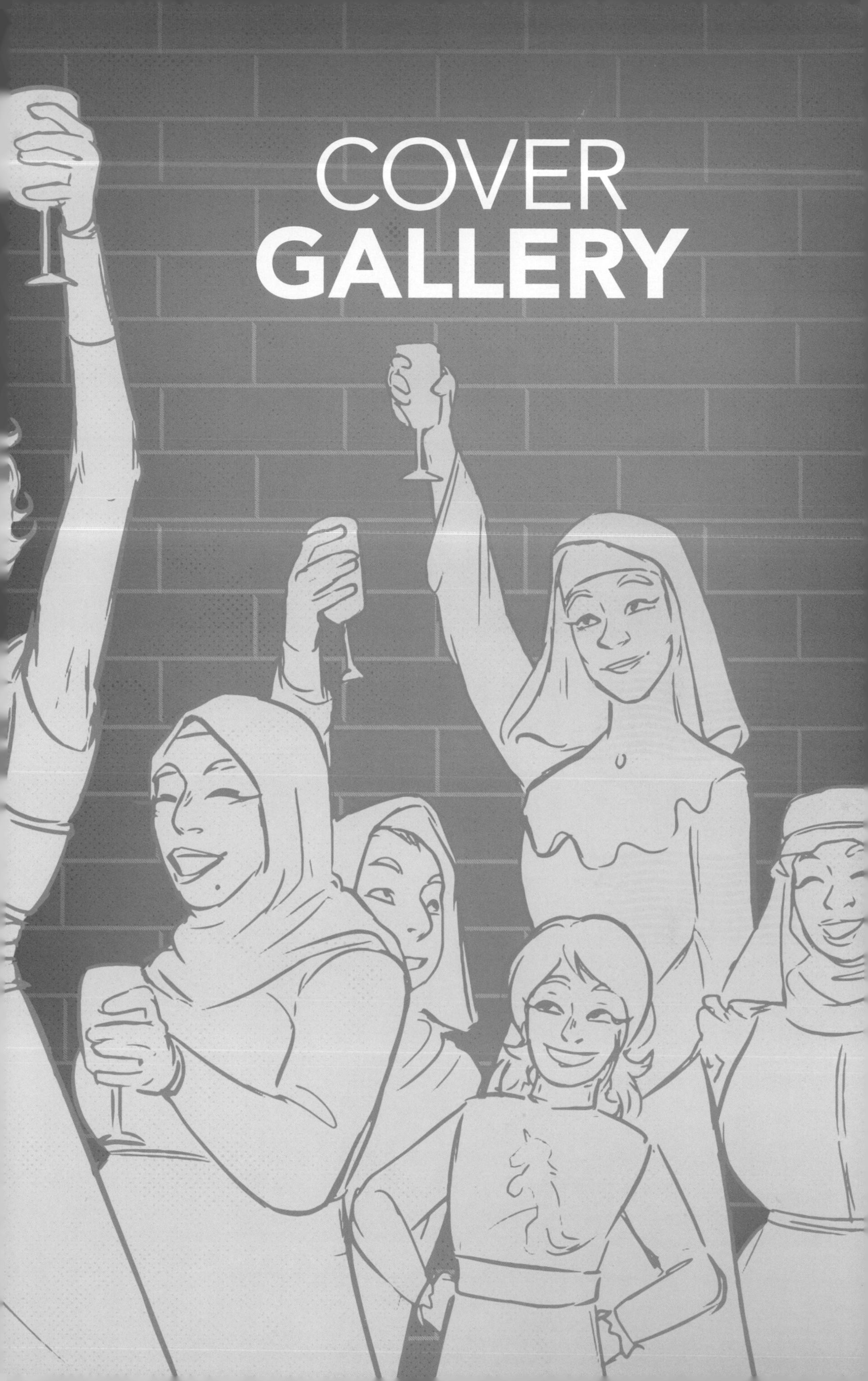

ISSUE ONE COVER
ASHLEY A. WOODS

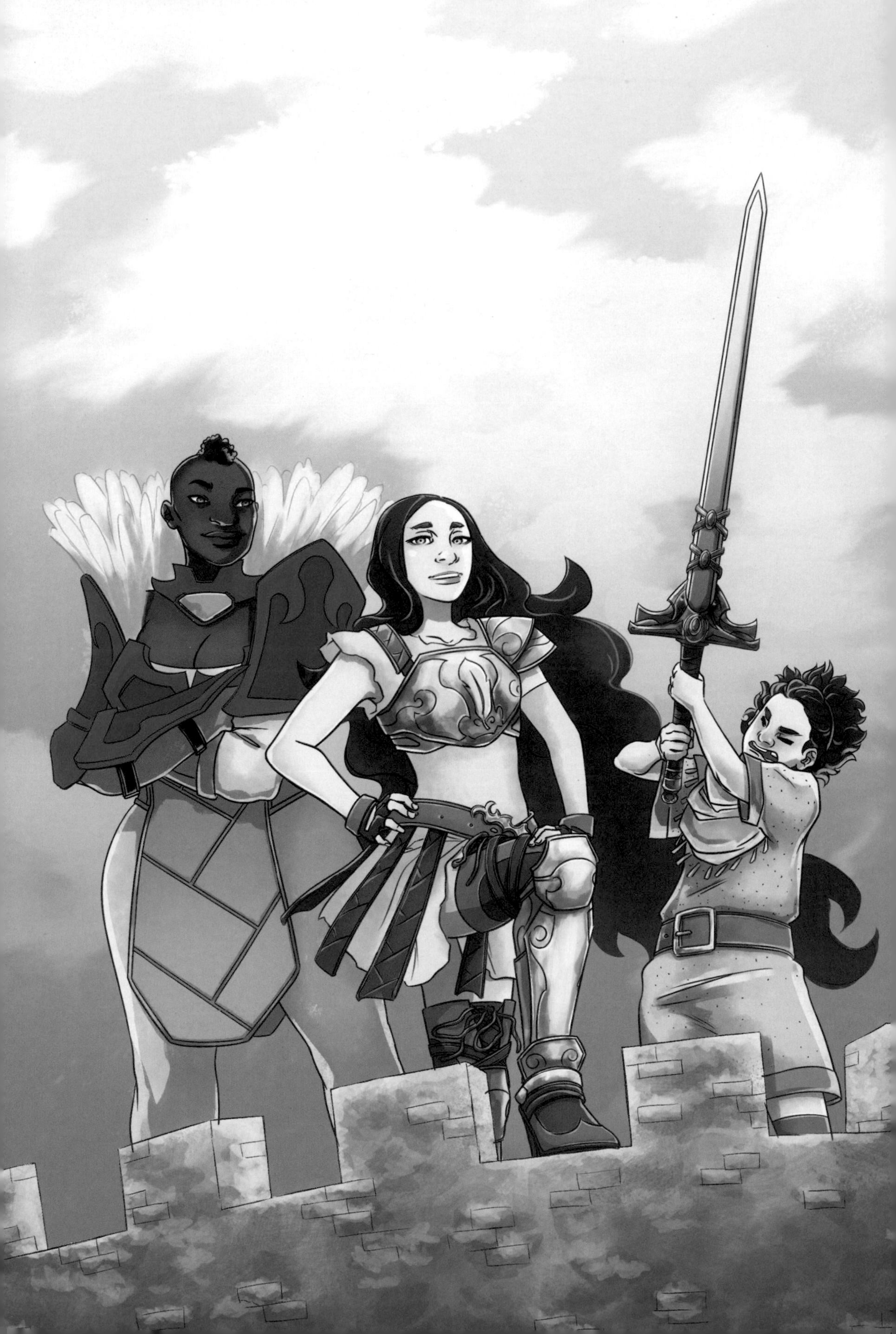

ISSUE ONE VARIANT COVER
ELSA CHARRETIER
WITH COLORS BY **MARGAUX SALTEL**

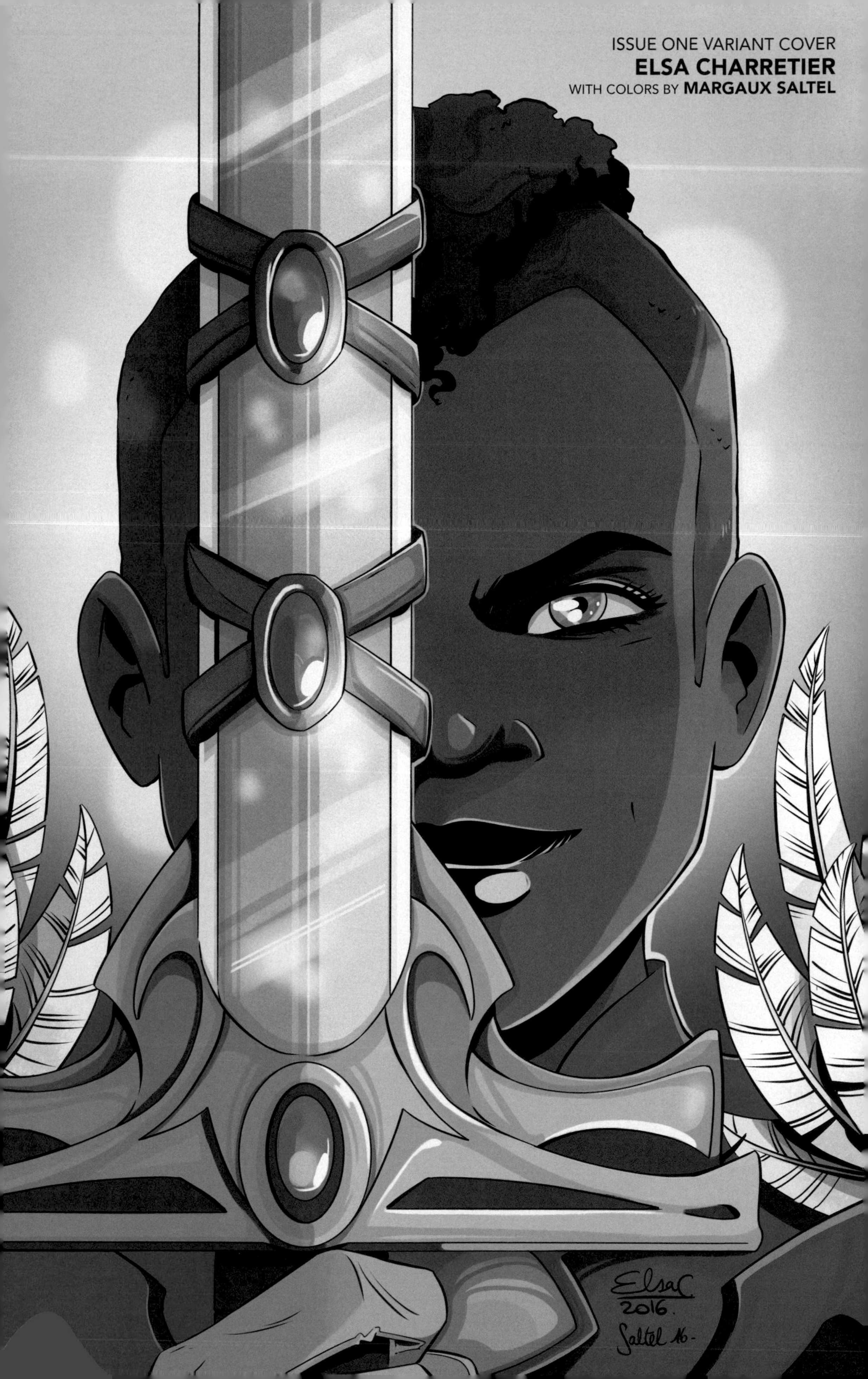
ElsaC.
2016.
Saltel 16-

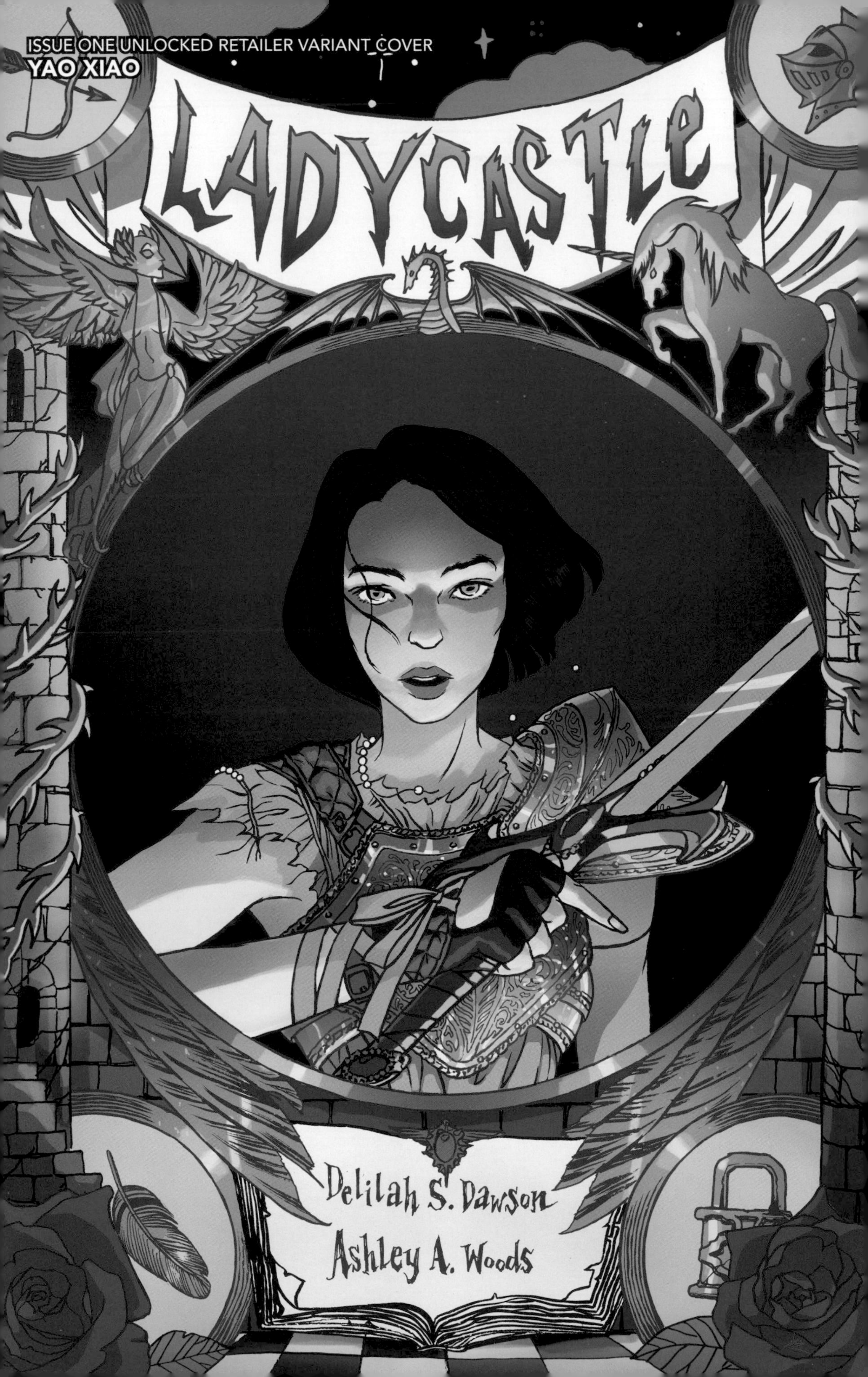

ISSUE ONE UNLOCKED RETAILER VARIANT COVER
YAO XIAO
LADYCASTLE
Delilah S. Dawson
Ashley A. Woods

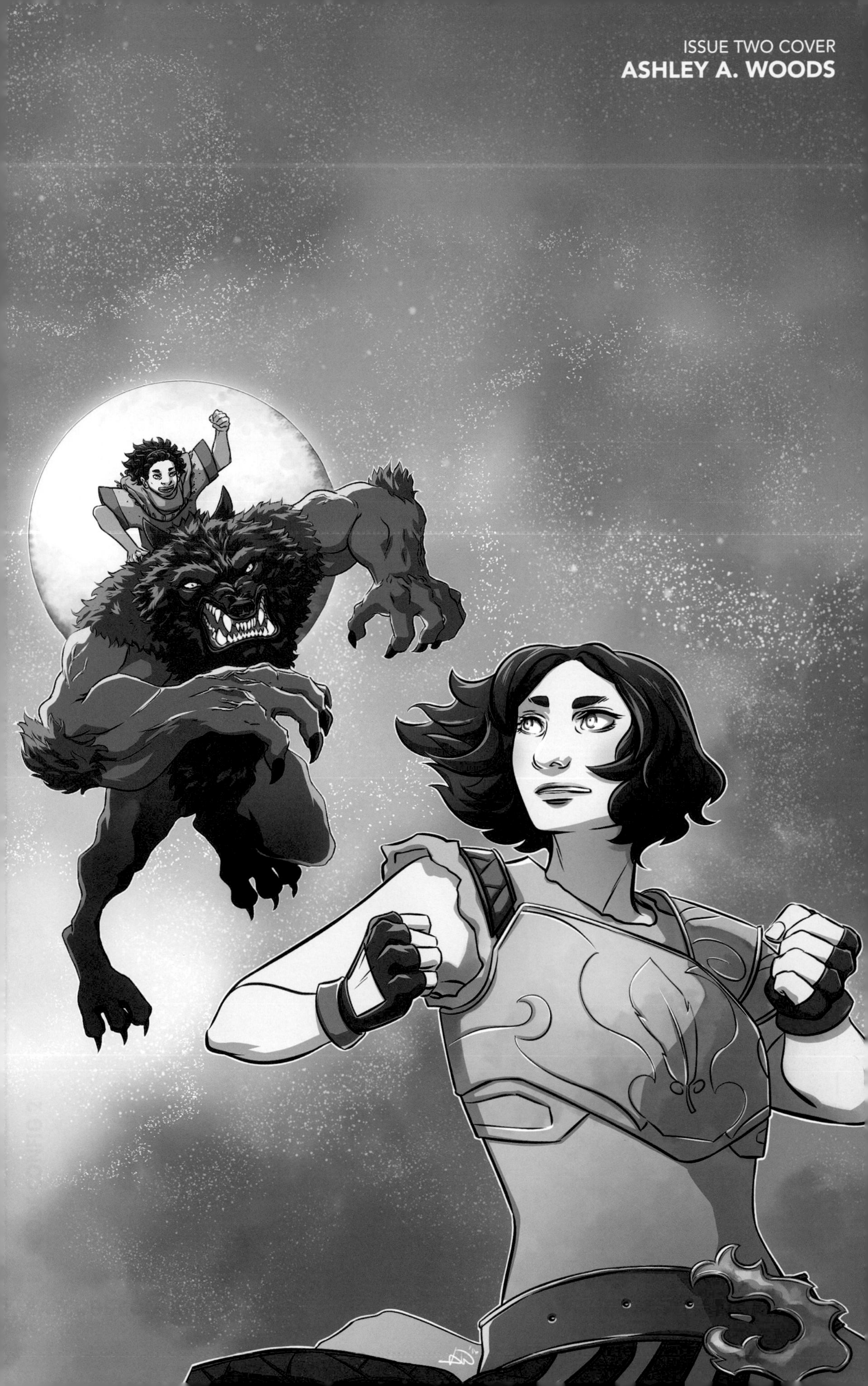

ISSUE TWO COVER
ASHLEY A. WOODS

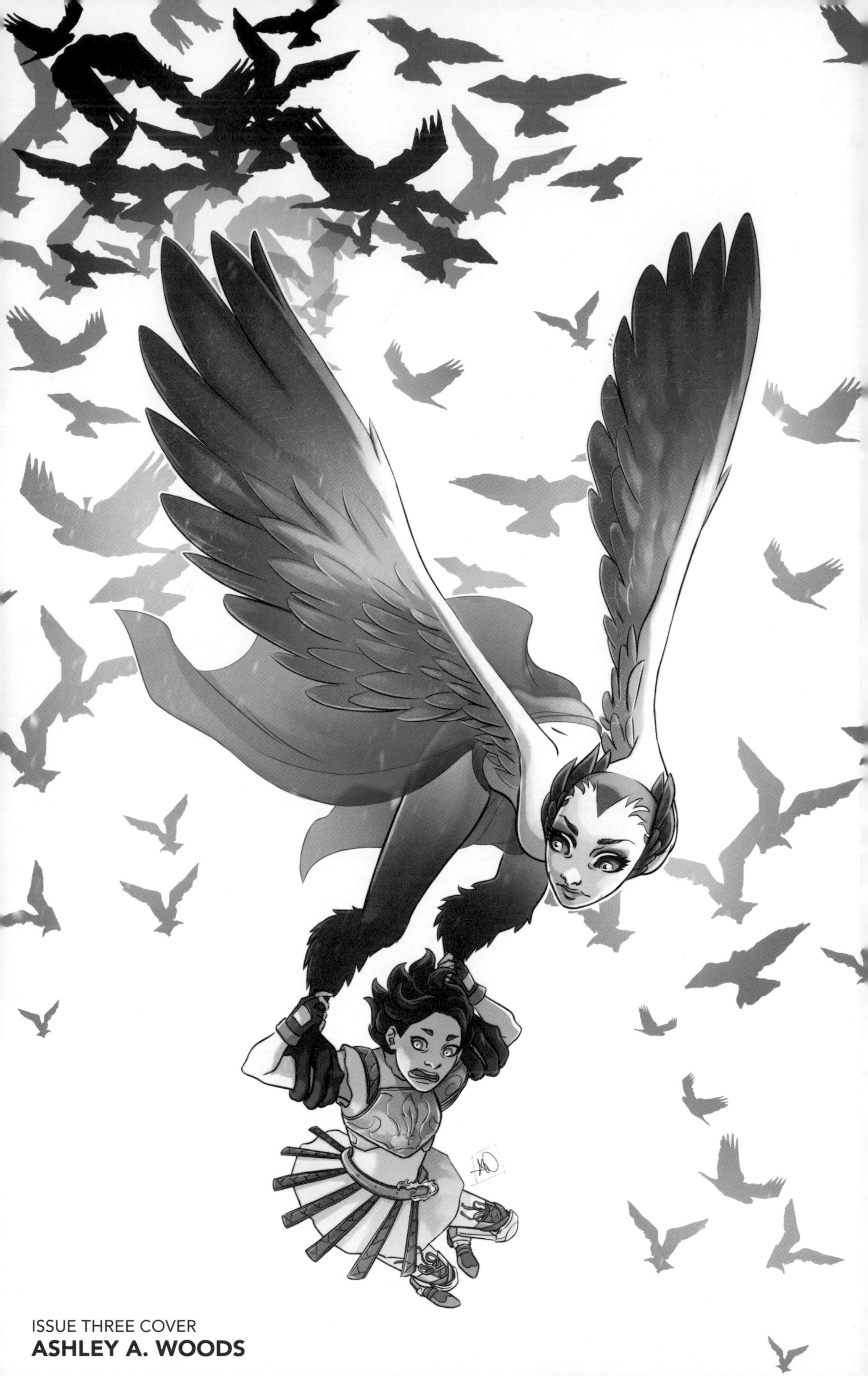

ISSUE THREE COVER
ASHLEY A. WOODS

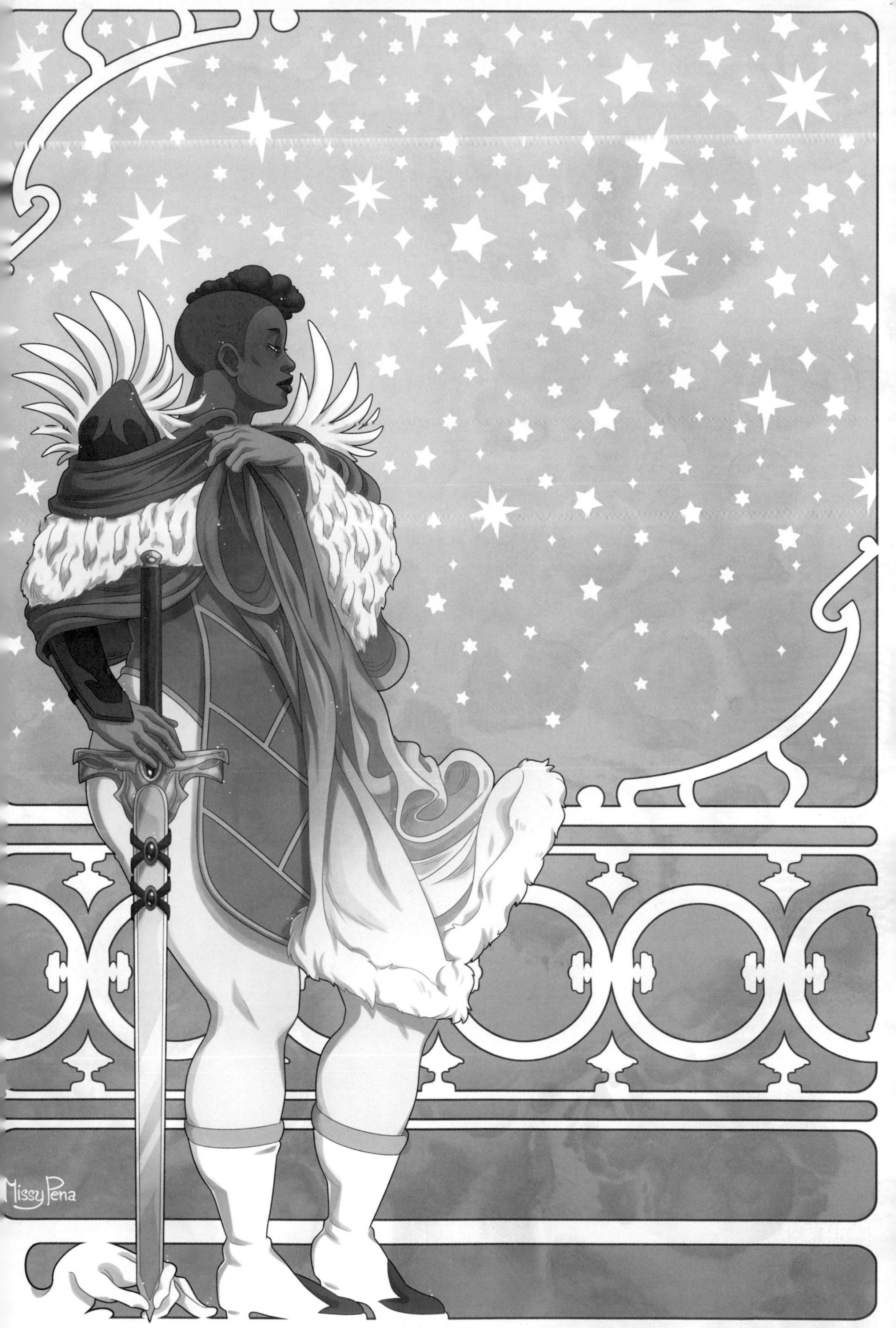
Missy Pena

ISSUE FOUR COVER
MISSY PEÑA

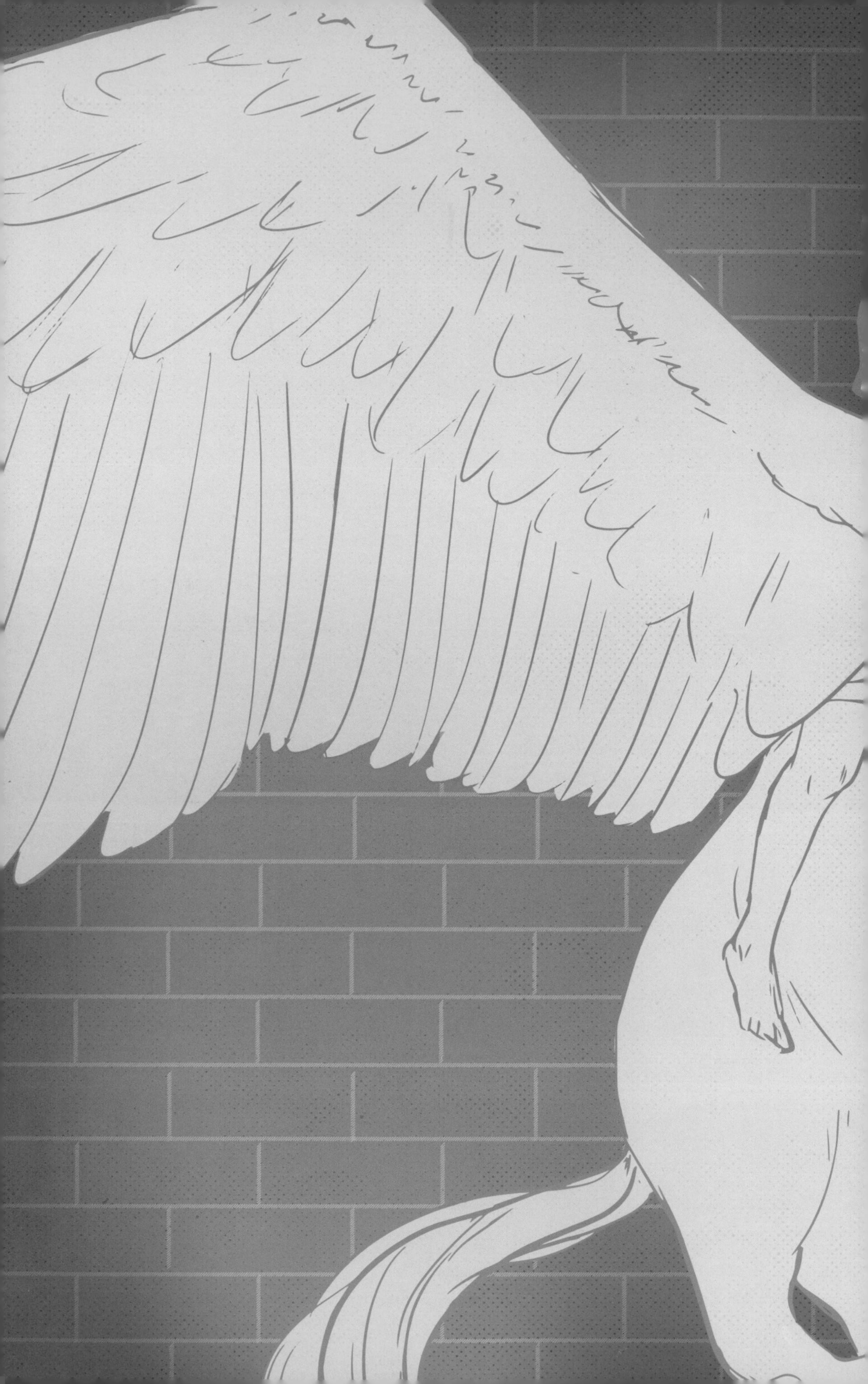